Living to Die

By

L.B. Kelly

1663 LIBERTY DRIVE, SUITE 200
BLOOMINGTON, INDIANA 47403
(800) 839-8640
WWW.AUTHORHOUSE.COM

First published by AuthorHouse 10/04/04

ISBN: 1-4184-9790-8 (sc)

Printed in the United States of America
Bloomington, Indiana

This book is printed on acid-free paper.

Chapter One

It was a cold, dark night he was all by himself with nobody to talk him out of what he was doing. Steven stood with his back against the wall outside of his house with the barrel of a nine-millimeter gun against his temple. He was shaking uncontrollably; he really was scared because he had convinced himself that he was actually going to do it this time. He was convinced that his life was not worth living another minute and that this was the only way out. Tears ran down his face as he thought of moments from his childhood. He thought of a day when he and his parents and his baby sister were a happy family. A day when his mother and sister were still around and his father wasn't a drunkard whom he barely knew.

It was a beautiful day; one made for the beach. Steven was twelve years old and his sister was eight. They were both so excited about going to the beach with their mom and dad. It had seemed like an eternity since they planned to go and it was like waiting for Christmas. That morning Steven and his sister, Brooke got up with the sun and got their parents up shortly thereafter. They were up late the night before packing their bag and making sure they had everything they would need, it would be a day to remember.

It was a Monday; they planned it that way in hopes that the beach in Biloxi wouldn't be so crowded the way it usually was on the weekends. Their mom and dad both took off work and Steven and Brooke skipped school. It had been so long since they all had done anything as a family. Steven's father worked as a foreman with a large construction company that often took him away from his family on the weekends and his mother was a legal secretary at an area law firm, so with such a hectic schedule this day was a welcome break for everyone.

The family lived near Pascagoula, Mississippi, but knowing that Biloxi offered such a beautiful beach they made the short trip west. They made a few passes up and down the coast along Highway 90, the gulf always looked so grand to Steven from the highway; it gave him butterflies every time that he saw it. After finding just the right spot Steven's dad pulled the car over into one of the parking areas and cut the engine. It was about eight o' clock in the morning so it wasn't extremely hot yet. Steven and Brooke hurried out of the car and stood over the beach on the wooden walkway and took in the sights and sounds for a moment. As the two scrambled down the sandy embankment, neither one of them thought to grab the buckets and digging implements that they had so carefully packed the night before.

"Slow down, be careful." They could hear their mother shout to them as they ran for the water. She might as well have told them to stop breathing; they were there for fun, plain and simple.

They had been there for a while and had gone back and forth between swimming and playing in the sand. Pretty soon Steven decided it was time for swimming again. He got up and went back into the water and like clockwork Brooke followed after him; as far as she was concerned anything her brother did was good enough for her.

Steven waded out about waist-deep, which was about chest-deep for Brooke. They splashed water at each other and Steven would dunk his sister under playfully. After a while Steven was becoming bored with the limit of the waist deep water that his parents had set for him. He looked out towards the open gulf and then back to his parents who were laid at ease on the beach.

"I'm going out a little deeper, you stay here. I'll be right back." Steven said to Brooke as she wiped water away from her squinted eyes.

"Dad said no." Brooke reminded her brother.

"It'll be okay, nothing's gonna happen." He assured her.

Steven moved a little deeper, about chest-deep and checked his foothold. He wanted to make sure that he could reach the bottom; regardless of his boasts he wasn't a great swimmer.

Steven felt comfortable so he bobbed around there for a minute while Brooke watched nervously between him and their parents. Feeling more confident, Steven decided to venture out a little further, about shoulder-deep this time.

"Be careful, Steven." Brooke said with concern.

"I'm all right." Steven said to reassure himself as well as Brooke.

Steven began to bob around as he did before, but before he knew it he had drifted out and he was literally in over his head. He floated around a little, going completely under the water's surface at times, more than he really wanted to.

Steven was starting to become worried that he would not be able to make it back to his sister if he stayed out there much longer so he went down one more time and tried to push off from the sandy bottom but lost his footing. He stayed down longer this time and felt his stomach knot up as a result of his panic. He flailed his arms and legs franticly and made it to the surface long enough to catch a gasp of air and a glimpse of his sister's horrified face.

"Steven!" Brooke screamed not really knowing what to do. She looked back at her parents who were oblivious to what was happening. Finally she decided Steven would just have to get in trouble because he needed help.

"Daddy, Steven is drowning! Help!" Brooke screamed as loud as she could.

Their dad and mom were alerted to attention by Brooke's cries and Steven's dad was on his feet and in the water, swimming towards them quicker than he ever thought he could. Their mother waded out almost as quickly to Brooke and grabbed her up and watched as their father dove down after Steven, who had gone completely under by this time. Steven could see the bright, blue-sky swirl around, distorted by the water as everything faded out.

Steven's vision and hearing faded back in and he saw his father kneeling over him with tears in his eyes. His father had preformed CPR and Steven realized how close of a call it really was as he coughed up the seawater. His father scooped him up and hugged him tightly.

"Don't ever do that again! I love you, son! Don't ever do that again!" Steven's father sobbed to his son as he cradled him while rocking back and forth on his knees.

Even though he had nearly killed himself and spent the rest of the day at the hospital under observation it was a happy day. Steven's father, who was never one to show his feelings showed his son how much he loved him that day at the beach. Steven never forgot it and he thought that maybe it would take death looming over them one more time for him to show it again.

Steven let out one final breath that made itself visible in the cold, October air as he prepared to squeeze the trigger. The next few seconds seemed like an hour. He noticed everything in that moment and it seemed surreal that his life was going to end this way. After his father saved him that day in Biloxi and his mother and Brooke were killed in a car wreck by a drunk driver and after learning to deal with his father's physical and verbal abuse it seemed so ironic that he would deliver his own demise.

He applied more pressure to the trigger and anticipated the bullet shooting through his head. Instead he felt a sense of reason, shoot through his head as he felt the cold steel of the nine millimeter's barrel lower from his temple. He just couldn't do it and funnier than that he couldn't figure out why. Did his mother touch him from heaven? Or did his baby sister, whom he missed so desperately, try to do what she could to save him once more?

Steven collapsed in a heap against the back of his house and began to sob. He regained his composure and caught a glimpse of the full moon shining so brightly down upon him. He stared at the moon for a minute and then looked at the gun in his hand. He tossed it on the ground a few feet in front of him and looked at it a few seconds more. He then reached up to his temple where he had the gun and felt a perfect, circular indention and a slight tenderness; he hadn't realized that he had pressed the gun so hard.

He looked down at his arms and saw the huge goose bumps and began to shiver. He didn't put on a jacket because through his logic he was going to die and what's the point of a jacket when you're dead, right?

Steven got up and picked up his gun and walked to the left side of the house. He looked at his neighbor's house that was about sixty, sixty-five feet away from his own and wondered if Mrs. Stiles had noticed anything. All of her windows were dark so he decided that she hadn't. He didn't want people to think he was crazy since he still had to look them in the eye.

He continued walking to the front of the house, looking at the other houses in the area. It wasn't a large community that they lived in but it was a close one and it had been his home all of his life and everyone knew him and his problems. Everyone at his school knew about his problems as well, from him losing his mother and sister to his father's often-obvious abuse. When Steven came back to school after the funeral the other kids and even some teachers treated him differently whether it was for the better or for the worse, either way it was uncomfortable to Steven to be the center of so much attention.

He made his way to the porch steps and then to the door, he opened it and went inside the house. The coldness of the house hit Steven hard every time he went inside, not just the physical coldness, but also the coldness in his soul as well. It seemed so empty since his mother and Brooke died. Every time he stood in the spot in the living room where he stood at this moment he could see Brooke lying in the floor with her coloring book and colors nagging him to color with her and he fought back tears every time, wishing he that still could.

To his left, in the kitchen he could see his mother watching the evening news from a small television set on the countertop as she made supper. Every single time he saw these things he wished that the bastard that killed them had died too instead of chipping away time from his twelve-year manslaughter sentence in a minimum-security prison, if it could truly be called prison. This guy is going to be with his family again and Steven's family was destroyed.

Steven looked straight ahead into the hallway at the mirror that hung there and saw himself holding the gun in his hand. He wondered what his mother would have thought of him, but he already knew. He could almost feel the disappointment in himself for her and he could certainly feel her disappointment for his father.

Steven's father simply went off the deep end after the deaths of his wife and daughter. He picked up an old drinking habit, only it was a hundred times worse this time around and he made Steven his whipping boy for all of his anger and frustrations, both verbally and physically. He was no more a father to Steven at this point than he could have been to a perfect stranger. He had devoted his life to the bottle, the same bottle that had robbed him of his family.

It had been just over a year since the accident. It might as well have been ten years as far as Steven was concerned, because that's what it felt like to him. It felt like a lifetime had passed since he last saw Brooke. It happened on a Thursday night, Brooke had just started taking ballet lessons and it was time for her first recital. Steven remembered how excited she was and he also remembered thinking how fast she was growing up. She was twelve years old and was starting to become interested in more delicate, lady-like things and Steven was fifteen and becoming more interested in delicate, lady-like girls, but they were still as close as any brother and sister could be.

That evening Brooke and her mother were already getting ready to go when Steven got home from whatever he was doing after school that day. Brooke asked Steven to go with them one last time, but of course he declined; ballet wasn't exactly his cup of tea and Brooke knew that and didn't hold it against him. They finally got ready to go and started out the door. Brooke gave Steven a hug and told him that she loved him; she was never one to let an opportunity go by to let everyone know how much she loved them. Steven wished her luck and they were gone, forever.

Steven's thoughts were interrupted by a set of headlights casting moving shadows on the wall in front of him. His father was home and Steven's stomach became uneasy with the thought of the inevitable confrontation. Steven looked at the clock on the wall above the fireplace; it was one twenty a.m. He had no idea where his father had been. They didn't even know each other any more. Steven's father, Tim made his way up the steps and went into the house. He stopped short at the door when he saw Steven and just stared at him for a minute.

"What in the hell are you doing with that?" Tim asked of Steven after noticing the gun in his hand.

"I, I thought I heard somebody outside. I went to check it out." Steven stammered a little hoping Tim would accept his excuse.

"Well, nobody was in the garage were they? I got a bunch of tools in there. That's all I need, some dope-head stealing my tools." Tim said with complete disregard for Steven's safety.

"No, I didn't see anybody." Steven replied. There was a short silence and then Tim took off his jacket and hung it on the coat rack that stood next to the door. He then made a beeline for the refrigerator to get his last beer of the night. He was already plainly drunk.

"Where ya been, Dad?" Steven asked of Tim, almost instantly wishing that he hadn't. Tim had already cracked the beer open and was gulping it down. His expression changed with disgust at Steven's question. Tim lowered the beer to his side and bowed his head. He took in a short breath and expelled it quickly. He turned and looked at Steven and then walked over to meet him eye to eye.

"I don't think that where I've been is any of your business. You know, I'm getting sick of your nosey ass snooping around in my business. I'm a grown man and having to answer to my son about where I've been." Tim spat out the slurred remarks at Steven who had his face slightly turned so as not to take in any more of Tim's repugnant breath than he had to.

"I was just wondering, Dad. I was getting worried." Steven replied flatly starring past Tim aimlessly into the kitchen.

"Well don't worry about me. I deserve to take a day off from work and kick back a little." Tim said taking a few steps towards the old radio that sat on the table by his recliner in the living room.

"You took off work again? Dad, if you lose you're job were gonna lose the house." Steven said to Tim, who had his back turned as he searched through the stations on the radio.

"I'll be damned, it's like I'm still living with your mother." Tim said uninterrupted and with a slight chuckle.

9

"Go to hell." Steven replied. He almost bit his tongue to keep from saying it, but he just couldn't hold back any longer. Tim was always making remarks like that about Steven's mother and he'd had enough.

Tim clinched his fist and then spun around and hit Steven across the right side of his face. Steven stumbled and dropped the gun before falling to the floor himself.

Tim stood over him, fuming, with his fists still clinched tightly. Steven was choking up and breathing heavily. He looked into Tim's eyes and was more afraid of his father at this moment than at any other. Before Steven would take his father's comments without saying anything at all. This time Tim was surprised and enraged all at once. Steven looked at the gun that lay on the floor between them and thought how easy it would be to just pick it up and put Tim out of his misery.

"What, you think you want to plug me with that thing? Well then go ahead and do it, please!" Tim yelled with his arms spread open at Steven after noticing his line of sight. There was a silence and Steven started breathing even harder as tears escaped from his eyes. Tim leaned over and picked the gun up and held it up to his own head.

"Hell, you want me to do it for you? Don't think I haven't thought about it before!" Tim yelled. Steven really thought he might do it. It was like time froze for a moment. Steven could see how vulnerable his father was and also how unstable he had become. Steven knew at that moment that something had to give.

"You know why I don't stay around here that much? Around you." Tim asked while relaxing the gun and gestured to Steven with it. Steven gave no reply; he just sat there nervously on the floor.

"'Cause every time I look at your face I see your mother's face or your sister's and it makes me sick!" Tim lowered the gun and started pacing back and forth in front of Steven. Steven then thought about how differently this night would have been if he had come in the house a little earlier or if he had gone straight to his bedroom when he came in, or even if he had actually blown his brains out in the back yard. He was starting to feel sick at his stomach, between Tim's ranting and the damned Oak Ridge boys counting flowers on the wall on the radio and at that moment he had never missed his mother so badly.

"I don't guess it's your fault, is it?" Tim said as he sat down on the edge of his lazy boy with a strange calm falling over him all at once. Steven still said nothing.

" Get up, Son. I love you, I'm sorry." Tim said as the gun dangled loosely in his hand.

Steven could see a small part of the man he used to know in that statement and then he had never missed his father so badly and he was certain that the man that he knew now didn't mean a word of what he just said. He stood up slowly and looked at his father.

"Go to bed." Tim said to him after another short silence. Steven wanted to say something, but he didn't know what. He just turned and walked down the hallway to his bedroom.

Steven shut his door behind him and sat down on his bed. He rubbed his right cheek gently and pains shot through his head and he winced slightly, it seemed to him that Tim was hitting him harder and harder every time. Steven moved his hand up to his temple where he'd held the gun. He thought about what he tried to do, but quickly dismissed the thoughts; he just didn't want to think about it any more.

L.B. Kelly

He got up and changed into a pair of shorts, took his shirt off and sat back down on his bed. He heard the front door slam and then heard his father's truck crank and leave few seconds later.

Steven reached over to his nightstand and cut his lamp off and then pulled the covers up around his neck and thought about Brooke for a little while and wondered if there would ever be happiness in his life again. It had become such an unfamiliar emotion that he wasn't sure he would ever be able to recognize it. Steven was alone and that's all he had known for such a long time and he hated it. He lay there in the darkness for the rest of the night with his thoughts, staring at the clock wide-awake.

* * *

The next morning Steven's room was cold and he was feeling groggy from the hour and a half nap that he had gotten the night before. He lay in his bed, trying to get his eyes focused. He quickly remembered the fight with his father from the night before when he tried to yawn and his jaw was so sore that he could hardly move it; it felt like someone had hit him with a baseball bat instead of a fist.

He got up and went down the hall to the bathroom. He had a sinking feeling in the pit of his stomach when he looked in the mirror. The lower right side of his face from his cheekbone down to his jaw line was darkened with bruises.

"What is today gonna be like?" He thought to himself; he got enough cold stares every day without having something to attract them.

Steven brushed his teeth and completed his normal, everyday routine and then headed for the kitchen. He didn't even bother looking in on his father because he was almost positive that he hadn't come in while he was asleep. He looked out the kitchen window and shook his head as he saw an empty driveway. He wasn't surprised at the fact that his father didn't come home it was just that first thing in the morning his father was almost normal and he was kind of sorry that he missed it.

Steven took a glass from the cabinet and then moved over to the refrigerator and poured himself some orange juice. He looked at the clock on the oven. It was five forty-five and Steven thought it funny that he had been getting up so early. He could remember his mother begging him to get out of bed right up until it was time to leave.

Steven chugged his juice down and set the glass on the counter and went to his bedroom and got dressed for school. He came back through the kitchen and grabbed a pop tart and reached for his key ring when he noticed that his father had left the gun sitting on the table by his chair. Steven looked at it for a second and then picked his house key up that was sitting next to it. He put the key in his pocket and opened his pop tart, picked up his book bag and walked out onto the porch leaving the gun where it was.

Steven stopped on the steps and took a look around at the sights of the morning. The ground was wet with dew, the sky was clear and blue and he thought 'this is what the day after my death would have looked like if I did it last night.' He didn't give it much thought, he just took in a deep breath, pulled his jacket's hood over his head covering his bruises and slung his back pack over his shoulder and went down the steps and started on his way to the bus stop. Steven broke off a piece of his pop tart and started eating it. He looked down at his watch; it was six o' clock. He wasn't in any hurry, as it would be at least an hour before the bus

13

came and it only took him about fifteen minutes to get to the stop.

Steven was about half way when a big, brown dog came running up to him, just like every morning. He knew that the only reason the dog was so friendly was because he knew Steven would share his breakfast with him.

Steven broke off a piece of the pastry and threw it down and the dog snapped it into his mouth in mid-air. Steven again thought about how things could have been different if he had pulled the trigger the night before. People would have said things like 'What a shame.' 'He was such a quite kid.' or 'The poor kid always did have a lot of problems.' There were so many rumors going around town about Steven and his father ranging form the truth about the beatings and tongue-lashings to complete lies about sexual abuse. Yeah, they would say those things and kick around the rumors for a little while but things would have gotten back to normal pretty quick. Steven also knew that the incident would have either caused his father to drink himself into the grave quicker than he was already or to get on the straight and narrow, of course a day late and a dollar short, if it would have affected his life at all. The last year Steven had felt like nothing but a burden to his father. The only real difference that Steven could see was that stupid dog would have missed out on the pop tart.

"O.K., this is it, you bum." Steven said to the dog as he dropped one last treat to him. "I'm hungry too."

Steven kept walking down the sidewalk and of course the dog followed. Steven could hear from behind him the sound of a car's deep, rumbling exhaust and he knew instantly who it was, John Larson. John was Steven's worst tormentor; from the time they were in first grade together up until now. When Steven came back to school after his mother and Brooke's wreck and the rumor mill got cranked up, John's torture became ten times worse. There were insensitive remarks about his mother and comments about his father, slaps to the head and John also spread a rumor that Steven was gay. John was much bigger than Steven, both physically and socially so Steven fought back the urge to stand up to him for the fear of taking a beating from him and then one from his father after he got home. John was Mr. Popularity, with any girlfriend that he wanted and a gang of friends. Friends were something that Steven didn't have any of, No one to back him up and no one to talk to. So Steven saw fit to just let John's words roll off his back and not say anything at all, just listen to the laughs and not make things any harder than they had to be.

Steven looked behind him to see what John would yell at him or throw at him today. When he did he saw John swerve the 67' Camaro up onto the sidewalk as if to hit him.

"Watch out, you faggot!" John yelled and honked the car's horn obnoxiously as he sped off.

Steven jumped out of the way and stumbled, causing him to drop his book bag and his pop tart, which the unshaken dog devoured quickly.

Steven stood there with his heart pounding intensely. Papers flew from his busted book bag and he stomped at the satisfied dog causing him to run away. Steven covered his face with his hands, inhaled deeply and then after a second began picking up his strewn papers.

* * *

Steven could feel the cold stares from everyone from the second he walked into the high school. He didn't look anyone in the eye; he just made his way to his first period class as quickly as he could.

Steven noticed when he walked through the door that most everyone was already there. He scanned the room and spotted a chair in the back of the class and headed towards it passing by John Larson who was sitting behind his girlfriend, Rebecca.

"You wait'n on a blizzard, freak?" John said to Steven as he passed by, referring to his heavy jacket and hooded face. Steven said nothing.

"Leave him alone, John." Rebecca said.

"That fag almost hit my car this morning. I ought to beat his ass." John continued ignoring his girlfriend.

"Just leave him alone." Rebecca repeated as the teacher walked into the room closing the door behind her.

Rebecca looked at Steven who had sat down three chairs back and one row over from them but quickly looked away when Steven peered out at her from under his hood. Rebecca and Steven were friends in elementary but now, just like everyone else she treated him as though he had some kind of communicable disease, but the truth was that Steven was a disease, a social disease. It wasn't only his peers thinking this way, it was their parents who had heard all the rumors and were telling their children to stay away from him. God forbid that someone should try to help him, as far as everyone in this backward town was concerned it was better to ignore the situation and hope it would go away rather than to dirty their hands trying to fix it.

The teacher, Mrs. Jennings began the roll call. Steven listened until she got to his name. He knew that she would make him take his hood off and then everyone would see what his father had done to him.

"...Steven Harris?" Mrs. Jennings said and then looked up to find him in the room.

"Here." Steven said hoping that she would just move on to the next name.

"Steven, please remove your hood in my class." The teacher said as she adjusted her glasses to see him. Steven paused for a moment. "Steven?"

Steven reluctantly pulled the hood back revealing his blackened cheek. Mrs. Jennings began to ask him what had happened but then figured it out and quickly continued with the roll call. Steven looked around the room and saw a few people still looking at him. He then he looked at John who was snickering at his embarrassment. Steven's eyes began to well up and he tightened his fists, wishing John's throat was in them. He just hung his head and waited for the end of the period.

Finally the bell rang marking the end of homeroom. Steven waited for everyone to leave the room before getting up himself to leave and as he did he briefly looked at Mrs. Jennings who really wanted to say something but only turned away and let Steven walk by.

Steven could hear whispers as he walked down the hallway to his locker. He turned the corner and saw John talking to one of his football buddies at their locker, near Steven's. Steven opened his locker and started unloading everything out of his busted book bag waiting for John to say something.

"Hey fag! What happened to your purse? I mean book bag?" John asked, with such an arrogant tone that it made Steven's stomach turn just to hear it. Steven again said nothing. John moved closer to continue his torture while laughter from his friends egged him on.

"Hey, I'm talkn' to you. What are you deaf, don't understand English?" John continued with amusement. Steven remained silent and continued putting books in his locker as the anger built inside of him.

"Naw, He's just scared." One of John's buddies answered for Steven.

More people were starting to watch what was going on and John wasn't about to slow down with such a big audience to entertain. He moved closer to Steven and began again.

"You know, you might want to put some make-up over those bruises so your dad will think you're pretty enough to pay you a visit tonight." John said, satisfied that he would get a reaction with that remark. The laughter continued.

Steven clinched his jaw tightly and was overcome with anger. He looked down at the History book that he held in his hand and thought about how heavy it was. He then sighed sharply and gripped the book with both hands. For a second he felt a sense of reason telling him to just take it in stride, but he was tired of doing that. Without giving it a second thought he spun around and hit John in the face as hard as he could with the book, changing his cocky grin into a look of astonished bewilderment.

The laughter came to a screeching halt. John took two involuntary steps back and fell on his butt as blood gushed from his nose and from around his loosened front teeth.

Steven felt such a relief and for once held his head high in the presence of his classmates who were all bound together with shock at what they had just seen. He even noticed

Rebecca, shaking her head as if to say to John 'You asked for it.' He then prepared for John's friends to take revenge for their fearless leader, but they just picked his limp, semi-conscious body up from the floor. Steven felt a hand on his shoulder and turned quickly to see who it was and he saw Mr. Stern's face.

"Get in my office now." Mr. Stern, the school's principal said to Steven with a notable lack of interest to deal with the situation.

All of a sudden reality came screaming back to Steven, not only the reality of him standing up for himself for once, which felt very good. But also that of knowing that he had just humiliated the captain of the football team in front of the entire school and that he would surely seek retribution. However the reality that Steven was most concerned with was the one in which his father would be informed of his actions. He knew that his father would be furious that Steven had drawn such unwanted attention. But the fact remained that Steven did what he did and now he had to face the music.

"Take Larson down to the nurse's station." Steven heard Mr. Stern say to John's buddies after he had already started on his way to Stern's office. Even though Steven knew that he was in deep, he couldn't help but smile.

Steven continued down the hall until he got to the administrative office. He opened the door and went in and went straight into Mr. Stern's office and sat down in the chair in front of the desk and waited.

Mr. Stern came in directly and shut the door behind him and walked hurriedly around Steven to his chair and sat down. He could barely contain his excitement for finally having an excuse to get rid of this unwanted blemish upon the school that made everyone so uncomfortable.

Mr. Stern was a tall, slender man who looked like a praying mantis seated behind the desk. He shuffled some papers around for a moment, trying to calm himself somewhat before giving that trademark Mr. Stern sigh before he began.

"You want to tell me what's going on, Harris?" He asked even though he already knew what the problem was.

"Nothing." Steven replied.

"Well something is going on, you don't just attack someone over nothing." Mr. Stern said, thinly disguising his awareness of the situation. Steven hung his head and leaned forward in the chair, placing his elbows on his knees. Mr. Stern squinted his eyes slightly trying to read what Steven was going to say next.

"Nothing. I'm just tired of being walked on around here. John asked for it." Steven explained.

"Well even if he did that does not give you the right to break his nose. I can't allow that kind of behavior." Mr. Stern said to Steven trying to figure out whether or not he would be able to expel him, or at least suspend him.

"But you can let him make me miserable day in and day out?" Steven asked letting his anger rebuild.

"I don't have any idea what you are talking about. If there have been any problems in the past you should have come to me with them instead of taking matters into your own hands. Now you've tied mine." Mr. Stern was really trying to convince Steven that he cared.

"Look I don't expect you to do anything to John. Just give me detention or the paddle or whatever and let me go back and wait for John to do whatever he's gonna do to get back at me." Steven said as he leaned back in the chair staring past Mr. Stern aimlessly.

Stern relaxed in his chair and felt a small twinge of guilt and pity for Steven as he studied the bruises on his face; he worked through both the guilt and pity effortlessly.

"I'm afraid it's not going to be that easy. I'm going to have to suspend you until the disciplinary committee can meet and decide what appropriate action should be taken. I'm going to have to call your father to come pick you up." Mr. Stern said capturing Steven's attention instantly.

"You don't have to do that, Mr. Stern." Steven said leaning forward in the chair again.

"I'm afraid you've given me no choice, Steven. I'm sorry." Mr. Stern said as he punched the intercom button on his phone to communicate with the secretary in the front office.

"Mrs. Turner, Get me Tim Harris' phone number at work, please."

Steven sat silently as he once again rested his elbows on his knees. Mr. Stern shared in the silence and remained still until Mrs. Turner came in with the number.

"Thank you." Mr. Stern said to her politely. She simply responded with a smile and cast a curious glare towards Steven as she exited the room.

Mr. Stern dialed the number looking at Steven briefly as it started to ring. Steven's mind began to wonder as he heard Mr. Stern talking to his father. What was Tim going to say? More importantly to Steven what was he going to do? His thoughts were interrupted when Stern handed him the phone.

"Your father would like to speak with you." Steven reached out to take the phone.

"Dad?" Steven started. Tim cut him off quickly.

"What in the hell have you done? That kid's parents are probably gonna sue me now! I can't believe this, I'm bust'n my ass to send you to that school and your gonna get kicked out!"

"Dad, I'm sorry."

"Yeah, your damned sure gonna be. Let me talk to Mr. Idiot again." Tim said with disgust.

Steven lowered the phone from his ear slowly and handed it across the desk with a trembling hand to Mr. Stern. Steven was terrified.

"Yes?" Mr. Stern said. He noticed Steven's fear and felt a real concern but ignored it.

Steven listened to them talk and was becoming shaky. He didn't know what to do.

"Your father wants you to go on home. He said that he would talk to you this evening." Mr. Stern said to Steven after hanging the phone up. He paused for a moment.

"Is there something you want to talk about?" Mr. Stern said giving in to his concern. Steven said nothing.

"Go collect your things from your locker and I will give you a ride home." Mr. Stern said after a minute.

Steven got up and left the office without saying anything. He headed down the hall towards his locker, but instead of stopping there he continued up the stairs that were near by. He kept walking, staring at his feet until he got to the south entrance of the school. He went outside through the door, stopped and took a look around and saw nobody.

He stood there with his back against the door looking up at the awning that hung above it. Tears rolled down each side of his face. He was afraid to go home. He had no idea what to do but he knew that he couldn't hang around there much longer before Stern would start looking for him.

He wiped the tears from his face and pulled his hood over his head. He walked down the sidewalk that led away from the building and into the parking lot. When he got to the parking lot he darted in between the parked cars quickly, almost running, hoping that he wouldn't be seen.

He finally made it across to the fence that separated the parking lot from the main road and climbed over it with ease. He turned around and took one last look at the school and then made his way down the main road that led into town.

After a good two and a half or three mile power walk through town that seemed to go by in a second Steven finally got to his house. He slowed his pace about thirty yards away to be sure Tim wasn't home. He didn't see his truck so he continued on. He ran up the steps in front of his house and unlocked the door and burst through it. He dropped his keys down on the table and picked the gun up that had been left there. He looked at it for a second and then went into the hall and down to the bathroom. He stood in front of the mirror and looked at himself and then at the gun again. He then looked out through the opened door into the hallway and saw the family photo that hung on the wall.

He looked at Brooke's smiling face and then let out a yell that hurt his ears.

He then busted out the mirror with the heel of the gun and then dropped it in the sink and turned and walked out of the bathroom.

He went straight to his bedroom and flung his closet door open and searched franticly for a small duffel bag. After finding the bag he moved to his dresser and started filling it indiscriminately with shirts and pants. He then went to his bed and threw his mattress out of the way, exposing his hidden stash of money. He had to hide it from his dad for the fact that he would drink it away if he had known about it. He counted the money and stuck it in his pocket.

Steven walked out of his bedroom and grabbed the family picture down off the wall and smashed the frame on the bookcase that it hung over and pulled the photo from it shaking off the broken glass at the same time. He folded the picture twice and put it in the inside pocket of his jacket and headed for the door.

He walked through the yard to the sidewalk and took his usual morning route. He had no idea where he was going. He only knew that he was tired of getting beaten up by his father and that he surely would have gotten a good one for what he had done and he surely didn't want to take a pounding from John and his cronies when he went back to school. The way Steven saw it, if he couldn't kill himself he could at least run away.

Steven walked for about two hours trying to build his courage. He was going in circles and he was growing tired. He started to question his decision, however he knew regardless of whether or not the decision was grounded he wouldn't have been able to go back home considering the condition in which he had left the house.

Steven came to an intersection. He stood there by the stop sign in the mid-day sun, the warmth of which counter acted the sharp, October wind. He looked up to the sky and saw the tops of the trees in the lonesome area being tossed around by it. He could almost feel himself being pushed forward by it as well, like a knowing hand at his back moving him in the right direction.

So forward he went down the desolate road that led away from town. He moved at a relaxed pace but also with a sense of awareness.

As he walked he thought of his father and how surprised he would be to find the house empty and in such a mess and for once he didn't care. As far as he was concerned Tim could throw the biggest tantrum in the world and tear the house down, because he wasn't going to be there to see it. He didn't know where he was going to be but the fact was that he didn't care as long as it wasn't with his father or even in this town.

After walking about two miles Steven passed a railroad crossing. He continued walking but then stopped all at once and turned around and looked at it for a minute. He then thought that by sticking to the main road he would eventually be found by Tim or maybe by the sheriff's department.

He went back to the crossing and stood in the middle. He looked to his right and knew that if he walked south he would end up right back where he started. He then looked to his left and could see a bend in the tracks ahead and decided that he might as well see what was on the other side. He knew that sooner or later it would lead to some sort of civilization.

* * *

Steven had walked for hours and his feet were so sore that he could hardly walk. He was starting to become a little worried, after walking all this way he hadn't seen any roads or pathways, only woods.

Over the past few hours he had thought of everything that was going on in his life and of what might lie ahead. So far he had no regrets over leaving. He had nothing but fond memories behind him and those, he could take with him anywhere.

Steven stopped abruptly after hearing a train horn bellow from behind him in the distance. He stood in the middle of the tracks and pondered for a moment. It was hard to tell how far away the train was, however he knew that it couldn't be far.

Steven looked around him at the ample trees on either side of the tracks. He walked down one side to the edge of the woods and surveyed the forest. Butterflies grew in his stomach as he took in the ominous sight of the timberland. The whole afternoon it felt to Steven as though he was being watched from the trees. He had ignored the feeling up until this point but in the dwindling daylight the mystery seemed to rise.

Steven walked about ten paces into the woods and turned around and watched the tracks. He squatted down and instantly felt the relief in his tired legs. Finally after convincing himself that he wasn't going to be attacked by anything that might be lurking among the trees he stretched his legs out and sat down flat on the leaf-covered ground.

He heard the train's horn again and could tell that it was getting closer. He began to think about the opportunity that it presented.

"People hop freight trains. Surely there will be an open door on one of the cars. How fast could it be going?" Steven said to himself out loud.

Steven could feel the ground rumbling slightly. He got up to wait for the train's arrival feeling confident that he had a winning plan.

"O.K. I'll wait for the train to pass, find an open door, run up and jump on. How hard could it be?" Steven continued to himself.

He stood there in the woods waiting for the train to pass, trembling from both nervous fear and the steadily dropping evening air.

The rumbling of the ground became more intense and he could now see the train. His fear then turned partially to excitement as the monstrous machine moved closer to him. Steven reached down and picked his bag up, gripped it tightly and he prepared to make his move.

The engine past by him, he was in awe at It's size and overcome by the noise. His heart was pounding fiercely. He could hardly hear himself think.

He waited for a few cars to pass and then spotted one that was open. He ran out of the woods and got as close as he could to the tracks and ran as fast as he could along side the train. By this time the car he had his eye on was terribly out of reach and his master plan was foiled as the train sped by him at forty-five miles per hour.

Steven slowed his pace until he came to a stop. He stood there hunched over with his hands on his knees, breathing heavily.

"There's no way in hell." He said as the train roared past him.

After a second Steven stood upright and looked behind him seeing nothing. He then looked at the train again as it shrunk out of sight.

"Well, I'm glad I didn't throw my bag on first." Steven said to himself as dusted his pants off and slowly started walking down the tracks.

Steven walked for another hour and a half. It was almost completely dark by this time and very cold. He was limping a little on the count of his sore feet and weary legs and he wondered how he was ever going to make it through the night.

He then came upon yet another bend in the tracks. As he rounded the bend he stopped short when he saw the train that had defeated him earlier stalled on the tracks. He looked all around and saw nobody.

"You gotta be kidding me." Steven said.

He then made his way down off the tracks with his butterflies returning. Steven trotted along the railroad and as he did his breath escaped from his nose and mouth looking like smoke before dissipating behind him.

Steven stopped near the end of the train and hunkered down trying to figure out why the train had stopped.

He couldn't see anything from where he was so he moved a little closer to the front of the train while dragging his bag behind him. The moon was bright this night as it had been the night before and it provided a dim, ambient light that Steven used to find his way.

He could now see the front of the train and also two separate flashlights investigating the lower part of the engine car.

Steven sighed a deep, cleansing breath and then looked up to the side of the train trying to find the open door that he had seen before. He spotted it a few car lengths up and ran to it, remaining low.

He stopped underneath the door and looked at the engineers. Satisfied that they were still preoccupied he looked up slowly into the car.

Inside he saw about twenty or thirty empty transport pallets, some were stacked neatly while others had fallen or had been just tossed in carelessly.

Steven inspected the car as carefully as he could with such little light. He wondered how safe it would be inside it and then thought that it would have to be as safe as taking the chance of freezing to death, which at this point seemed to be his only other alternative.

He then took another look ahead to the engineers and then tossed his bag into the car before climbing in himself.

Steven looked around the car and then walked over to the far side. He picked up a couple of pallets and stacked them against the wall and sat down on them.

He began a steady shiver and then leaned forward and pulled his bag to him. He opened it and pulled out a sweatshirt. He then took his jacket off and pulled the sweatshirt over his head, put his jacket back on over it and then pulled his hood up tight around his face.

Steven leaned back against the wall and crossed his legs in front of him and put his hands in his jacket pockets. He felt something in his right pocket and remembered the picture he had taken from the house. He pulled it out and unfolded it.

He looked at the picture by the moonlight that poured in through the door and studied each face individually. Tim's had a forced smile across it that Steven hadn't noticed before now. His mother's face was beautiful as always and he missed the love that he could feel just by looking at her and Brooke, her face was always so full of joy and life that it was hard to ever be angry with her, or even around her. Steven remembered thinking at her visitation, after she died that she still looked so content and peaceful even then. Steven then looked at his own face and could remember for a second what it felt like to be normal. He thought about the normal problems that teenagers deal with all the time and what he was dealing with then and he realized how oblivious to misery he really was despite what he thought.

Steven jumped to attention instinctively as the train jerked into motion. He watched the dark tree line through the door and as the train gained speed it became a moonlit blur. He then looked down at the picture again and traced over Brooke's face with his finger.

Steven then all at once folded the picture and put it back in his pocket and then folded his arms in front of his chest. He sat there on the pallets staring out the door enjoying the relief that his legs and feet were feeling. Steven then moved his bag to the corner of the stacked pallets and the wall and laid his head on it as a pillow and allowed the train to rock him into a light sleep.

* * *

Steven jumped into awareness when he heard the loud screeching of the train coming to a halt. He stood up and looked around and then walked to the door and took a look outside. They were arriving in a city, he had no idea which city he was in but he did know that his father or John Larson or anybody else in that stuck up town wasn't there and to Steven that was all that mattered.

The train slowly rolled to a stop as it entered the freight yard. Steven wondered what he should do. He didn't know whether or not he would be found, if he stayed where he was .If he did stay put how long would it be before the train would go out again?

He finally decided that the best thing to do would be to get off and try to find out where he was.

Upon leaving the train he looked around and saw a world of freight cars and a couple of engines sitting cold. He could see some sort of terminal office about a hundred yards away. He then looked up at the engine of his train and saw the engineers getting off and he then looked for a quick hiding spot.

He ran out, away from the train across two sets of empty tracks that were laid close together. He could see his shadow being cast on the ground by the florescent lights that hung high above the yard and it yielded such a strange feeling inside him, like he was watching a movie or he was watching all this happen to some one else.

He ran behind an old freight car and peered back out to see if he had been noticed. As he watched, he saw the engineers walking towards the terminal office.

Steven relaxed a bit and was then able to take a more detailed look around. The yard was full of trains, freight cars and empty tracks as far as the buzzing lights would allow him to see.

Steven walked around the end of the freight car at a slow, cautious pace scanning every direction as he went along, he moved across sets of tracks and weaved through the maze of cars.

Steven stopped between two lines of freight cars when he saw a figure of a man ahead of him in the feeble light. He appeared to Steven to be a security guard, as he was walking along the same route as Steven shining a flashlight into and underneath the cars.

The security guard walked along the tracks, dispatching his nightly duties with a complacent whistle. He headed towards a motionless Steven, who was frozen with the fear of being caught.

The guard carried on with his routine, completely unaware of Steven's presence only twenty or thirty feet in front of him. The keys on his belt jingled and jangled as he waddled along, with his corpulent gut jiggling in rhythm. Steven thought to himself after observing the sight of the guard, that he should be glad that he didn't have to investigate his feet.

Steven knew that he was caught. The guard was now only seconds away from shining his light upon him. He didn't know what to do, if he ran now he would be heard. Steven then thought that once the guard spots him the only thing he would be able to do would be to run or get caught and be sent back to Tim. He had come too far now to be sent right back.

In the midst of Steven's attempt to rationalize the situation his face was set aglow by the guard's flashlight. The guard let out a startled gasp. Steven looked like a deer, caught in a pair of headlights and he acted upon his first instinct, which was to run.

As Steven ran he could hear the keys on the guard's belt jingling in a more expeditious rhythm than before. Steven didn't look back but he knew that he was leaving the guard behind, as the jangling of his keys became more faint, Never the less Steven ran as hard as he could.

Steven made a couple of turns throughout the labyrinth that was the train yard. He could hear the rumbling of a train's engine. It grew louder as he moved closer to it and he finally spotted it several yards in front of a line of cars.

He ran along side the train looking up at the doors, trying to spot one that was open while also trying to keep an eye out for the roly-poly guard, who had probably already given up, or given out by this time.

Steven spotted a door that was about a quarter of the way open. He took another look behind him and then, with a slight effort, he opened the door enough for his body to fit through and then climbed in.

He shut the door, leaving it cracked open a bit so that he could still see out. He crouched down and watched out the door for the guard, hyperventilating as quietly as he could.

After a minute Steven decided that he had lost the guard and began to calm down a little. He then stood up to take a look around the car to see what he would be riding with. When he did he found himself looking down the barrel of a nine-millimeter pistol. Steven pulled in a startled breath and he felt an odd familiarity.

Steven tried looking past the gun to see who was wielding it, but the gunman's face was lost in the darkness.

"This car's full." The gunman said calmly from within the void. Steven opened his mouth to speak but didn't quite know what to say.

"I said that this car is full. Get out, now." The gunman said as he moved closer to Steven. He could now see the right side of his face, as the light that poured into the car through the door revealed it.

Steven could then hear from behind him a commotion, as if there were at least one more person in the car. Steven didn't look he only darted his eyes to the right and tried to listen more closely.

The gunman's patients had now been tested to its limit. He cocked the gun and put it to Steven's head.

Steven's eyes widened and he began to shake. He thought to himself "Maybe I've killed myself after all. At least this way I won't have to pull the trigger myself."

"Get out now, or die. I will kill you." The gunman said through his clinched teeth. He was only inches away from Steven's face. The gunman had a foul stench upon his breath that reminded Steven of his father.

The gunman appeared to be in his early twenties, with a hard look upon his unshaven face and a slender but muscular frame, however his eyes were empty and seemed to lead to a much older and unhealthy soul.

As the gunman prepared to follow through on his threat a sudden movement from outside captured his attention. It was guard; he had finally caught up with Steven.

The guard stood outside the freight car, looking around blankly. He had no idea where Steven had gone and was too fat to do anything other than shine his flashlight at the trains, so he wasn't about to attempt to open any doors or climb in any cars.

The gunman stood there in the car, watching the guard closely with his gun still pressed firmly against Steven's head.

The guard then concluded that he was the only one who had seen the kid and it wouldn't hurt his feelings, or his reputation for that matter, if he just kept the whole thing to himself. So with a slight blow to his pride, the guard turned and walked back towards the terminal office for another cup of coffee.

As the guard walked away the gunman turned to meet Steven eye to eye. He then thought that in his present situation it would be unwise to draw attention to him with a gunshot.

"When is this damned train gonna move!" The gunman shouted out loud as he removed the gun from Steven's head and began to pace anxiously.

Steven took a look around the car and saw two other men who seemed to be about the same age as the gunman, though not nearly as rugged or as mean. They were clearly subject to the gunman and seemingly just as paranoid.

The gunman then cut his eyes towards the two lackeys and was obviously becoming enraged.

"This is your fault, Jimmy." The gunman said as he bolted past Steven who was nervously watching and keeping quiet.

" 'Lets go hop the train.' 'I know all about it.' Hell, I could have been halfway to Jackson by now!" The gunman ranted as he held Jimmy down to the floor by his throat, while the other guy just looked on.

"I ought to pop you right now, just like I did that old man." The gunman continued while pointing the gun at Jimmy's head.

Just then the vibrating in the floor increased and the train jerked into motion. The gunman jumped and looked around as he slowly got up from over Jimmy.

"See, I told you." Jimmy said with an empty tone.

"What are we going to do about him?" The gunman's second flunky, Jake asked after the tension finally died down. The gunman looked at Jake and then at Steven, whom he had referred to.

"I don't know." The gunman said, as he looked Steven over. Steven remained quiet and very aware of what was happening.

"Jake, open the door so I can see out." The gunman sat down on one of the large pipefittings that were being hauled in the car as Jake opened the door fully.

"We could just throw him out." The gunman continued while staring coldly at Steven.

"Sit down." The gunman said. Steven dropped his bag to the floor and then sat down.

"What's in the bag?" He continued.

"Clothes." Steven answered simply.

The gunman looked at Jimmy as if to tell him to check the bag. Jimmy got up and walked over to Steven, unzipped his bag and began to look through it. Steven didn't say a word.

"You shouldn't have shot that guy, Michael." Jake said to the gunman.

"Shut up!" He replied.

"Nothing. Just clothes." Jimmy said as he dropped the bag down in Steven's lap.

"You got any money?" Michael asked.

"No." Steven said.

"You wouldn't lie to me, now would you?" Michael continued.

"If I had any money I wouldn't be here." Steven said this in hopes that it would make sense to him and he wouldn't want to search his pockets.

"I can't believe you killed that guy." Jake said as he stared aimlessly into space.

"You'd better shut your dumb-ass brother up, Jimmy. I gotta know he's gonna keep his mouth shut once we get off this train, or else something bad might happen to him." Michael said as Jimmy went over to comfort a plainly shaken Jake.

"What the hell are you looking at?" Michael asked Steven who had been watching intensely. Steven didn't say anything he only looked away.

For the next hour and a half nothing was said. Steven just sat there by the door and watched everyone in the moonlight and he couldn't help but wonder what these guys had done. He pieced together a few possible scenarios with what little information he had collected, but the truth was that Steven really didn't want to know and he figured he was probably better off not knowing.

Steven kept a careful eye on everyone, more especially Michael. He noticed that Michael hadn't set the gun down the whole time; he just sat there holding it as if he thought someone would attack him at any moment. Michael took a swig of whiskey from a bottle that he kept nearby and then set it back down on the floor next to a large grocery bag.

"What's your name, man?" Michael asked, breaking the silence. Steven looked at him with a bit of surprise. Was this guy trying to be his friend now?

"Steven." He replied after a second.

"Well, Steven where are you headed?" Michael asked as if he were leading up to something.

"I don't really know. Where ever this train takes me, I guess." Steven said as he looked over at Jake, who was still spaced out. Michael looked also and as he did a smirk found it's way across his face as a result of his amusement.

"You leaving anybody behind who will miss you?" Michael went on. Steven thought for a minute.

"Not likely." Steven said as he thought of Tim.

"Good, good, because I'll tell you it would be wise of you, once you get off this train to forget you ever saw us. Forget our names and forget our faces. I promise if you speak a word of this to anybody I will find and end you. Do you understand?" Steven could tell that Michael meant every word.

"Forget what?" Steven said nervously.

"Smart man. You want a drink?" Michael said as he offered out the bottle to Steven who just shook his head. Michael shrugged his shoulders and the gulped down much of the whiskey.

All of a sudden Jake struggled quickly to his hands and knees and threw up on the floor.

"Aww Jake, you nasty bastard!" Michael said as he picked his feet up off the floor.

"It's alright." Jimmy said as he rubbed his brother's back and looked coldly at Michael.

"I can't get that guy's face out of my head. Why did you have to kill him, Michael?" Jake said as he leaned back on his knees, breathing heavily.

"Shut up, Jake. Just forget about it." Michael said as he sat up to the edge of the pipefitting.

"I can't. Maybe you can, but I can't. You said we were just gonna rob the place and not hurt anybody." Jake said through tears. Steven just watched on, his palms became sweaty as he detected Michael becoming unstable.

"It's alright, Jake. It's gonna be alright." Jimmy said, trying to comfort his little brother.

"No it's not, I'm gonna turn myself in, Michael I'm sorry but I can't handle it." Jake said as he rocked back and forth on his knees.

"I'm sorry too." Michael said as he got up and pointed the gun at Jake's head and pulled the trigger. The shot delivered a bright flash that illuminated the car for a second. Steven couldn't believe what he had just seen.

"You son-of-a-bitch!" Jimmy yelled as he dove into Michael, spearing him to the floor.

Steven got up from the floor quickly and stood, dumbfounded as he clinched his bag tightly. He didn't know what to do.

Jimmy and Michael wrestled over the gun on the floor of the car. Steven looked over at Jake and was horrified at the sight of the partially decapitated body.

Steven jumped when he heard another shot escape from the gun. He looked at Jimmy and Michael who were still fighting on the floor and then another shot was fired randomly.

Steven looked out the open door and then back at the struggle. He knew that he had to get out and the only way was the hard way.

Steven stepped up to the door and crouched slightly as if he were preparing to skydive from an airplane. He then took a second to build his courage and dove out the door. He looked back quickly, on his way out as he heard another shot fire. He saw Jimmy lying motionless on the floor and Michael was getting up aiming at him. He fired a shot and missed.

Steven hit the sharp, loose rocks on the side of the tracks and felt pain in his shoulder as it scraped across the ground. Steven let out a cry of pain after his knee popped as he rolled down the small incline.

He came to rest in the cold, wet grass along the side of the tracks. He lay there staring up at the bright moon trying to compute what had just happened. After a minute or two he got up and hobbled a little until he gained his balance. He took a few steps back towards the tracks and leaned over and picked his bag up.

He walked back onto the tracks and watched the train disappear into the night. Steven looked behind him and then straight ahead again. He then brushed his pants off and took in a deep breath. He was sickened by what he had seen and couldn't get rid of the image of Jake's dead body.

He shook his head in disbelief of the day's events and started limping slowly down the tracks trying to figure out where he was.

Chapter Two

The early morning light poured over Michael Rowan's face, gently pulling him out of a chemically induced slumber. He opened his eyes and then closed them quickly as their exposure to the sun intensified the pounding pain inside his head. After a moment's composure he looked to his alarm clock that was beside his bed, it was nine a.m.

Michael was two hours late for work. He knew that it would be useless to go in with any excuses or even to call in. According to his supervisor the last time he was late, if Michael couldn't come in at seven from then on, he needn't bother coming in at all, don't call, don't write, don't do anything.

Michael just rolled back over in his bed and buried his head in his pillow and felt a bit disappointed with himself, having lost another job. He couldn't count on one hand the jobs he had gotten and lost over the past year. His current job at an area plant was one of the worst he had ever had in terms of pay. He had also held it the longest and was becoming uncomfortable with his position. Maybe that was the problem, he was becoming bored with playing the straight, sun up to sun down kind of guy that his mother wanted him

43

to be and he was starting to miss the dusk to dawn misfit that he really was.

Michael sat up in the bed and stretched his arms out wide while rolling his neck from side to side. He reached over to his nightstand and took a cigarette from the almost empty pack that was there and lit it.

He looked around his filthy, one room apartment as he blew the smoke from his lungs. He got up and walked over to the kitchen sink and found the least dirty glass that was in amongst a pile of dirty dishes and TV. dinner trays. He filled the glass with water and then took three aspirins from a bottle that was always readily available on the countertop and swallowed them down, followed by the water. He made a terrible face as the water settled on his stomach along with the whiskey and beer he had consumed the night before.

Michael dropped the glass back down into the sink and let out a belch that smelled as though it could have gotten him drunk all over again.

He looked around the apartment once more and wondered what he was going to do with his life. At this point it seemed to Michael to be a hopeless and pointless existence, he was simply being.

He walked over to the closet and opened the door. He stepped inside and reached above the door and pulled a loose panel away from the wall. He reached inside the recess and pulled out a small canvass bag.

He took the bag over to the kitchen table and set it down atop a pile of unopened bills and junk mail that had accumulated there over the weeks. He opened the bag and looked inside and pulled out a small bag of marijuana. The small amount in the bag shrank from over a pound to just about ten dollars worth with no profit to show for it, no tangible profit anyway.

The bag was given to him to sell by a local thug who promised Michael a small payoff in return. Michael had bought marijuana from the dealer many times for his own use and now gained enough of his trust to sell some for him and join in the spoils of the profits, both the financial profits and also the favors that certain female clients were willing to provide. However at this point the favors were outweighing the dollars and it was time to settle up.

Michael knew that the dealer would have ready a harsh punishment for such a disregard for his interest. Michael already owed him some money, which was to come off the top of his earnings. So while on such thin ice already, he wasn't even thinking of meeting the dealer empty handed.

Michael stood in thought for a moment. He finally came to the conclusion that if he had to explain the loss of three-quarters of the dealer's weed that he might as well explain the loss of all of it. So with that notion Michael opened the sandwich bag and looked around the cluttered table for a pack of rolling papers.

After finding the papers he took one sheet of the thin wrapping out and creased the middle of it. He then took a pinch of marijuana out of the bag and sprinkled it over the paper and then repeated the process. He then rolled the joint tightly and lit it using the cigarette that he was already smoking. He then dropped the cigarette in the ashtray and went into the small bathroom and shut the door.

He sat down on the edge of the bathtub and tried to think of a way out of the mess that he found himself in as he puffed away.

* * *

Michael left the apartment around eleven o' clock that morning. He went downstairs and got into his '77 Monte Carlo and sat there for a minute as the thought of selling the car crossed his mind. He then pushed the thought back in his mind, reserving it as a last resort.

Michael cranked the car and took off. He drove aimlessly down the main street of the small city in which he lived. He was trying to think of someone whom he could borrow money from but as he thought of each person he knew to ask he was reminded of his past transgressions and debts already owed to them.

He then came to a red light at an intersection. As he sat there he looked around and noticed the liquor store that sat on the corner and the wheels inside his head began to turn.

After the light turned green Michael whipped his car around the corner and parked on the street about three or four spaces down from the liquor store. He got out and walked down the sidewalk to the entrance of the store and walked in nonchalantly.

Upon entering the store he noticed immediately a camera above the clerk pointed at the counter. He looked around the rest of the store and saw only one more camera in the far-left corner above the cooler. The clerk made eye contact with Michael and gave a nod of acknowledgment.

Michael walked on back to the rear of the store trying to take in as much of the layout as possible. He noticed the back door was locked tight with a pad lock and all of the windows were small and rectangular, about eight feet off the floor anyone would be hard pressed to see in or out.

He took a single twenty-four ounce can of beer from the cooler and started back towards the front. He walked to the counter and set the beer down.

"That'll be all for ya?" The old man behind the counter asked.

"Pack of cigarettes, shorts." Michael said flatly as studied everything behind the counter.

"I.D." The old man said. Michael didn't respond.

"I.D., son." The old man repeated.

"What?" Michael said with a slight annoyance.

"I.D. I'll need to see your I.D., damn it" The old man was becoming angry.

Michael took his wallet out and showed the old man his driver's license. The man looked at it for a second and then proceeded to ring everything up. Michael paid and then left the store.

"I can wait till tonight and that old man will be gone, I can knock this place off and that will be that." Michael said to himself as he walked back to his car.

He opened the door of the old red Monte Carlo and cracked the beer open and took a good, long drink. He took a look around trying to memorize anything that he thought might be helpful.

He got into the car and took off along the route that he thought he might take later that night. He felt a little uneasy about the situation but the more he thought about it the better he felt.

He was positive that he was going to do it but he knew that he was going to need some help. He went over a list of people in his head that he thought could be talked into such a stupid thing to do and only one name came to mind, Jimmy Dent.

Jimmy was an old friend of Michael's, they went to high school together and when Michael moved to the city Jimmy followed soon after. Yes Jimmy would be the perfect choice. Michael had always been able to talk him into anything. Now it was only a matter of finding him.

Michael made his way over to Jimmy's apartment. He got out of his car and stood on the sidewalk looking the building over thinking how much of a dump it was, but the truth was that it wasn't any worse than the building he lived in.

Michael took a cigarette from his jacket pocket and lit it and then walked into the building and up to the third floor.

Michael stopped at 3b and rapped on the door, there was no answer. He hadn't seen Jimmy in two or three weeks and didn't know if he still had a job or not. Michael knew the secret combination to the door so he pushed against it in the middle and it came right open.

Michael walked inside and took a look around. There were empty beer cans strewn across the coffee table, dirty clothes in the floor and the smell of rotting food sitting out in the kitchen. Michael scanned the room briefly for an ashtray and then thought that a few ashes in the floor wouldn't make a difference in this place so he just dumped his ashes right on the carpet.

Michael walked over to Jimmy's bedroom and looked inside. He saw an empty, unmade bed and debris similar to what was in the living room. He then turned and walked down to the second bedroom and looked inside. He saw Jimmy's brother, Jake fast asleep in his bed. Michael walked into the bedroom, which was somewhat neater than the rest of the apartment and stood at Jake's bedside and watched him for a second thinking how easy it would be to rob them blind while he slept. Michael couldn't bring himself to rob his friends, as they say there lies an honor among thieves, besides there wasn't anything of value in the apartment to bother with.

"Wake up!" Michael shouted causing little reaction from Jake.

"C'mon, I could steal your bed out from under you and you'd never know it." Michael said as he shook Jake.

"What the hell do you want?" Jake asked as he slowly came to life and covered his face with his pillow.

"C'mon, where's your brother? It's important." Michael asked while pulling the pillow away from Jake's face.

"I don't know, or care." Jake said through a growing aggravation.

"Is he at work?" Michael asked as he dropped his cigarette in an almost empty beer can that sat on a table next to the bed. Jake gave a laugh as if it were absurd for anyone to think Jimmy was at a job.

"Naw, he ain't had a job in almost two weeks. I don't know where he is. Why?" Jake asked as he sat up in his bed, looking very much as if he were suffering from a hang over.

"I need his help with something." Michael replied.

"What is it?" Jake asked as he rubbed his head.

49

L.B. Kelly

"Just something. C'mon, your gonna help me find him."
Michael said as he pilfered through a pile of clothes in a
chair near the bed. Michael threw a pair of pants and a shirt
at Jake, hitting him in the face.

"Hurry up, I'll be downstairs in the car." Michael said as he
left the apartment.

* * *

"Pull over up here." Jake said pointing at a gas station.

"You think he's here?" Michael asked.

"No, But they got coffee." Jake said as Michael rolled his
eyes. Michael pulled the car into the parking lot of the small
convenience store.

"Tighten up, Jake. I ain't got all day." Michael said as Jake
got out of the car.

Michael sat anxiously there in the car wanting to find Jimmy
so he could get everything planned out. He looked around
the parking lot and spotted a large man walking towards his
car. It was the dealer.

"Shit." Michael spat out to himself as he looked around
instinctively for a way out. But there would be no way out,
he had been seen and it was unavoidable.

"Ain't seen you around lately, you're not trying to duck me
are you?" The dealer asked while knowing the answer he
would hear.

"Naw, Trey. I've been busy. You know, trying to make
it." Michael said being visibly nervous while rolling his
window down.

"Man, cut it. What you got on my weed, Michael?" Trey said getting right to the point.

"I've gotten rid of almost all of it." Michael said trying to reassure Trey.

"Well give me my money." Trey said flatly.

"You know I ain't got it with me." Michael said.

"Let's go get it, then." Trey said as he started to walk towards his car.

"Trey, I'll bring it by to you tonight, I promise. I just got something I really need to do right now." Michael said hoping he could get out of the situation.

"Michael, I hope for your sake that you're not lying. Because you're messing with my money and I got people I gotta pay too. You already owe me money, so I know you're not stupid enough to try to screw me over, at least you better hope you're not. Listen to me close, if I don't see you with my money by midnight, I'm coming to find you and you will pay one way or another." Trey calmly explained everything to Michael as he pulled his thick flannel shirt back to reveal a thirty-eight-caliber pistol stuck in the waistband of his jeans.

No other words were said. The two shared a silence for a moment and Trey walked away feeling confident that he had gotten his point across.

Michael took in a deep breath feeling a reinforced motivation to find Jimmy and get a plan mapped out because he knew that Trey meant what he said.

Jake got back into the car and settled into the seat with a cup of coffee in his hand.

"Who was that?" Jake asked. Michael said nothing; he just cranked the car and took off.

"I think I know where Jimmy might be. Take a Left at the next light." Jake continued as he took a cautious sip from his hot coffee.

Jake gave direction through the city until they reached the outskirts and arrived at Jimmy's girlfriend's place. It was an old, well-lived in house trailer that was a top of the line mobile home in its day, but was now showing its age.

Michael got out of the car and looked around the trailer park and felt infected by its filth. There were bags of garbage torn open and strewn about in the yard. A couple of houses down sat a burnt out trailer; its smell made his stomach turn.

"I know my place is messy but damn!" Michael said to Jake who was getting out of the car with his coffee still in hand.

Jake walked up the front steps and onto a small stoop that was in front of the door. Michael followed after and noticed that there were few stable spots on the steps so he stepped with care.

Jake knocked on the door and it was answered a second later by a young, blonde haired girl with a Kool-Aid ring around her mouth, she couldn't have been any older that four or five.

"Hey Becky, Is Jimmy here?" Jake asked the little girl.

"Mommy!" Becky yelled as she ran through the house.

Jake walked into the house followed by Michael who noticed that the inside of the house wasn't a bit cleaner than the outside. There was so much dirt and sand in the carpet that it just sat on top and would get kicked up as it was walked upon. There were dirty dishes in the floor of the living room and holes punched in various spots of the walls.

Just then an unattractively thin woman who appeared to be a bit older than both Michael and Jimmy emerged from a dark bedroom. She had dark circles under her eyes and stringy, unwashed hair. She was obviously a slave to some sort of chemical substance.

"Jake?" The woman said as she rubbed her sleepy face.

"Jimmy, your brother's here!" The woman yelled as she went into the bathroom.

Michael could hear a rustling in the bedroom and then a few minutes later a shirtless Jimmy spilled from the room and stopped to see who was calling on him so early in the afternoon.

Jimmy's already dim expression dropped further when he saw his brother being accompanied by Michael. He knew that Michael had something up his sleeve because he never showed up unless he needed something.

"What time is it?" Jimmy asked as he continued down the narrow hallway into the living room.

"Twelve-thirty." Jake replied.

"What's up, Michael?" Jimmy said as he shook Michael's hand as he always did.

"I need your help with something." Michael said as Jimmy looked around for a cigarette.

"I'm shocked." Jimmy said with thick sarcasm.

"Look, seriously we need to go somewhere and talk." Michael said as he gestured towards the door.

"Breakfast." Jimmy said after thinking for a second.

After finding his shirt and shoes Jimmy walked outside past Becky, who had made her way back into the living room, Michael and Jake followed directly.

* * *

Michael sat across from Jimmy and Jake in a small booth at the local diner. His stomach began to churn as he watched Jimmy inhale his meal of runny, fried eggs, half-raw bacon and soupy grits.

Michael took a drink of his black coffee and a drag from his cigarette as he prepared to explain his plan.

"So, what's up, what do you need help with?" Jimmy asked through a mouth full of food. Michael paused for a moment and then began to speak.

"I need some money in the worst way." Michael started.

"Well I sure as hell don't have any. I barely have enough to pay for this meal, so don't ask me." Jimmy said, cutting him off.

"Don't worry, I've got something better in mind." Michael said as he leaned in closer.

"What?" Jimmy asked as he put his fork down and lit a cigarette and sat back to listen to what bright idea Michael had cooked up this time. Michael looked around to make sure no one else was listening. He then lowered his voice and started again.

"You know that liquor store on the corner of Main and Locke?" Michael asked.

"Oh no, you're crazy if you think I'm helping you rob a store. That's all I need, to get my ass shot off over a couple hundred dollars." Jimmy said firmly.

"Yeah, you're gonna help me and so is Jake." Michael said, as he looked Jimmy deep in the eye.

Jake sat there stunned trying to figure out whether or not Michael was actually serious. Jimmy knew he was serious and that there would be little he could do to get out of it if Michael had his mind set on doing it, which he seemed to have.

"Look, it's too easy. I went in there this morning and looked around and I don't think it would be any problem. We go in there, stick a gun in their face, tell them to empty the register and we're out of there before they know what hit 'em." Michael made it all sound too easy as he explained it.

"Well what's gonna keep them from sticking a gun in your face?" Jimmy asked, presenting a possibility to Michael that he hadn't really thought of.

"Yeah, what's gonna happen if we go in there and one of us gets killed?" Jake added.

"That's not gonna happen. We get in and out; don't give them time to react. Look it's Friday, we wait until just before they close. I figure there will be at least eight hundred or a thousand dollars there. Jake can dial my cell number in his phone and go in first. If there's no one in the store he hits send and we come in. We get paid and nobody gets hurt, it's as simple as that." Michael had it all figured out.

"A grand's not gonna go very far after it's split three ways. Even if it's that much." Jimmy said while curiously wondering what would be in it for him and his brother.

"Well that's where the favor comes in." Michael said still feeling confident that he could talk Jimmy into it. As long as he could talk Jimmy into he knew that Jake would follow suit.

"Oh, that's where?" Jimmy asked.

"Yeah, look I got about fifty dollars worth of weed at my place. If you guys will take a smaller cut, I'll throw it in." Michael bargained.

"How small?" Jimmy asked.

"Quarter." Michael said.

Jimmy shook his head. He could feel himself giving in. He looked over at Jake who had a nervous look in his eyes that was almost begging Jimmy not to say yes. Jimmy then looked at Michael and sighed softly and against his better judgment gave in.

"Okay." Jimmy said.

* * *

All night long it seemed to Michael as though eleven-thirty would never come and when it finally did he could feel the excitement grow inside him and he loved it.

The only time the three had parted ways all day was when Jimmy left to break into his girlfriend's dad's house to steal a gun. They spent the rest of the day in Michael's apartment smoking weed and going over their plan, mapping out the route that they would take.

Jake desperately wanted to back out but he knew that if he did he would never hear the end of it, besides he wanted to partake in the reward so that's what he thought about whenever he felt the ensuing guilt tugging at his conscience. Jimmy felt no guilt whatsoever about the idea. He simply saw it as a slightly inconvenient way to get by and Michael of course didn't know the meaning of the word guilt and didn't care about anything but getting the money that he needed.

Finally the time came. Michael sat up from the couch where he had been lying and picked the gun up and checked it once again to make sure it was loaded. He then looked at Jimmy with a certain determination, but all the while perfectly relaxed. Jimmy took in a deep breath and then looked at Jake, who was more nervous at this time than he had been at any other and Jimmy was sensing it. He gave a second thought to Jake's involvement, but dismissed the thought and began to look at it as a sort of right of passage for him.

"Let's go." Michael said all at once as he got up from the couch and headed for the door.

* * *

Jake started to feel nauseous as they neared the liquor store. He stared out the window at the street- lights and he couldn't believe what he was about to do. Sure he smoked weed and had stolen a couple cartons of cigarettes but never anything on the level of armed robbery.

Michael stopped the car at the red light at the intersection. There was a dead silence in the car. Everyone was feeling the tension and Jake just wanted to get it over with.

The light turned green and Michael drove calmly around the corner and parked close to where he had earlier that day and cut the engine.

"Alright Jake, dial the number." Michael said as he looked around for anything that might present a problem. Jake keyed the numbers into his phone nervously.

"If there's nobody in the store hit send. When my phone rings me and Jimmy will come in, get the cash and then we haul ass." Michael continued looking around as he instructed Jake.

"Okay." Jake said anxiously.

"It's okay, it'll be over before you know it." Jimmy said to him with solace. Jake gave him a short nod and then stepped out of the car.

Jake walked down the sidewalk to the store. As he walked he thought of every reason why he should just keep walking past the store, but he knew if he did that Michael would just find him and make him do it any way.

Jake made it to the door and stopped. He took a deep breath and pushed the door open and entered the store with forced steps. He walked past the counter looking around the store apprehensively.

"Can I help you?" The man behind the counter asked.

"Just looking around." Jake stuttered. He scanned the store and saw no one. The man studied Jake suspiciously as he observed the way he was inspecting the store.

"You got an I.D., son?" The man asked.

"Yeah, I got it, one second." Jake said as he searched the surface of his phone inside his pocket for the call button.

"Well bring it here." The man said sternly.

Jake was becoming extremely flustered at this point. He finally found the button and pressed it. Jake's sick feeling was now almost overwhelming and sweat was starting to form across his face.

"What in the hell are you up to? Are you on something?" The man asked becoming highly irritated.

Jake opened his mouth to stall the man a while longer and just as he did the door burst open and Jimmy entered the store followed by Michael who was holding the gun, which he already had out and ready for the intimidation.

Without saying a word Michael raised the gun and fired two shots at the camera above the clerk, destroying it with the second shot. The man sprang to attention and had a confused look of fear upon his face.

"Watch the door!" Michael shouted to Jake as he switched places with him.

Jimmy proceeded further into the store and began to select the most expensive bottles of whiskey and liquor he could find. He froze for a second as he found himself starring at the video camera in the back of the store. The camera's sight didn't extend to the front of the store so Michael and Jake hadn't been detected by it, but he knew that he had. He was bothered by this realization but there was little that he could do about it at this point so he continued to pick through the bottles.

Back up front Michael had his gun drawn down on the man and he realized that it was the same old man from earlier that morning, but he wasn't convinced that the old man recognized him.

"Don't look at my face! Empty the register into one of those bags!" Michael ordered the old man after a short pause.

The old man opened the register and began to remove the money with shaky hands. Michael took a quick look to the door and at Jake who looked to be doing all that he could to keep from crying. Michael wanted to laugh at his inability to handle the situation.

Michael looked back to the old man who was now looking him in the eye. A look of fruition poured over the old man's face as he placed Michael's scowl.

"You were in here this morning, I looked at your I.D." The old man said while trying to think of his name. Michael stood there in a daze with the gun pointed at the old man and he didn't know what to do. He was sure that the old man would have been gone by now, but the fact remained that the old man was there and he remembered his face and now he had to decide what to do.

"Rowan." The old man said as he recalled the name. The old man knew instantly that he had made a mistake. Michael automatically pulled the trigger three times hitting the old man in the chest and time seemed to freeze for a moment. The action was instant, almost instinctive and Michael knew before the bullets hit the man, as they were leaving the gun even, that he had made the biggest mistake of his life.

After hearing the shots Jimmy dropped the bottles he was holding and Jake turned a pale white and started hyperventilating. Michael just stood, holding the gun up as he looked into the old man's frightened eyes as he fell to the floor clutching his chest.

"What the hell are you doing? Are you crazy?" Jimmy yelled as he ran up to the counter and looked over to see the old man who was lying on the floor with his eyes wide open and no breath in his body.

"He knew who I was. I'm not going to jail." Michael said as he ran around the counter.

He stood over the old man collecting the rest of the money out of the cash drawer. He threw the money in the bag and then moved to the door, grabbing a bottle of bourbon on the way out.

Michael ran out the door past Jake who was inanimate with shock.

"Come on!" Jimmy said to Jake as he grabbed him by his jacket and pulled him along as he also exited the store.

Michael cranked the car and as he did he thought to himself that he should have left it running, but that was a small detail that was no longer relevant at this point. Now he had to find a way out of the newer, bigger mess that he found himself in. He looked around to see if they had been seen. Seeing no one, Michael put the car in drive and drove away as if nothing had happened.

"Shit! What are we gonna do, Michael?" Jimmy asked as he contemplated the possible penalties for what they had done. He couldn't believe it; he had ended up just like his father said, just like these losers on the news that didn't think things through.

"It's alright." Jimmy said to Jake as he noticed that his hyperventilating had increased.

"Why? Why did you do that?" Jake asked with a shaky voice.

L.B. Kelly

"Shut up, I'm trying to think." Michael said as he kept his eyes sharply focused on the road.

"We weren't seen and the old man's not talking and I popped the camera." Michael continued.

"I got caught by the camera in the back." Jimmy said, reminding Michael of it. "Besides Jake got caught by the one in front when he went in to start with. What were you planning to do about that?" Jimmy continued. Jake heard that and knew it was true. He had a feeling overcome him as though he had been hung out to dry.

"Whatever, man. We are all in this together, now let's get out together and quick." Michael said as he drove. He looked at the fuel gauge and felt discouragement when he saw the needle was sitting on the empty mark. There was a short silence as every one tried to think of what to do.

"Let's head over to the freight yard and jump a train." Jimmy suggested.

"Yeah and get caught trying to sneak in." Michael retorted.

"No, it'll be fine. I know all about it. I've done it before." Jimmy said reassuringly.

Michael thought for a second and then decided that it made sense. Surely the sheriff's department would be searching the highways after the body is discovered. It would be a straight shot, if Jimmy knows what he talking about.

"Alright, let's go." Michael said as he steered the car towards the freight yard.

* * *

Michael drove down the street adjacent to the freight yard in downtown. He looked the yard over quickly which seemed to be very quiet, as did the rest of the city. He then pulled the car into the parking lot of a small fast food place that was closed for the night and cut the engine.

"I guess we'll cut through there and try to find a way through the fence." Jimmy said after a moment.

"Well let's do it." Michael said as he looked around. He picked the gun up from the seat and stuck it down the front of his pants and then grabbed the bag of cash and the bottle of whiskey and got out of the car, leaving the keys in the ignition.

Jimmy and Jake got out of the car and followed Michael who was already making his way to the small, wooded area that separated the restaurant from the train yard.

They moved through the woods with caution, communicating with whispers in the bright moonlight. After reaching the edge of the yard Michael and Jimmy surveyed the opposing fence and considered their options.

The fence was easily ten feet tall and apparently quite sturdy. They looked up and down for an inconspicuously silent method of entry. Jimmy walked down the fence and found a few broken links in it about two feet off the ground. It was just enough to allow the fence to be pulled up enough to crawl under.

Jimmy reached down and picked up a pine- cone and threw it at Michael, hitting him in the back. Michael's attention turned to Jimmy, who motioned for him to come. He then followed the fence to Jimmy and took a look at the find.

They took another look at the train yard for any movement. Upon further investigation they spotted a guard walking the tracks inside the fence swirling his flashlight on the ground in random patterns as if to alleviate boredom. They watched steadfastly as the obese guard disappeared behind a line of cars that looked as if they were being prepared for departure.

As soon as the guard was gone Michael kneeled down on one knee and pulled the fence up and Jimmy quickly crawled under. Michael then looked back at Jake who was still in a state of shock and motioned for him to come, but he remained still.

Michael was becoming frustrated with Jake. He got up and walked back down to where he had left him and grabbed him by his jacket and slung him towards the opening. Jake fell to the ground about half way there and Michael picked him up and slung him again.

"Don't jerk me around, Jake. Now is not the time. Now get your ass under that fence." Michael said calmly to Jake who was lying on the ground at the opening trying to hold back tears.

Jake didn't say anything, he only moved under the fence to join Jimmy on the other side. Michael threw the bag and the whiskey under the fence and joined them as well and they proceeded to the line of cars that they had been watching. After reaching the train they walked along side it looking for an open car to climb into.

Finally they came to a car with the door cracked open slightly. Michael looked around the yard then he and Jimmy pushed the door open. Jimmy looked inside and could make out shapes of some sort of fittings inside the dark car.

"I think it's okay. Boost me in." Jimmy said as he looked back at Michael.

Michael pushed Jimmy up into the car and then grabbed Jake once again by the jacket and lifted him into the car while Jimmy pulled him in by his arms. Michael jumped slightly and hoisted himself into the car and then stood up and looked around.

Michael shut the door, leaving it cracked slightly. He then moved to the far side of the car and took a seat on one of the pipe- fittings and cracked open the bottle of whiskey and turned it up. A shiver shook his body as he swallowed the sour mash down. Michael wiped his mouth on the sleeve of his jacket as he held the bottle out to Jimmy who shook his head in refusal.

"It's good. It'll warm you up, you sure?" Michael asked.

"No, I'm sure." Jimmy said calmly.

"Jake?" Michael said with a smile holding the bottle out to him. Jake didn't respond, he just sat in the same spot against the wall staring aimlessly.

Jimmy watched Michael as he taunted Jake and he couldn't figure out why he wasn't more concerned with what he had done. Michael wasn't showing the slightest bit of remorse for ending the old man's life. He was also showing little interest in where he was going or what he was gonna do once he got there. Jimmy kept telling himself over and over, "You dumb ass! I told you! Stay away from him!" Jimmy always would breath a sigh of relief whenever he would make it to the end of one of Michael's big ideas, However there appeared to be no relief in sight this time and now he had ruined his little brother's life along with his own.

Michael set the bottle down on the floor of the car and picked the bag up and pulled the money out and began to count it.

"How much?" Jimmy asked.

"Six fifty." Michael replied as his shoulders dropped in disappointment. Jimmy shook his head and let out a sharp breath.

"You killed that man over six hundred dollars?" Jake said flatly, breaking his silence as if all the money in the world could have made a difference. "You bastard." Jake continued.

Michael cut his eyes to Jake as he prepared to move to retaliate with physical reinforcement as well as verbal, just as he did they were all alerted by a movement at the door of the car.

Michael sprang to attention, pulled the gun from his waistband and stepped back into the shadows and Jimmy and Jake both disappeared into the dark corner just to the left of the door.

A skinny, dirty blonde haired boy pushed the door open. He looked to be no older than Seventeen or Eighteen. The boy climbed inside the car and immediately pushed the door shut, leaving a small crack to see through. Without even looking around, the boy crouched down and peered out the door as if to see if he was being chased. Michael thought to himself that would be all he needed some idiot punk to lead a security guard to him.

The hyperventilating boy seemed to relax a bit. He stood up and began to turn around and as he did Michael raised the gun to meet him when he turned around. The boy jumped when he found the gun's barrel pointed at his face.

"This car's full." Michael said as he held the gun firm. He could tell that the boy wanted to say something, ask who Michael was, ask why he was holding a gun on him or something, but he didn't say anything he just stood there.

"I said this car's full. Get out now." Michael said as he moved closer to the boy.

Jake made a small movement from the corner and the boy cut his eyes towards the sound. Michael was growing tired of the boy quickly. He then cocked the gun and pressed it against his head.

"Get out now or die. I will kill you!" Michael said sharply.

Michael thought to himself "I've killed somebody already, I'll kill this kid too. Who's gonna miss a runaway?" He was a second away from pulling the trigger when he heard some one approaching the car. It was the obese guard that they had eluded earlier.

Michael held still, watching the guard. He concluded that the guard had been chasing the boy and had lost him. Michael shot a glance at the boy and then pressed the gun harder against his head as if to tell him not to say or do anything. After looking around for a minute the guard lost interest and walked away. Michael stared the boy in the eye for a minute trying to decide what to do about him. He thought it unwise to draw the guard back to the car with a gunshot.

"When is this damned train gonna move?" Michael yelled out loud as he removed the gun from the boy's head. Michael was now becoming anxious and was beginning to question the train hopping idea.

Michael glared at Jimmy and was becoming angry at the fact that he had gone along with the idea. The way Michael saw it they were wasting time hanging around on a train like some kind of damned hobo.

"This is your fault, Jimmy." Michael said as he flew past the boy.

L.B. Kelly

"Lets go hop the train, I know all about it. Hell, I could have been half way to Jackson by now!" Michael continued as he pinned Jimmy to the floor by his throat. Michael then cocked the gun and pointed it at Jimmy's head.

"I ought to pop you right now, just like I did that old man." Michael said, looking into Jimmy's confused eyes as Jake looked on in disbelief. Jimmy could tell that the reality of the situation was starting to get to Michael and he was starting to come apart. Then just as if by cue the vibrating in the floor of the car grew more intense and the train jerked into motion. Michael then relaxed a bit and rose to his feet.

"See, I told you." Jimmy said flatly.

"What are we going to do about him?" Jake asked about the boy as the thick situation began to lighten. Michael looked at Jake as if his toleration of him began to weaken.

"I don't know." Michael replied. " Jake, open the door so I can see out." Michael continued as he sat back down.

Jake reluctantly got up and opened the door and then sat back down. His mind was flooded with so many thoughts. He couldn't get the frightened man's face out of his head. He kept wondering about the man's family, was he married? Did he have any children, or grandchildren? He didn't know how he was ever going to be able to live with himself or even face his own family knowing what he helped to do.

Jake could hear Michael talking to the boy, but was tuning him out for the most part. His mind was wandering, he was thinking of turning himself into the police when he got off the train. The only thing holding him back, of course was the fear of prison and knowing that he will send his brother to prison as well, but they had made their bed and now they had to lie in it. He was still in shock over the whole thing.

"I can't believe you killed that guy." Jake said as he stared into the darkness in the other side of the car.

"You better shut your dumb-ass brother up, Jimmy. I gotta know that he's gonna keep his mouth shut once we get off this train or else something bad might happen to him." Michael said. He was really becoming concerned that he wouldn't be able to trust Jake to keep silent. Jimmy moved closer to his brother and tried to comfort him.

The next hour or two was quiet; everybody just stared at each other as the train rumbled down the tracks. Jake had replayed the scene from the liquor store in his head over and over until he couldn't stand it any more. He finally made his decision, he was turning himself in whether Michael and his brother like it or not.

Michael began to question the boy again, trying to rattle him. The boy had given the impression that he wasn't particularly afraid of Michael, just cautious of him and that angered Michael a little as well as intriguing him somewhat.

Suddenly Jake began to feel nauseous from the unsettling experience. He began to sweat and shake a little. He then brought himself to his hands and knees and threw up on the floor.

"Aww Jake, You nasty bastard!" Michael yelled through laughter.

"It's alright." Jimmy said as he rubbed Jake's back.

"I can't get that guy's face out of my head. Why did you have to kill him, Michael?" Jake said as he leaned back on his knees.

"Shut up, Jake. Just forget about it!" Michael said as he poised to get up.

"I can't. Maybe you can, but I can't. You said you were just gonna rob the place and not hurt anybody." Jake said as he began to cry.

"It's alright, Jimmy. It's gonna be alright." Jimmy said trying to comfort him further.

"No it's not. I'm gonna turn myself in. Michael, I'm sorry but I can't handle it." Jake said as he rocked back and forth soothingly. Michael was seeing red; he was enraged. There was no way he was going to let Jake send him to prison just because he had a guilty conscience.

"I'm sorry too." Michael said calmly as he got up from his seat and put the gun to Jake's head and then pulled the trigger.

"You son of a bitch!" Jimmy yelled as he sprang up, tackling Michael to the floor.

Jimmy and Michael struggled over the gun; firing off several wild shots until Jimmy's body went limp on top of him after the last one.

Michael pushed Jimmy off of him and he saw the boy jumping out of the door. Michael raised the gun and fired a couple of shots at him but missed. He locked eyes with the boy for a second before he vanished from the car and shared with him a feeling of incompleteness.

Michael got up from the floor and ran to the door and looked out. He saw the boy tumbling in the loose gravel along side the tracks as he disappeared in the distance.

Michael sighed deeply and then looked back at Jimmy who was lying on the floor writhing in pain. He walked over to him and loomed over him with a neurotic gleam in his eyes.

Jimmy had a look of realization mixed with despair upon his face, as he looked Michael in the eye for the last time. Michael aligned the barrel of the gun with Jimmy's face and then squeezed the trigger, releasing Jimmy from his pain.

Michael had never felt such disdain for anyone as he felt for himself at that moment. He walked back over to the door and gazed out at the moon as he felt his heart and soul transform from that of a petty hoodlum's into that of a full blown thief and murderer's. He couldn't believe that his life had come to this. No matter how he tried he couldn't quite put his finger on when, or what particular event sent his existence into a downward spiral. One that would eventually lead him to dispatch the closest thing he had ever had to a true friend and commit unforgivable acts towards people that he didn't even know.

Michael looked back at the bodies of Jimmy and Jake and then down at the gun in his hand. He then began to wipe his fingerprints from the gun with his shirttail. He walked over to Jake and picked his right hand up and placed the gun in it, carefully shielding it from further prints with the continued use of his shirt.

He wrapped Jake's stiffening fingers around the trigger and fired another bullet into Jimmy's body. He then placed Jake's arm on the floor as though it may have come to rest there after shooting himself, as it may appear to whom ever discovers the bodies.

Michael sat patiently and waited as the train entered another city in the early hours of the morning. The train let out a bellow of its horn as it neared a crossing. He once again moved to the door and worked up his nerve and with one last look back to the carnage he had left in his wake he leapt from the door and rolled to rest on the edge of the tracks.

He stood up and looked around the new city in the slowly increasing morning light. He had always felt alone but never with such solitude. He then looked up at the cloudy sky and wondered how his life would be from now on.

Chapter Three

Carrie Anderson woke up early on the morning of October 17, the second anniversary of her father's death. She thought of him every day and most days around six in the evening she subconsciously expected him to come in after a day of hard work and tell her about it. She could still smell his cigarette smoke in the house and hear his laughter after a heart felt joke. She missed him badly, aside from her brother he was all that she had. Her mother died after giving birth to her and she had no other family to speak of.

Carrie lay in her bed and watched the sun come up. She paid particular attention to the sunrise that morning as if she were using it as a backdrop for her dreams, dreams that she dare not speak out loud to anyone, not even her brother.

Carrie's brother, David, had been raising her for the past two years and was hell bent on sending her to college. He was always on her to keep her grades up and was very protective of her when it came to guys asking her out, as any brother should be. However, Carrie was of the opinion that he was a little too overbearing at times, especially when it came to the latter.

L.B. Kelly

Carrie had her own dreams mapped out and the fact that they changed from week to week didn't matter to her. All that mattered was that her life was her life and she wasn't sure that her plans included college, if they did, fine and if they didn't that would be fine too.

Carrie sat up in her bed, dreading going to school. She did well, making excellent grades and even greater impressions upon her teachers and peers, but lately she found herself uninterested in the subjects and most of the people.

Carrie had a few close friends. Her closest friend was Lisa Carter. Lisa was the complete opposite of Carrie, she drank and smoked and was quite promiscuous. Carrie was no saint but her escapades were far less exorbitant in comparison. Lisa's yearning for David first fueled their friendship, but it became genuine after the crush turned tame. For the past year and a half they were almost inseparable.

"You up?" David yelled through the door, making Carrie jump slightly.

"Yeah, I'm up." Carrie replied.

"Well Let's go, we're running late." David said as he continued down the hall.

"It's Friday, just make it through today." Carrie said to herself as motivation.

Carrie sighed deeply and got up from the bed and completed her normal routine. She made her way into the kitchen where David was sitting at the table, drinking a cup of coffee.

David was twenty-five years old, but he was wise beyond those years. He had been working in his father's auto repair shop ever since he was old enough to know the difference between a ratchet and a screwdriver. At first it was to spend

74

time with his father and learn something, but eventually it evolved into necessity because of the increasing business and his father's dwindling health.

"You don't have to do that this morning." David said to Carrie as she took down a skillet from the cabinet to make breakfast.

"Why? Today is no different from any other day." Carrie said. David paused for a moment, not knowing quite what to say.

"Yeah, but we're running late and you need to get ready." David continued.

"I am ready. Do I look that bad?" Carrie asked.

"Of course not, you look great as always. Remember you got the looks and the brains, I'm still trying to figure out what I got." David said with a slight chuckle.

"You got dad's nonchalant way of sparing someone's feelings. I'm fine, I promise. It's only six- thirty, let me make you something to eat." Carrie said as she continued to make breakfast.

"I know. I'm sorry, I just know how hard it was on you last year and I just want you to take it easy. Maybe you ought to stay home today." David suggested.

"It's hard every day. Dad is gone and we're just going to have to learn to deal with it, both of us. Just because you never talk about it doesn't mean that you hide it all that well and I would much rather sit through school than to sit here doing nothing all day." Carrie said as she took a carton of eggs from the refrigerator.

"Yeah, you're right. Besides, you need to keep those grades up anyway." David said, changing the subject from his inability to cope with the loss of his father.

Carrie cooked the breakfast of scrambled eggs, toast and bacon in silence. She then sat down at the table with David and ate in continued silence. As Carrie prepared to once again bring up the subject of David's suppressed feelings there was a knock at the door. Carrie's expression dropped a bit.

"That's Ran. He's early." David said as woofed down the rest of his breakfast.

"I wonder why." Carrie said as she got up and began to clear the table. Ran worked for David at the shop and was an excellent mechanic for being only nineteen years old and he was madly in love with Carrie.

"Hey David. What's going on?" Ran greeted as he walked into the kitchen, after letting himself in.

"Not much." David replied as he got up and walked down the hall and into the bathroom to brush his teeth again.

"Hey Carrie." Ran said as he moved to the counter beside her and grabbed a left over piece of bacon from the plate just before Carrie took it away.

"Hey Randy." Carrie said.

"You coming out to Eddie's tonight with Lisa?" Ran asked eagerly.

"I don't know. I doubt it." Carrie replied as she kept with what she was doing.

"Oh, come on. It'll be fun, everybody's gonna be there." Ran continued, trying to convince her to go. As Carrie began to consider it she heard the front door open and close and Lisa appeared from around the corner.

"Lisa, tell Carrie she needs to go to the party tonight. You are going, right?" Ran said, hoping he could count on Lisa to get Carrie to go.

"You know I'm going and so are you, Carrie." Lisa said as she sat down at the table.

"Going where?" David asked as he came back into the kitchen.

"Hey, David." Lisa said, still fighting twinges of the former crush for David.

"Hey, Lisa. Going where?" David said without missing a beat.

"Just a little get together. No big deal." Carrie said as she finished rinsing off the used dishes.

"I don't know, maybe you ought to go. Get out of the house for once." David said as he thought it over.

"I'll think about it." Carrie said as she gave a look to Lisa as if to say "Thanks a lot, now I guess I have to go". Lisa just returned a wry smile for the fact that she knew that Carrie thought that David would have said no or discouraged her in going.

"Well come on, Ran. We need to hustle." David said as he went over to Carrie and kissed her forehead. "Be careful, I love you." David continued as he and Ran left the house. Ran sent one last, toothy smile to Carrie as he left the kitchen. After hearing the front door close Lisa got up and walked over to Carrie.

"He is so into you, why don't you give him half a chance?" Lisa asked as if she knew what she would do if she were in Carrie's shoes.

"I don't know He's just too cocky. Would you go out with him?" Carrie asked before she realized with whom she was talking.

"I'd do more than go out with him." Lisa said with a devilish grin.

"I should have known better. Come on, we're gonna be late." Carrie said as she made her way into the living room to gather her books and purse.

* * *

David gripped the steering wheel of his 1970 Dodge Charger tightly as he negotiated perfectly every slight curve and twist that the road had to offer. The car was his pride and joy, he loved driving it and he loved letting it drive him. At times it seemed to David as though the world stood still while he opened up the dual four-barrel carbs that sat atop the massive 442 engine. It was cheap therapy as far as he was concerned. Any time something troubled him all he had to do was get into the car and fire the engine up and let the rumble of the exhaust sooth his worried mind.

David's father found the car nearly ruined and bought it for him before he was even old enough to get a driver's license. They spent months building the engine, taking time with every small detail. They spent many nights painstakingly renewing every detail of the body and replaced every button and every stitch inside the car. They were times David would never forget.

"How could you stand to get all those tattoos on your arms." Ran asked out of the blue.

"What do you mean?" David said as he looked down at his ink-covered arms.

"Well didn't it hurt?" Ran inquired further.

"No, you gotta be a man, son!" David playfully said.

"I was thinking about getting one." Ran said as he rubbed the tops of his legs uneasily.

"What's wrong, Ran?" David said after a slightly awkward silence.

"Nothing. Why?" Ran said as though David was way off base.

"Ran we've been working together almost two years, I've gotten to know you pretty well. Something's on your mind now spit it out." David said, stating the obvious. Ran squirmed in his seat as he began to speak.

"You know I've been trying to patch things up with my dad and well things have been going pretty good and he offered me a job down at his lumberyard as a supervisor. I'd be making more money and I'd have some benefits too." Ran explained as he stared out the passenger window.

"Well, It sounds pretty good. What did you tell him?" David asked while trying not to sound too disappointed, although he was extremely. Ran's talent and ability to learn was not easy to find and he didn't want to stand in the way of his mending fences with his father or the opportunity for him to make more money, not for such a selfish reason anyway.

"I didn't tell him anything. I wanted to talk to you first, I don't want to leave you hanging." Ran said as he looked to David.

L.B. Kelly

"You need to do what's best for you, don't worry about me. I knew when I hired you that you weren't going to work for me forever." David said with encouragement.

"I know I just feel like I'm letting you down." Ran said feeling disappointed with himself.

"Don't even worry about it, I'll probably find somebody better than you any way." David said with dry, offbeat sarcasm that only a friend would recognize.

"He said if I wanted the job I could start Monday. Is that okay with you or do you need me to wait a while?" Ran asked, as the tension died down a little.

"Whenever. I guess you're going to move out of the trailer, huh?" David said even though the truth was that it did bother him somewhat that he was going to leave so quickly. They had a shop full of cars to repair and Ran's car was one of them.

David's father had bought a mid-sized camper trailer shortly before he died. He was always talking about cutting back on work and start traveling so that he could see the country and spend time with Carrie and David, but that was on the bottom of a long list of things that never got done.

David ran water to the trailer and Ran moved into it after he and his father had a falling out over Ran quitting school to work in David's shop.

"Yeah, but I'll go ahead and pay you for next week too." Ran said, hoping it would ease the guilt that he felt.

"You don't have to do that." David said as he stared at the road.

"You Sure?" Ran asked.

"Yeah." David replied.

The remainder of the trip was spent in silence. David's mind was already busy with thoughts of the work backing up and the prospect of having to break in some one new, but the cards had been stacked against him before and he wasn't going to think about it, not then anyway.

* * *

The house was cold and void when Carrie got home from school. The whole day her mind was filled with empty thoughts of her father. She relived every worn out memory and every warm moment from her childhood. She looked forward to staying at home and locking herself away with a box of photographs and nothing else, but Lisa was intent upon dragging her out and pushing her on Ran. Carrie just wasn't into it. She liked to have fun as much as Lisa did but she wasn't willing to sacrifice her dignity for it.

Ran was a good-looking guy and any girl would proud to date him but dating him came at a price. According to Ran in his own words, any girl that dated him had to "Put out or get out" and Carrie wasn't looking for that from anyone.

She wasn't opposed to sex, but she saw it as more than just five seconds of ecstasy followed by a nap. To her it was something that began before the first button was opened or even before the first kiss was felt and lasted long after the awkward physical part was over, lingering in the eyes of her lover. It would become something that could be shared between them with a simple look, even in the presence of others. To Carrie it was more than just fun.

Carrie had been on a couple of dates with Ran. Apparently to obtain the privilege, as Ran saw it, to share with him a bed, backseat or wherever convenience may happen to lie at the time it was necessary to sit through mindless ramblings about his car or his ability to work on cars. It was enough to Carrie to make a four-hour date seem like a four-hour root canal gone bad.

Carrie looked at the clock that hung above the couch in the living room; it was three forty five. Lisa said that she would be back around seven and that gave Carrie about three hours to get David's supper cooked and get herself ready.

Carrie went into the kitchen opened the freezer and looked everything over, trying to decide what to cook when the phone rang. Carrie walked back into the living room and picked up the phone that sat on a table next to her father's chair.

"Hello?" Carrie answered.

"Hey, what are you doing?" David asked from the other end of the line.

"I just got home. I was about to cook your supper." Carrie replied.

"Don't bother. I'm going straight to Julie's after I close up." David informed Carrie.

"Okay." Carrie said slowly, felling a slight bit of jealousy. Julie was David's girlfriend of about three months with whom he had been spending more and more time with lately. On a sub conscious level Carrie was afraid of losing David to her and it was becoming harder for Carrie to hold the fear to herself.

"What is it?" David asked.

"Nothing." Carrie said after a second. David knew that something was bothering her and he was pretty sure of what it was, however the risk of opening up a new can of worms kept him from accepting Carrie's subtle invitation to delve into the subject.

"Alright. Are you going with Lisa?" David asked before the subject was mentioned.

"I guess." Carrie said dryly.

"Do you need some money?" David continued.

"No, I have a little." Carrie said.

"Okay, I've got my cell if you need me. I love you, be careful." David said.

"Okay, I love you too. Bye." Carrie said as she hung up the phone. She took a long look around the house, she felt so alone and cold. It no longer felt like a home, ever since her father died it was just a place to eat and sleep.

Carrie walked down the hallway and into her bedroom to try and figure out what she would wear later that night. She stood in the middle of her room, where she spent most of her time and took another long look around. It didn't seem quite as cold to her in there, but the emptiness followed her everywhere in the house. She then looked to her father's picture that sat upon her nightstand beside her bed. She sat down and began to think.

Tom Anderson was forty-eight years old when he died. He died of a heart attack after a month filled with stressful days and late nights at work. The night that it happened, Carrie waited and waited for her father to come home. Six o' clock had come and gone and there was no call from him as there usually was when he was working late. Carrie finally gave in to her fears and called David who was living alone in an apartment in the city at the time. She asked him to go back to the shop and check on their father. David called her back about forty-five minutes later and confirmed her fears. He had found their father slumped over the fender of a car, dead.

Carrie shifted her forlorn gaze from her father's picture to one of her mother that also sat on the nightstand. A totally unequal array of feelings poured into Carrie's heart when she saw her mother smiling back at her from the photo, feelings of guilt for not being able to know her enough to feel a loss and guilt for being the reason that she was gone. She felt this guilt despite her father's almost constant reminders that it wasn't her fault. On her every birthday and on her mother and father's wedding anniversary the guilt consumed her.

Each time that she looked into her father's eyes she saw a warm, loving parent who knew her every detail and in photographs of her mother she only saw a stranger about whom she had heard so many fond stories. David was eight years old when his mother died and he still had many vivid memories of her. He and his father would often reminisce over times that they shared and every time they did Carrie felt like such an outsider.

Carrie broke free from the painful thoughts and sighed deeply. She thought to herself that she should get up and start getting ready to go, but instead she laid her head down on her pillow and looked at her father's picture again. Her eyes became heavy and she drifted off into a peaceful sleep with thoughts of her father still busy in her mind.

* * *

Carrie was awakened by Lisa's presence in the room. She rolled over in the bed and looked at her clock, it was seven o' six.

"What are you doing?" Lisa asked as she walked into the room and discovered Carrie fast asleep.

"I was just tired." Carrie said groggily as she sat up.

"Come on, let's go. There are guys waiting!" Lisa said excitedly.

"I don't care. I'd rather sleep." Carrie said through a yawn.

"I'll ignore that, besides there's one guy in particular waiting for you." Lisa said as she opened the door of Carrie's closet and began matching up outfits.

"Lisa, please leave it alone. I'm just not into Ran, we went on a couple of dates and it just didn't work." Carrie said as she got up and went into the bathroom that connected to her room.

"You guys are just so cute together." Lisa said as she turned to look at Carrie.

"So I should go out with him just because we look good together?" Carrie asked as she prepared her toothbrush.

"That and the fact that you could wash your clothes on his stomach." Lisa said as she continued looking through the closet.

"Of course, what have I been thinking all this time?" Carrie said with heavy sarcasm as she paused her brushing. The two shared a laugh for a moment and then Lisa continued.

"Well if you don't come around soon I might just have to steal him from you." Lisa said facetiously.

"You can have him." Carrie said as she continued brushing. A fleeting desire fell over Lisa's heart and she quickly dismissed the thoughts, as she looked an outfit over.

"How about this one?" Lisa asked as she moved over to the bathroom door showing the outfit to Carrie. Carrie took the outfit and held it out and studied it, it was exactly what Carrie would have picked out herself.

"Perfect." Carrie said while sending a smile to Lisa.

"Well hurry up and change, we gotta go." Lisa said as Carrie shut the door.

* * *

Carrie and Lisa turned into Eddie's driveway about ten till eight. Eddie's parents were out of town on what they described in their own words as 'A well overdue Eddie vacation.' Eddie was a loveable, fun guy and his parents were the same way. The truth was that his dad had won a weekend stay at one of the hotel casinos over in Vicksburg and so using normal logic Eddie concluded that the right thing to do would be to throw a party. Lisa drove her Pontiac grand am past the house and into a large, open field surrounded by an infinite, dark tree line. In the middle of the field she and Carrie saw a large bon fire blazing with about eight or nine cars and trucks parked randomly around the fire. Lisa pulled the car up and parked nearby.

"I don't know about this, Lisa." Carrie said nervously as she surveyed the crowd of about twenty people who were mingling around the fire and the cars. Some of them she knew and some she had never seen before.

"I know there's a lot of people here that we don't know. Just relax and don't worry about it, it'll be fun. Besides I think we've already been spotted." Lisa said as she noticed Ran walking over with three beers in hand and a big smile on his face.

Ran walked to Carrie's side of the car and opened the door. Carrie forced a smile and got out of the car while Lisa gave one final check of her make up in the rearview mirror before getting out herself.

"Hey, Carrie. I'm glad you made it. Here." Ran said with his ever-present smile as he handed Carrie a beer.

"It's cold." Lisa said as she shivered under her very sheer topper after meeting Carrie and Ran on the other side of the car.

"Why didn't you wear a real jacket?" Carrie asked.

"And cover this body up? I don't think so." Lisa said with a comedic tone as she took the other beer from Ran. Lisa was no slouch, but she couldn't touch Carrie as far as beauty and she knew it and it ate her up inside. Lisa had to work so hard to make herself beautiful and it just came naturally for Carrie and everyone thought so.

"Come on over by the fire and warm up." Ran said as he led the way.

They darted through the crowd of people to a log that had been rolled up near the fire and sat down on it. Carrie looked around and could already feel the boredom creeping up.

She had been to these parties before, if they could truthfully be called parties and the most exciting thing that might happen would be the occasional fight or maybe someone's parents crashing the party. For the most part it was an entire night devoted to drinking, the smoking of different things, sex and passing out.

"Ooo, there's Ricky! I'll be right back." Lisa said as she got up and trotted towards him. Lisa had her eye on Ricky for a while and she felt that this night would be the perfect opportunity for her to finally snare him.

"Okay." Carrie said as she watched Lisa go, thinking that she might have set a personal record for finding a guy so quickly. Ran took Lisa's place next to Carrie.

"Here, let me get that." Ran said as he took the beer from Carrie's hands and cracked it open for her.

"Thanks." Carrie said as Ran handed the beer back to her. Carrie wasn't much of a drinker and she thought to herself then that the can of beer would probably last her the whole night.

"I told David that I was leaving today." Ran said over the music that was bellowing from one of the cars that was close by.

"What did he say?" Carrie asked even though she was almost positive of what he said.

"Ya know; he just wished me the best of luck. I mean I had to; I don't want to spend the rest of my life in a mechanic's shop. I want to make something of myself." Carrie's expression dropped as a result of Ran's remarks and he didn't even seem to notice. A year and a half earlier the job with David was the best thing that ever happened as far as Ran was concerned and now all of a sudden he was too god to do it. Things like that were what bothered Carrie so badly about Ran and she just couldn't get past it.

"You know you could do a lot worse, Ran. You should think about things before you say them." Carrie said as she got up and walked away as Ran followed directly after.

"Carrie, you know what I mean." Ran said to Carrie who was standing in the far reaches of the fire light with her back turned to the crowd.

"I know what you said." Carrie retorted with a growing anger towards Ran's indirect implication that her father never amounted to anything.

"Well I didn't mean anything by it. It's just a chance for me to make more money, that's all." Ran stammered.

"Well say that. Don't belittle what my father did and what my brother does just to try to make yourself feel better about something your daddy is pushing you into." Carrie spat at Ran with conviction. There was a brief stillness between them.

"I'm sorry. Do you forgive me?" Ran asked finally, while playfully nudging Carrie.

"Sure." Carrie said after a second, not having calmed her anger at all. She thought of something her father used to say; "You just have to overlook some people. Some people just can't help it." He would say that whenever someone's ignorance would shine through.

"Good, now let's get back in there, I need another beer." Ran said as he gulped down the last of his beer.

"How many have you had? You might need to slow down a little." Carrie asked as she started to recognize the effects of too many already.

"I don't know, four or five. Yeah, you got some catching up to do don't you?" Ran said, completely missing the point that Carrie was trying to make. He then made a beeline back into the crowd and to the first cooler he saw. Carrie just shook her head.

L.B. Kelly

"Yeah." Carrie said as she took a sip of her beer. 'You just have to overlook some people.' Carrie repeated to herself in thought.

The next couple of hours were spent talking to people Carrie really didn't know and some she really didn't want to know. Occasionally Ran and Lisa respectively would find their way back to Carrie. Lisa would fill her in on how things were going with Ricky and Ran would ramble on about how he finally finished working on his car and got it out of David's shop. He also mentioned how he felt a little guilty about leaving him high and dry as if he had been carrying David for the last two years.

At one point Carrie found herself momentarily free of Ran's smothering affection and was able to sneak away over to Jeff Tate's truck. She sat down on the tailgate beside Jeff and struck up a conversation. Jeff was one of Ran's best friends and one of the few people Carrie had known since kindergarten. From a distance Ran took notice of Jeff and Carrie's chat and of course he felt the need to break it up because in his mind Carrie was his.

"What's up, Jeff?" Ran asked as he approached the truck.

"Not a whole lot." Jeff replied.

"It's getting kind of lame around here." Ran said as he took a look around through intoxicated eyes.

"You getting ready to cut out?" Jeff asked.

"Yeah, probably before too long." Ran replied.

"Where's Lisa? I haven't seen her." Jeff asked.

"She's over there talking to Ricky. Why are you still in love with her?" Carrie asked in a teasing way. Jeff blushed slightly.

"I don't know, I'd like to talk to her but she don't seem interested." Jeff said as he stared at her.

"Well your not trying hard enough." Carrie said.

"You don't have to try very damned hard. I think as long as you got a pulse your good to go." Ran interjected with a smug laugh. Carrie looked at him, slightly disgusted but didn't say anything.

"Is that Dwayne over there with'em?" Ran asked focusing his sight harder.

"Yeah, his truck's over there. They haven't been here long." Jeff said as he pointed at Dwayne's 78' Ford pick-up. Ran stared at Dwayne sharply as he noticed how self-contented he seemed as he was talking to Ricky and Lisa. Ran then noticed Stacy, who was Dwayne's girlfriend and Ran's ex-girlfriend, was watching him as he watched them. She rolled her eyes and snuggled up to Dwayne as if to let Ran know that she still hated him.

"He's a dick, I hate him." Ran said as he leaned against Jeff's truck.

"Why, because he beat you in the quarter mile that time?" Jeff asked tauntingly of Ran. Ran just shook his head and remained silent and then drank down the rest of his current beer.

"Who wants to break something?" Eddie, the host of the party asked as he walked down the hill away from his house carrying a can of hairspray under his arm and a sack of potatoes one hand and a large odd looking device made of

PVC plastic in the other hand. The device had a four-inch chamber that was about a foot long and plugged on one end with a lantern striker screwed into the side. The chamber led to a smaller barrel that was about three feet long.

"What is that?" Carrie asked.

"A potato gun." Ran said as though everyone should know what it was.

"A potato gun." Carrie repeated. She rolled her eyes and shook her head as Ran and Jeff moved towards Eddie, as did every other guy to get their turn with the new toy.

"They actually have a potato gun." Lisa said as she sat down on the tailgate next to Carrie shaking her head as well.

Eddie twisted and bumped a potato down into the end of the barrel of the gun and bumped the gun on the ground until the potato reached the other end of the barrel. He then flipped the gun around and unscrewed the plug out of the chamber and sprayed a generous amount of hairspray into it and quickly plugged it again. Eddie gave a smile to the captivated crowd and then put the butt end of the gun on his hip and aimed up into the dark sky and twisted the lantern striker causing a boom that made everyone jump. The blast sent the potato hurling into the somber reaches of the night at an extremely high rate of speed. Every guy burst into laughter at the sight and every girl shook her head in disbelief at the fact that they're significant others were so easily amused.

As the laughter subsided every guy wanted his turn at the helm of the gun and of course Ran took his turn first. Ran took the gun and repeated the process as Eddie had done and launched another potato into the heavens causing more laughter.

"Give it up, it's my turn." Dwayne said as he reached out to take the gun.

"No, that wasn't a good one. I want to do it again." Ran said as he held the gun tight. If looks could kill Ran would have dropped dead as Dwayne glared at him. Dwayne was just as pretentious as Ran was and the animosity between them was mutual. At this point it was just a matter of time and opportunity before the ill will came to a head.

"Come on, man. Give somebody else a chance." Dwayne said as he tugged on the gun.

"Let go of it." Ran said as he jerked it away from Dwayne.

"Just let him do it again. There's enough for everybody." Eddie said, sensing the escalating tension. Ran repeated the loading and priming of the gun once again and took aim at the sky.

"Little bitch." Dwayne mumbled under his breath. Ran heard Dwayne's remark and he was in no mental condition to combat the anger. Ran's first instinct was to drop the gun and take a swing but then he thought about what he had in his hand and wondered how much damage the gun would inflict on a human body. Ran wasn't quite drunk enough to take a chance of killing anybody, not even Dwayne so he did the next best thing. Ran turned to his right and aimed the gun towards a few people who were standing in front of Dwayne's truck. They quickly cleared out of the way and a smile spread across Ran's face.

"Don't do it!" Dwayne yelled, but before he could move a muscle to stop him Ran twisted the striker. The potato slammed into the side of the truck, perfectly centered in the door leaving an impressive dent and the splattered remnants of the potato.

L.B. Kelly

"You asshole!" Dwayne yelled as he took a swing at Ran, hitting him squarely in the jaw. Everyone present took a collective gasp. Ran dropped the gun and managed to slug Dwayne in the stomach a couple of times before the two fell to the ground in a tangled heap of drunken stupidity. After a moment of entertainment from the fight Jeff and Ricky peeled Ran off of Dwayne. Dwayne then rolled around the ground, cradling his bloodied nose in his hand and making noises as if he were dying. Eddie helped Dwayne to his feet and he gained an uneasy balance.

Ran, who was steadily thrashing about broke free from Ricky and Jeff and planted another firm shot to Dwayne's face, sending him sprawling to the ground once more. Eddie pulled Dwayne up from the ground again as Ricky recaptured Ran.

"Ran, chill out! What the hell is wrong with you?" Eddie asked through choked-back anger at the situation.

"Nothing, I just get tired of little punks running their mouths." Ran said as he began to calm down.

"You're an asshole, Ran." Stacy said as she rushed to Dwayne's side for consolation.

"Maybe you ought to just take off." Eddie said to Ran somberly.

"Fine, piss on all of y'all!" Ran said as he was still trying to compose himself. Carrie just shook her head as Lisa watched on, appearing to be excited by the confrontation.

"Y'all coming?" Ran asked of Ricky and Jeff as he looked around and was becoming a little embarrassed by the ordeal.

"Yeah." Ricky said as he grabbed another beer for the road.

"Yeah, let's go." Jeff said as he started walking back to his truck. Carrie and Lisa got up from the tailgate and Jeff closed it behind them.

"Come on let's go too." Lisa whispered to Carrie.

"We might as well. Where are we going, Ran?" Carrie asked as everyone looked at them as though they had the plague.

"You and Lisa and Jeff go down to the bridge. Me and Ricky will meet y'all there in a little while." Ran said and then sent one last glare at Dwayne and Stacy before he and Ricky took off to his car.

"I'll follow y'all." Jeff said to Carrie and Lisa as he got into his truck.

"Hey, Carrie! You tell your boyfriend to watch his back, this is not over." Stacy yelled as Carrie and Lisa were getting into the car.

"Whatever, Stacy. If you think you want to start something with us go ahead. You'll be sorry." Carrie said before getting into the car. Despite the mixed feelings that she had for Ran the fact remained that she had known him for sometime and he would stand up for her and David would stand up for him as well. David had a reputation for not beating around the bush when it came to someone threatening his family or friends, whether they asked for it or not.

"He's not my boyfriend." Carrie reaffirmed to Lisa as they drove away from the field.

* * *

Lisa slowed the car down as they came to a deep curve in the road. Ahead was a large bridge that was about two and a half miles outside of the small town. There was a well-beaten path, just wide enough to accommodate a car or a truck that led away from the road to the underbelly of the bridge. Some of the area kids laid claim to it years back and would hide out under there and do what they would do. There was a kind of understanding between the kids and the county deputies that if the kids didn't bother the deputies the deputies wouldn't bother the kids, since most of the deputies hid out under there as teens there wasn't much they could say in good conscience.

Lisa turned off the road slowly, followed by Jeff. They made their way to a small clearing and parked their vehicles and got out.

"Do you have a flashlight, Jeff?" Lisa asked, a little spooked by the darkness.

"Yeah, I think so." Jeff replied as he searched behind the seat of his truck for the light.

Jeff turned the flashlight on and led the way down a smaller path to the sandy creek bank. There was a huge amount of space under the bridge and despite the low status of the creek it was rather humbling.

"Who the hell is that?" Jeff asked as they noticed a small campfire on the other side of the creek.

"I don't know. A drifter maybe." Carrie suggested.

"He's a serial killer." Lisa said with laughter as she shook Carrie, making her jump.

"I don't know, just keep your eyes on him." Jeff said as they stood there in the darkness.

"Well quit staring at him and let's build a fire of our own." Carrie said as she started looking around for wood to burn. Jeff went down to the edge of the creek and collected some wood that had washed up.

In no time Jeff had a decent fire burning. Carrie sat down next to it and began to warm her hands as Jeff noticed Lisa rubbing her arms in an effort to warm them. Jeff looked at Carrie as he stoked the fire and she motioned for him to go sit beside her and warm her himself. Jeff looked at Lisa and felt a slight nervousness fall over him and he looked at Carrie again who motioned to him once more. Jeff slowly got up and moved over next to Lisa. She gave a brief surprised look and then appreciated the warmth. Jeff then looked to Carrie yet again for further encouragement, which she gave him in the form of a smile that would ease anyone.

"Hey, Lisa." Jeff started anxiously. But before he could say another word he was interrupted by the sound of Ran's car.

"We got more beer, we need help." Ran yelled from his car. Lisa got up from the ground and ran to help them; leaving Jeff with his words idle on his tongue. Jeff looked at Carrie again, looking as though someone had just pulled the ground out from under him.

"I'm sorry." Carrie said with a genuine sympathy.

"What the hell?" Ran said as he stopped short on his way to the fire. "Hey hobo, beat it!" He continued.

"Stop it, Ran. Just leave him alone. He's not hurting anything." Carrie said as she studied the derelict more closely this time and wondered concisely about his plight.

"Hobo." Ran repeated, lowering his volume a bit this time.

L.B. Kelly

Jeff got up and took one of the three twelve packs that they brought as Ricky and Lisa neared the fire.

"You think y'all got enough?" Carrie asked after seeing the wealth of beer that they had gotten.

"That's just a little less that we'll have to get tomorrow night." Ran said as he sat down near the fire.

"What do I owe on this?" Jeff asked politely as always.

"Nothing; it was a donation." Ran said with a suspect smile. Jeff, knowing Ran, didn't have to ask any questions.

"What time is it?" Jeff asked.

"Eleven forty-five." Carrie answered as she looked at her cell phone. Jeff nodded his head in acknowledgement. Jeff's heart sunk as Lisa and Ricky sat down on the opposite side of the fire and got very snug with one another. Carrie's sympathy deepened as she witnessed the change of expression on Jeff's face.

"I gotta take a leak." Ran said brutishly.

"Oh, be still my heart." Carrie said jokingly as ran got up and walked out of the light. Ran's boorish charm was starting to wear off on her.

"Gimme a cigarette, Ran." Jeff said as Ran was coming back from a lengthy break with nature.

"I thought you quit." Carrie said as Ran handed him a tattered pack of smokes that looked as if a drunk had handled it.

"Yeah, I just got an urge for one." Jeff said as he lit one of the cigarettes with the lighter that he already had. Carrie didn't say anything.

Ran sat down close next to Carrie and she didn't instinctively shy away this time she wasn't exactly sure how she felt about it, but one thing she was sure of was that he was warm.

"I'm gonna take off." Jeff said as he got up and threw his cigarette into the fire after Ricky and Lisa started kissing heavily.

"You out?" Ran asked.

"Yeah, I'm out. Bye Carrie." Jeff said as he walked away.

"Jeff." Carrie said without effect.

"What's his problem?" Ricky asked as he and Lisa both seemed oblivious to what was going on.

"I don't know." Carrie said as she leaned deeper into Ran's warmth.

The next half-hour or so was spent with Ran gently rubbing the back of Carrie's neck and breathing into her ear. Ricky and Lisa were going much further than that and finally began whisper back and forth for a moment.

"Hey, Carrie. Is it okay if I take Ricky home?" Lisa asked after some deliberation with Ricky.

"Yeah, I'll take her home." Ran answered for Carrie. Carrie gave Lisa another 'thanks a lot' look as Ran and Ricky got up and started to leave.

"Do we need to put this out?" Carrie asked of the fire.

"Naw, it'll burn out." Ran said as he and Ricky walked away.

"Thanks, I owe you one." Lisa said as she brushed sand from her pants.

"Yeah, yeah, yeah one more." Carrie said as she gave Lisa a hug. "Be careful." She continued.

"I will, you too." Lisa returned.

* * *

Carrie gripped the armrest nervously as Ran drove, swerving occasionally. She knew David would have a fit if he knew she was riding with Ran after he drank as much as he did, but it was too late, now she was just hoping nothing would happen.

"Ran, slow down." Carrie said as she turned the blaring radio down.

"Okay, okay." Ran said as he backed off the accelerator a bit.

"Where are we going anyway?" Carrie asked knowing no short cuts home on the route that they were taking.

"I just want to check out the cotton field down by the tracks. See if there are any deer moving." Ran said being inconspicuous only to his self.

"It's getting late, Ran." Carrie said.

"It won't take long, I promise." Ran assured her. Carrie just sighed and agreed.

Ran drove a few more miles and turned off the road to the left and began down a long gravel driveway that led to the cotton fields that also served the local kids as a make-out spot. Ran pulled the car off to the side of the road where it overlooked the massive cotton fields and just as if they were in cahoots with him, there were two beautiful deer standing about a fifty yards out in the field.

"Oh, Ran look!" Carrie said excitedly as she was taken with the beauty of the animals.

"See, I told you." Ran said with a satisfied smile on his face.

Ran then moved closer to Carrie on the seat and put his arm around her and began to kiss her neck gently. Carrie's heart was flooded with so many different emotions all at once. Her initial instinct was to pull away. She felt a closeness that she hadn't felt from anyone in a long time and it felt good, but it wasn't right, she didn't love him and Carrie had to admit it to herself. Ran moved from her neck to her lips and started kissing her softly and then became more intense.

Ran placed his left hand on Carrie's thigh and slowly worked his way up to her waistline. He found his way underneath her shirt and started rubbing her stomach tenderly.

Carrie's breathing was becoming heavy and she knew she couldn't let this go any further, but she was giving in.

Ran's hand traveled slowly from Carrie's stomach to her breasts and his touch felt more like groping rather than caressing and a chill shook Carrie's body.

"Stop." Carrie said pulling away.

Ran ignored her. Things just became more intense and he pulled her bra away.

"Randy, Stop it!" Carrie screamed and then slapped him with everything that she had.

Ran's eyes widened in shock of what had just happened. He paused for a moment and then slammed his fist into the stirring wheel and let out a frustrated yell.

"I don't get it! You go out with me and tease me all this time, it's time to pay up!" Ran ranted as he moved in to her. Carrie slapped him again, harder this time.

"Take me home, Ran!" Carrie demanded.

"I love you, Carrie. You owe me this." Ran continued.

"No you don't! I don't owe you anything, Take me home!" Carrie continued. There was a long silence.

"Do I need to call David?" Carrie threatened. She then felt the outside of her pocket for her cell phone but it wasn't there, she had lost it.

"No you don't have to do that." Ran said quickly.

After a moment Ran put the car in reverse and backed out, recklessly and tore down the driveway.

Finally without a word said along the way they arrived at Carrie's house. Ran put the car in park in front of the house.

"You're not gonna say anything to David are you?" Ran asked nervously.

Carrie didn't say anything, she just got out and slammed the door and stormed into the house. Carrie stood in the living room until she heard Ran leave the driveway. She didn't hear him pull into the back yard to the trailer so she breathed a little easier. She locked the door and went into her bedroom. She had so many things running through her mind ranging from her anger about what had just happened, to her wondering about what happened to her cell phone.

Carrie sat down on her bed and looked once again to her father's picture. She picked it up and held it close to her chest and lay down and cried softly until she fell asleep.

Chapter Four

Steven hobbled down the tracks dragging his lame leg behind him. His feet ached and his shoulder was becoming stiff after slamming it into the ground when he jumped from the train, which he still couldn't believe he had done.

The surroundings of the tracks seemed to loose its mystery as the sun started to peak over the trees, however it also revealed the lengthy walk that Steven had ahead of him. As he walked, Steven relived moments from the past forty-eight hours of his life. He thought of Wednesday night when he was prepared to kill himself and then of Thursday morning when he felt more alive than he had in such a long time when he finally gave John Larson what he had been asking for all those years. Then his stomach turned when he thought of the most recent hours on the train. He felt sickened on top of his fatigue when he thought of Jake's body lying on the floor of the car with the upper right portion of his head missing. Steven kept thinking that it was nothing like he had seen in the movies. It was something that no matter how many times he saw in his mind he would never become desensitized to it and he knew that no matter where he ended up he would never be the same.

"How much trouble would it have been to grab a box of cookies or something?" he asked himself out loud as his stomach roared with hunger. He pressed on thinking of the nice, hot meal he knew he would eventually get his hands on.

Steven was covering ground slowly. The flat, open track ahead offered no motivation to pick up the pace. The track eventually led him through the middle of a large cotton field with nothing but cotton and railroad as far as the eye could see.

Steven walked for hours and along the way he thought about Tim and what he must be thinking and how it would be impossible for him to ever face him now. He also thought about what John Larson must have felt like that morning, walking into school with a broken nose and with everyone knowing who broke it. It was something that Steven would have loved to see, but the fact that he knew it was happening was reward enough.

About mid-morning Steven was ready to give up. He had made it through the cotton field and into another tree-shrouded stretch of tracks. His feet were barely movable and his legs were sore and beyond weak. He then stopped and leaned over with his hands on his knees and took a good look behind him, being surprised at the amount of ground that he had covered. He then looked to the sky and noticed the sun, increasingly bearing down and warming things up considerably. Steven then pulled off his sweatshirt and stuffed it into his bag. He then looked straight ahead and took an excited breath and felt a renewed vigor after spotting, some distance down the tracks what appeared to be a road crossing over the track. He put the every ounce of pain that he was feeling into the back of his mind and walked quickly to the crossing, never taking his eyes from it.

Steven stood in the middle of the railroad at the crossing and looked both ways down the blacktop road, neither direction offered solace. He then looked straight ahead down the track and then left and right again, as the choice hovered in his mind and he finally decided to go left.

Steven walked down the desolate road with spirit at first, but as the road endured his feet once again became heavy. He began to entertain himself by thinking that somehow he had fallen into an episode of some cheesy science fiction show about some kind of never-ending road and the more he thought about it, the more reasonable it seemed.

Finally, as Steven emerged from a sharp curve in the road a large bridge came into view, stretching impressively across a massive gap, he was in awe at its length. He then walked to the middle and peered over the side rails and was further stricken at the height of the bridge. It was about eighty feet to the diminished creek below and he felt butterflies grow in his stomach as he studied the commanding sight. Steven then looked down to the concrete base of the rail and couldn't resist sitting down. The comfort that he felt in his legs was indescribable. He sat there for a while, enjoying the relief and then thought to himself that if he stayed there much longer he wouldn't be able to move so he forced himself to get up and continue his aimless journey.

Steven walked another mile or so and was starting to notice a greater number of houses than he had been seeing and as the houses thickened he could see ahead what he hoped would be civilization. Steven continued walking and ahead in the distance he could make out a line of buildings. As he made his way towards the buildings the road evolved into a narrow street and crossed over another Small Street ahead. Sidewalks replaced the grassy shoulders of the road and the silence of the country had given way to the humble commotion of a small town. As Steven walked down the decrepit sidewalk his weariness and the pain in his knee and shoulder became secondary thought as he studied his knew surroundings as if he were coming into the world for the first time.

He looked across the street from where he was and saw a bank and next door to it was a barbershop and separated from them by another Small Street was what looked to be a town hall and police station. He noticed the soft flow of traffic through the town and saw a few people strolling about and felt comfort fall over him as he sensed how content everyone seemed to be and he also longed to be content.

Steven stopped at the end of the sidewalk and took a look around. He stood on the corner in front of a doctor's office and he wished that he could go in and tell them to give him some of everything. At least he would ask for some painkillers and something to make him sleep for a week, but his first priority to himself was to find something to eat and drink, he would worry about the pain later.

Steven then looked in both directions of the adjoining street and saw a small chophouse about a quarter of a mile down to the left. He crossed the town's main street and made his way to it, quickly.

As he opened the door of the diner and stepped inside he was taken over by the smell of the food and his stomach responded with a wanting growl. Steven scanned the restaurant and spotted an empty stool at the counter and walked over and sat down.

"Hey, how are ya?" Steven asked of the old man on the stool next to him. The old man responded with only a nod. Steven grabbed the greasy, plastic-covered menu that sat in front of him and began to look it over.

"What'll ya have?" The waitress asked as she laid out a napkin and then silverware.

"How big is this cheeseburger?" Steven asked as he pointed to the item on the menu.

"About that big." The waitress said without gesture and in a wise tone.

"Okay, can you make it a double with fries?" Steven asked without letting her tone bother him. He was too hungry to be bothered.

"Yeah, what do you want to drink?" The waitress asked sharply.

"Coke." Steven said.

"We got sweet tea, coffee and water." The waitress said as though Steven should have known that already.

"Tea's fine." Steven said as the waitress walked away without saying anything else.

Steven looked over to the old man who was staring at him and gave a short smile to which the old man simply looked away. The waitress then brought Steven a large glass of tea and sat it down and walked away again. He took the glass and turned it up and didn't put it down until it was empty. He then set the glass down and exhaled a satisfied breath and then looked around for the waitress.

"Excuse me, ma'am. Can I get some more tea please?" Steven asked the waitress, who was talking to someone at the end of the counter. She gave no response.

"Ma'am?" Steven said again as he held his empty glass up. The waitress cocked her head to the side and lowered her shoulders in disgust and walked down to Steven.

"Refills are twenty-five cents." The waitress said.

"Okay." Steven said, becoming a bit agitated.

The waitress brought Steven's refilled glass to him and hurried off again. He then picked his glass up and took a conserving sip and then took a look around. The place was about half-full, there were a few people staring at Steven, trying to figure out what he was doing in their town but most everyone were minding their own business, or at least pretending to do so. He then turned his attention back to his glass and took another sip and then noticed the old man next to him was staring at him again.

"Is there something wrong?" Steven asked the old man, who remained silent. Steven stared back at him for a moment and then looked away to his glass feeling rather uncomfortable.

"Where you from?" The old man asked with a heavy drawl.

"The coast." Steven said after a second's pause.

"I knew you wasn't from around here, lest I'd been seeing you before. What you doing up this way, you got kin here?" The old man inquired.

"No sir, I'm just traveling. To be honest with you I really don't know where I'm at." Steven said as his tension began to ease.

"You're in Fanning, Mississippi." The old man said.

"Fanning." Steven repeated to himself.

"How in the hell does a man come to be somewhere and don't know where he is? You in trouble with the law?" The old man asked suspiciously.

"No sir, it's a long story." Steven said becoming slightly amused.

"What you got in that bag, dope?" The man asked as he looked to the floor at the bag. "You up here trying to sell it?" He further questioned.

"No sir." Steven said as the waitress delivered his fully dressed cheeseburger. It looked so good to him that he decided the rude waitress and the loopy old man were worth dealing with for it. Steven picked the burger up and began to devour it with delight.

"Well you never know with the way things are now days. It won't be long before all the kids around here will be trying to smoke that dope and drink corn whiskey and start going with one another, we got to watch who's coming in and out of here." The old man explained.

"Yes sir." Steven said as he enjoyed his meal.

"How old are you?" The man asked.

"Eighteen." Steven replied as he took a breather from eating to get a drink of his tea.

"Eighteen, when I was eighteen I didn't know if I was coming or going. I didn't know weather I ought to scratch my watch or wind my ass and I've spent the rest of my life trying to figure it out. Before I knew it I was seventy-five years old and right back here where I started, winding my ass." The old man said as he stared ahead, deadpan over his cup of coffee.

"Yes sir." Steven said again as he continued eating.

"Where is there a store around here?" Steven asked after a moment as he turned to look at the old man.

"Hattie's is on down a little ways at the end of this street here and around the corner. If you get anything to eat make sure it's in a can or that it come out the refrigerator, they got rats down there as big as dogs, dumping and chewing on everything. They gonna fool around and make somebody sick one of these days, selling that mess." The man advised Steven.

"Oh, alright I appreciate it." Steven said.

"What's your name, son?" The man asked.

"Steven Harris." Steven replied.

"Well my name is Sam Timmons. If you hang around long enough you'll probably see me again. I better get on, have a good one." The old man said as he got up and headed to the register.

Steven sat there at the counter thinking of the old man and then about how strange his life had become in such a short period of time. The reality of his situation became clear as he tried to figure out where he was going to sleep that night and his thoughts were further vexed when he realized that he had no idea what he would do the next day and then the day after that. He had one hundred fifty dollars in his pocket and though it would carry him for a little while, it wouldn't make miracles happen.

* * *

The ragged, wooden door slammed behind Steven as he entered Hattie's store and as it did a bell that dangled from it announced his arrival. Steven stood at the front of the store and checked the place out. There were no other patrons in the store, only the clerk who was standing behind the old counter looking at Steven with suspicion. He made his way to the other side of the store away from the clerk feeling a bit unwelcome. He walked along between the wall and a row of tables that were set up with washing powder, bath soap and other household items. He then moved on to another table and upon it, set out neatly were cans of luncheon meat, and beans with weenies among other things. Steven picked up a couple of cans of the beans and weenies and he grabbed some of the potted meat. He then moved down the row and picked up a small box of crackers and inspected it closely with the words of Mr. Timmons ringing in his mind. He saw no obvious fault to the box so he kept it and continued looking.

After picking up a six-pack of canned soda he moved to the counter and set everything down and made eye contact with the clerk.

"Hey." Steven said the clerk, who appeared to be in her late forties.

"Hey." The clerk returned dryly while continuing her suspicious look.

"Let me get one of those tooth brushes too, please." Steven said after spotting the brushes behind the counter. The clerk turned and picked up one of the brushes and set it upon the counter.

"Can I get some toothpaste too?" Steven asked.

"We don't have any." The clerk replied.

"You have a tooth brush, but no toothpaste?" Steven bewilderedly asked.

"That's right, we out okay. Use some baking soda." The clerk suggested.

"Baking soda?" Steven asked as he raised his brow.

"Yeah ain't you ever brushed your teeth with baking soda? Try it, it'll make'em shiny." The clerk said as she pointed him in the direction of the baking soda. Steven slowly made his way to the baking soda and picked it up and looked it over. After careful thought he decided to try it. He moved back up to the counter and set the box down.

"That's gonna be it?" The clerk asked.

"Yes ma'am." Steven responded.

"Is there a hotel around here?" Steven asked as the clerk added Steven's total up on an old adding machine.

"No baby, not for quite a few miles." The clerk said with a short laugh. Steven's expression dropped a bit as he eliminated a warm hotel bed from his mental list of possible options.

"Let me get one of those lighters too." Steven said as the prospect of having to camp out entered his mind.

"Thirteen eighty-five." The clerk said as she added the lighter to Steven's total.

"Damn, y'all are proud of this stuff." Steven said, stunned by the cost.

"Well, you sure welcome to try the grocery store, but it's about Ten miles yonder way, but if I ain't mistaken I didn't hear you drive up in no car." The clerk said, making Steven realize that it was either Hattie's or another long walk and there was no way he was going to walk that far.

"Okay." Steven said as he handed the clerk a twenty-dollar bill.

"Let me get you a bag." The clerk said as she gave Steven his change.

"Just as long as it doesn't cost extra." Steven said wisely.

"Look baby, I don't make the prices so don't get mad at me." The clerk said as she put Steven's things in a paper bag.

"I'm sorry, It's been a long day." Steven said as began to feel sorry for snapping at the lady.

"It's okay baby, it'll get better." The clerk said with a smile.

"It would have to." Steven said as he took the bag from the counter and then reached down and picked up his duffel bag.

Steven left the store and began to walk through the town; looking for somewhere he might be able to spend the night. He walked and walked until he found himself back where he began, in front of the doctor's office; he rubbed his hand over his face and closed his eyes tightly as the frustration grew inside him. The whole situation was becoming surreal to Steven, being in this strange place and seeing the things that he had seen was starting to wear upon his mind.

Steven sat down on a bench that was in front of the office and continued to ponder his current plight. He hadn't seen any motels or boarding houses anywhere in town and he was ready to throw his hands up when he thought of the bridge that he crossed on his way into town. He started telling himself that it may not be so bad, sleeping under a bridge; at least it would be a roof over his head. Besides he needed to make what little money he had last and a motel certainly wasn't the way to do it. After agreeing with himself that he had chosen the best course of action Steven took in a deep breath and looked out at the small town. His heart was filled with a certain excitement mixed with an obscure trepidation for the thought of making a new life for him, should it be in this town or perhaps some other town along the way.

Steven walked the mile and a half out of town to the bridge. As he approached the bridge Steven thought of vagrants that he had seen before, walking about aimlessly, as he was and he suddenly felt constraint for himself and then sympathy for them when realized that he was now one of them.

Steven stopped at the beginning of the bridge and looked to either side. He then moved to the right side of the bridge and looked behind him to be sure that he had no audience. He gripped his grocery bag and his duffel bag tightly in one hand as he grabbed the end of the rail for support with the other and lowered himself down the hill and walked a short distance down the slight incline towards the creek.

Steven was impressed at the space under the bridge. He felt like a child discovering a new hideout and he began to feel better about the idea as he walked in further underneath the bridge. He looked around studying the area as he gained his footing on the sandy ground. He reached the middle and slowly sat down as he continued looking the place over.

Across the creek Steven could see where others had built campfires and had littered the ground somewhat with beer cans and bottles.

Steven set his bags down beside him and began to relax a bit as he stretched his legs out. He rolled his neck from side to side in an attempt to loosen his tense muscles. He then pulled his feet in and untied his shoes and took them off as well as his socks. Steven's eyes rolled into the back of his head as he massaged his tired and blistered feet.

Steven felt an undeniable urge to close his eyes and just shut down. He reached to his left and picked up his duffel bag and dropped it behind him for use as a pillow. He laid his head down on the bag and stretched his bare toes and worked his body comfortably into the sand.

"I'll just rest my eyes." Steven said to himself as he closed his eyes, feeling a little nervous about sleeping there.

Steven fell fast asleep as he rested his eyes and as he did he found himself back in the train car in the presence of Michael, Jimmy and Jake. Things were moving in slow motion and there was no sound. He wanted to jump off the train, knowing what was going to happen, but he felt cemented into place. His feet were heavy, his arms were dead weight and his throat was tight with fear. Steven cried warnings to Jake, but his voice had no volume.

Steven scanned the car from his dark point of view. He could recognize, even without sound that the macabre events were happening just as they had before. Right on cue Michael got up from his seat and put the gun to Jake's Head and pulled the trigger and as Jake's body came to rest on the floor, what was left of his face became Steven's face and Michael became Steven's father, Tim. Tim then turned the gun to Jimmy, Who now had become Steven also. He pulled the trigger and smiled as the body fell. Steven was screaming at the top of his lungs with still no sound. His chest felt tight as though there were a ton of bricks on top of him. He had never felt such fear. After cutting Jimmy down Tim set his sights upon Steven and with a sinister grin and clinched teeth he fired a bullet into Steven's face. Just as the bullet would have made contact Steven jumped into awareness and took a look around.

Darkness was falling and the evening air was cooling off considerably. Steven brushed off his sore and now cold feet and quickly put his socks and shoes back on while trying to gain his bearings. Steven stood up and as he straightened out his injured knee he winced at the unbelievable pain that tore through his leg. Steven's body shook with the chill of the air and he felt nauseous when he thought of the dream that he had. He ran down towards the edge of the creek and made it about half way before throwing up. He fell to his knees in the sand and the pain in his leg disappeared momentarily as he began to heave again.

After a moment Steven rose to his feet and started moving slowly back to where his bags were. He was shivering harder now and was near tears. The vomiting mixed with the gruesome detail of his dream and the fact that he had painted his father as a killer, much less his own killer created a pit in his stomach and a fear of the question mark that loomed as his future. It caused him to yearn for the comfort of his mother's embrace or the warmth that his sister could offer through one of her amorous smiles. It was then that he finally realized that his mother and sister were gone and were never coming back.

Steven kneeled down over his bag and unzipped it. He searched inside until he found his hooded sweatshirt. He took it out and pulled it over his head and pulled the drawstring of the hood tightly around his face. He then stood up and looked around searching for something he could use to build a fire.

Steven walked to the edge of bridge's cover and found some old, dry limbs and branches that had been washed up by the creek. He drug them over to his camp sight and began to break them up and form them into the makings of a campfire, all the while trying to suppress the unsettling images that had haunted his dream.

Building a fire, a real campfire was something that Steven had never done in his lifetime and he found it to be quite a challenge. Steven struck his lighter and held a small twig over it until it began to burn on it's own. He lowered the twig slowly to the mound of wood and expected it to ignite on contact but was somewhat disappointed when the tiny flame simply flickered and disappeared. After a few more fruitless attempts he threw the twig and the lighter down in frustration and began to sulk. Steven sat there for a moment in disappointment. His stare settled upon his grocery bag and the thought clicked in his head. He reached over and tore a piece of the paper off as the vale of obliviousness was lifted from his eyes.

Steven pushed himself up from the ground and kneeled beside the pile of wood and made a small opening in the middle. He tore the piece of the bag into smaller portions and dropped them into the opening. He then picked the twig up once more and lit it and guided it through the sticks and lit the paper. It smoldered and then started to burn and Steven placed a stick over the flame and watched as it began to burn. He followed it with another, slightly bigger stick and then another, before he knew it he had a fire, a real campfire.

Steven sat back and relaxed a bit, feeling proud of himself for having built the fire and he briefly wished that building a new life could be so easy. He decided that he had wallowed in enough self-pity for one day; he had to figure out what he was going to do and do it.

Steven slid his lighter into his pocket as he looked around for enough fuel to keep his fire going through the night. He got up and began to walk the area and collected what he hoped would be enough wood.

After bringing the wood back to the camp sight, he sat down and began to settle in. He had no idea what time it was, all he new was that it was dark. He took one of his sodas from the bag and began to drink it; seeming not to mind at all the fact that it was lukewarm, at this point it had become a luxury.

The next few hours were spent in thought with topics ranging from his father and the train ride to wondering what in the hell all those strange noises were that were coming from the surrounding woods. Steven was starting to think that the night would never end and he was becoming tired of his own company.

The sickness in Steven's stomach was fading and was being replaced with hunger. He searched inside his bag and took from it a can of the potted meat and a sleeve of the crackers. It was then that he realized that he had no utensils, but then he concluded that the crackers would work alone nicely. As he ate Steven continued to think of the events of the past couple of days and was actually starting to enjoy the adventurous feeling that was coursing through him.

Steven was starting to appreciate the natural beauty of this new place and was now becoming used to the odd sounds that were emanating from the darkness. He was also no longer startled by the clacking sound of the passing cars on the bridge. His alertness however was heightened by the sound of oncoming vehicles slowing down as they approached the bridge. His jitteriness grew even higher when he saw headlight beams swirling spastic over a small landing, several yards from the edge of the bridge on the opposite side of the creek.

He heard two vehicles park and a short time later he heard three doors slam. Steven could make out the outlines of a car and a truck in the pale moonlight and could hear muffled conversation. He then noticed three people walking down towards the base of the bridge being led by a flashlight. They appeared to be a guy and two girls. After noticing Steven's fire they stopped and peered across the creek.

"What the hell are they staring at?" Steven asked himself as his nervousness came full-circle.

He set his food down and sat up from his relaxed, lying position and briefly considered leaving.

After a moment's gawking the three dispersed and began to look for wood to build their own fire. After regaining his comfort Steven laid back a bit and continued to eat his food while keeping a careful eye on the people across the creek.

Steven stood up and then kneeled down by the fire, stoking it with a long slender stick that he had found. He concluded that the strangers meant him no harm and he was coming to revere the break in monotony that they had provided.

Steven grew envious of the three as he longed for similar camaraderie in his own life, someone with whom he could share the smallest, most simple things or even confide in them the inner most secrets of his lonely and dejected heart. If he could have that back he would never take anyone or anything for granted again.

Steven's attention was called upon once again when he heard another vehicle slowing down as it approached the bridge above. He watched the landing again eagerly as the car parked and two more guys spilled out and began to call for assistance. One of the girls at the campfire got up and ran to their aid. As the new arrivals made their way to the fire, carrying enough beer to make a small army drunk, the tallest, most obnoxious looking of the two stopped and looked across the creek at Steven.

"Hey hobo, beat it!" The guy yelled to Steven. The anger grew inside Steven immediately and then the reality of the statement soon followed. Steven could see, but not hear that the girl that was still seated by the fire was saying something to the belligerent fellow in Steven's favor.

"Hobo." The guy repeated before resuming his business.

Steven took a broken piece of wood from his stockpile and threw it on the fire as the taunt from the drunken buffoon still rung loud in his head. "Where in the hell does he get off saying that to me? He doesn't know me." Steven thought to himself. As the statement replayed in his mind it became clear to Steven that that's what he was, a hobo, and that's how people were seeing him.

As the night wore on, the strangers across the creek left and Steven remained, thinking about his screwed up life. He thought about how stupid he was to think that he could have bettered his situation by leaving. Since he had been gone he had walked what seemed to him to be every inch of railroad in Mississippi and was chased by the fattest security guard in the world. He had witnessed a murder, maybe two and was nearly killed himself. Steven began to think that maybe he was better off dead.

Steven lay there in the sand by the fire starring at the bridge above, wondering what would happen if he jumped off of it. Would it be high enough to kill him or just low enough to break every bone in his body and add another highlight to his adventure. Steven drifted off to sleep as the conversation with himself faded away in his mind.

* * *

Steven awoke shivering in growing early morning light. He looked to his fire that was dwindling greatly. He got up quickly and found his stick and began to stoke the fire. He set another stick of wood over the fading embers and willed the fire back. Steven laid more wood over the fire as it began to perk up. He rubbed his hands together and moved closer to the fire and looked around.

After warming himself Steven felt the call of nature and walked over to the edge of the bridge and began to relive himself. As he stood there looking up at the bridge he resumed his thoughts from the night before. He then looked to the shallow water and studied the rocky creek bed.

"That would hurt too much." He said to himself as he observed the jagged stones.

The ringing of a phone interrupted his thoughts and activity. Steven looked around and thought he was losing his mind. He pinpointed the noise on the other side of the creek and concluded that one of the strangers from the night before must have lost a cell phone.

Steven walked back to his fire and began to warm himself again and as he did his stomach growled and grumbled with

123

hunger. He took another can of the fine potted meat that he'd gotten from Hattie's and began to eat as the cell phone finally quit ringing.

He finished eating and as the morning ever so slowly progressed he was becoming tired with boredom. He had been watching the other side of the creek, thinking of the strangers that had been there the night before. He was thinking about the cell phone, wondering if someone would come back there to look for it. He thought to himself that perhaps he should go and look for it. Maybe he could find out whom it belonged to or maybe put it to his own use, either way it would provide a distraction from the humdrum tediousness he had found himself in.

Steven set another log on the fire and pulled his hood over his head and made his way to the edged of the bridge where he entered the evening before. He climbed back up to the road and looked around and began to walk towards the other side of the bridge. His sore leg and feet were becoming useable again despite the tenderness that he still felt.

He came to the other end of the bridge and found the beaten path that the cars had used the night before. He walked down the small road to the landing where the cars were parked and continued walking underneath the bridge.

He stopped about where the strangers had and looked across to his lonely campfire and felt a fleeting twinge of pity for himself as he took in the lament sight. He continued on to the smoldering coal bed and looked around. The ground was littered with beer cans and cigarettes butts and empty cigarette packs that appeared to be from the night before as well as many other nights. He walked around to the other side of the coals and kneeled down where he found the cell phone.

He picked up the phone and looked at the screen and upon it was the message: Missed Call. He pressed the keys in a certain sequence and found the caller I.D. options. The call was received from "Home" so Steven concluded that the owner must have called the number to try and find it. Steven cleared the information from the screen. The banner on the main screen read "Carrie".

Steven felt a little disappointed after seeing it. He was hoping that phone belonged to the buffoon, if it had Steven would have taken great pride in busting it into a million pieces and throwing it into the creek, but he was pretty sure that the buffoon's name wasn't Carrie.

Steven stood there with the phone in his hand trying to figure out what he should do with it. He thought about looking through it to try and find the owner's number and letting them know that he had it. The thought of calling his father briefly crossed his mind and then as if his fingers were working independently from his body he found himself dialing the number. Steven put the phone up to his ear as it started to ring.

"….This might be him now. Hello?" Tim said as he answered the call. Steven froze when his father actually answered. He then wondered who Tim was talking to and could think of nothing to say.

"Hello?" Tim repeated disgustedly. Steven panicked and then hung up the phone. Steven stared at the phone and felt the emotion build inside him. He was trying desperately to figure out who was at his house with Tim. He could hear in the background, a woman's muffled voice and he could feel anger mix with the building emotion as he thought of another woman sleeping in his mother's bed and lounging in his mother's house.

Steven shook his mind free of the thoughts and put the phone in his pocket. He started towards path to return to his side of the creek when he heard the now familiar sound of a car slowing down to turn into the road leading under the bridge.

Steven was now very anxious. He felt like a cornered animal with nowhere to run. The only thing he could do was greet whoever was coming and hope that they were friendly.

He saw an old car come to rest on the landing. He couldn't tell what kind of car it was but he knew it was old and he liked it. A girl stepped out of the car that appeared to be close to Steven's age. She was just a little under his height and very beautiful, not in a blonde haired, blue eyed kind of way, but in a more natural and flattering way. She had walked about half way towards Steven before noticing that he was there. She stopped short when she saw him and appeared to be wondering whether or not he could be trusted.

"I'm sorry, I didn't know anyone was down here." The girl said coolly as she pulled her long brown hair away from her face and then turned to leave.

"Wait, are you Carrie?" Steven asked as he moved towards her.

"Yeah." Carrie said, as she turned around looking a bit shocked and confused.

"I have something of yours." Steven said as he pulled the cell phone from his pocket and handed it to her.

"Yeah, that's it, that's what I was looking for. Thanks." Carrie said as she reached out cautiously and took the phone.

"I was over there and I heard it ringing." Steven said awkwardly as he pointed to his camp sight.

"Was that you over there last night?" Carrie asked as she looked across the creek.

"Yeah." Steven said with shame as he looked away from her.

"Hey, I'm sorry about what Ran said last night, he's an idiot." Carrie said.

"Oh, It's okay. I've been called worse. Tell your boyfriend there's no hard feelings." Steven said truthfully.

"He's not my boyfriend." Carrie said very quickly.

"I'm sorry, I didn't mean to presume." Steven said apologetically.

"It's alright, how could you know? Besides I'm not sure if he'll even be my friend anymore." Carrie said suddenly realizing that she was becoming all too comfortable with this perfect stranger.

"Well look I gotta go, thanks again…" Carrie continued.

"Steven, my name is Steven." He said.

"Maybe I'll see you around, Steven." Carrie said as she turned and walked away. Steven watched her until she was out of sight.

"Wow." Steven said as he started walking back to his side of the creek thinking of the beautiful girl.

* * *

Steven sat in the sand staring into his campfire, which was quickly losing its usefulness as the heat began to rise. The boredom had returned and was now more than he could stand. He started to rundown a list of things he could do, but the list was short.

Steven started thinking about the cheeseburger he ate the day before and decided it was time for another one. He pulled his wad of cash out of his pocket and counted it. He had one hundred thirty dollars and fifteen cents left, more than enough not to feel guilty about eating another big lunch. Steven scooped up some sand and poured it over the fire, smothering it. He then got up and gathered his things and headed for the road and started walking back into town.

The walk seemed to go by a little quicker this time. His leg felt a little better, however his shoulder was still as sore as ever but the only thing on his mind now was the beautiful girl that he met under the bridge. He kept repeating her name over and over again in his mind and couldn't help wanting to see her again.

Steven found himself back in front of the diner. His mouth was already watering at the thought of eating another cheeseburger. He went inside and headed to the counter and saw a familiar face.

"Hey Mr. Timmons." Steven said as he sat down on a stool next to the old man.

"Hey uh…. Harris, right?" Mr. Timmons said as he found Steven's name in his memory.

"Yes sir." Steven said as he looked for the waitress.

"What's going on with you today?" Mr. Timmons asked sincerely.

"Nothing really, I'm just trying to get something to eat right now." Steven said as the waitress came and took his order with what seemed to Steven to be a little more warmth than the day before.

"Well what do you think of our little town so far?" The old man asked.

"Oh it's fine, what I've seen of it." Steven replied.

"Well you hang around long enough it'll be so fine to you that you ain't gonna want to leave." Mr. Timmons continued. Steven just smiled and nodded.

"I wouldn't know where else to go anyway." Steven replied. The old man paused and then began to speak.

"Well I guess what I've learned over the past seventy five years is that you end up where you're supposed to be even if you don't think it's where you ought to be." Mr. Timmons said wisely.

Steven mulled over the old man's words as he finished his meal. He began to look at his situation differently with the new enlightenment provided by Mr. Timmons. Maybe this was where he was supposed to be; maybe Steven's father actually helped him through his abuse. Perhaps happiness would find him in this place.

"I reckon I better get on, I got a bunch to do today and I been putting it off long enough." Mr. Timmons said as he got up and started to leave.

"Okay, Maybe I'll see you around." Steven said feeling somewhat disappointed over the ending of the conversation. Mr. Timmons took a few steps away and then stopped and looked back at Steven and thought for a moment.

"Hey, you want to make a little money today?" Mr. Timmons asked as he walked back over to Steven.

"I could probably stand to make some money." Steven said after a minute. He didn't know what he would be doing, but for a little company he would do just about anything.

"Now I can't pay much, but I have been known to be a pretty good cook and I can throw in supper tonight if you want it." Mr. Timmons Explained.

"It sounds good, Mr. Timmons." Steven said.

"Well come on then and, uh call me Sam." Mr. Timmons said as he walked out of the diner. Steven hastily paid for his meal, collected his bags and met Sam at his truck.

"You ever split wood?" Sam asked of Steven as he put the truck in gear and began to drive modestly down the road away from town.

"No sir." Steven said honestly.

"It ain't nothing to it, but it ain't a whole hell of a lot of fun either." Sam said as he watched the road carefully.

"I'll be glad to try." Steven replied.

"I used to be able to cut and split wood all day long, but the older I get the heavier that wood seems to get so any help is welcome." Sam said, mostly longing for the company as much as Steven was.

They drove about four or five miles outside of town and pulled into a pasture that was separated from the road by an iron cattle gap. The truck rattled and vibrated as it crossed the gap and began to rock from side to side as it crawled over the rough driveway. Steven felt a calm fall over him as he looked over the pasture laid out majestically under a perfect, blue sky. A few random trees broke its open flatness and the rest of the land was dotted with cows.

"This land has been in my family for four generations, my great grand daddy bought it when he settled here years ago. It's been many a cow raised on this place." Sam said while staring out over the land, reminiscing over childhood days in his spotted memory.

"What does your family do?" Sam asked. Steven cringed at the thought of talking about his father, but Sam didn't know Tim and therefore he didn't know how evil he could be. Never the less Steven gave no response to the question as he tried not to let his mind wander over the subject.

"I'm sorry. I didn't mean to pry." Sam said. Steven and Sam shared a silence as they arrived at the edge of the pasture. Sam parked the truck at the tree line and cut the engine.

Sam got out of the truck and walked to the massive wall of trees and began to look it over. Steven joined him at the end of the truck as he chose the tree they would bring down.

"Grab that chainsaw up." Sam said as he motioned to a saw in the back of the truck. Steven stepped up onto the truck's bumper and then stepped over the tailgate and into the back of the truck. He walked to the front of the truck bed and bent over to pick up the massive chainsaw. Steven discovered it to be quite heavy as he pulled it up, with some effort from the truck bed.

Steven walked back to the tailgate and set the saw down. He then jumped over the side of the truck to the ground and then pulled the saw out. He hobbled towards Sam, who had moved over to the tall oak tree he had picked out. As Steven walked the saw's weight pulled him over to one side and he was trying to ignore the pain that was pulsing in his sore leg.

"Just set it down right there." Sam said as he pulled an old pair of leather gloves from his pocket and then kneeled down beside the saw and began checking it out.

The old man stood up with the saw that looked as though it could have weighed as much as he did. He pulled the rope on the side of the saw with no result. He then adjusted the choke and tried again. This time the saw roared to life and Sam fed it fuel as he approached the tree.

The old man dug the saw into the side of the tree and rocked it back and forth as it chewed fiercely through the bark. Sam made one long cut, slanting down towards the ground and then another level cut underneath the slanted one, together the two cuts formed a wedge. Sam fed the saw more fuel as he jerked and pulled it from the tree.

"Grab that splitting maul out of the truck and bring here." Sam said to Steven, who was watching intensely.

Steven returned with the maul a short time later and handed it over to Sam who in turn handed him the chainsaw. Steven suddenly felt a little uncomfortable holding the running saw as it rumbled and shook his body. This was the closest that he had ever been to real work in his life.

Sam took the heavy maul in both hands and cocked it back as if he were a major league baseball player in the batter's box. He released the maul and knocked the wedge out of the tree.

"Move back." Sam said as he and Steven backed away. Steven watched the tree in awe as it crackled and popped on its way to the ground. As the tree settled it blew dried leaves up from the ground and Steven could feel the wind that was made from the tree's limbs as it made impact.

"I think you ought to get a feel for that old saw." Sam said as he motioned for Steven to join him next to the fallen tree.

"You see all these limbs sticking out? I want you to cut'em all off, like this." Sam continued as he took the saw from Steven and showed him the proper procedure. After making a few cuts Sam turned the saw over to Steven, who was visibly nervous but also very eager to take control of the saw. Steven made the first cut and felt a slight thrill as the saw cut through the wood like a hot knife through butter. The thrill increased as he made the next cut and then the next. Pretty soon he was free of the nervousness and preoccupied by the thrill.

Steven fell into a rhythm as he went up and down the tree, relieving it of its limbs when suddenly his train of thought was derailed by a loud bang. Steven looked up quickly from his work and saw Sam standing near the truck holding a smoking twelve-gauge shotgun in his hands.

"What are you doing?" Steven asked with a startled tone. Just as the words came out of his mouth he heard a thud from behind him.

"Run over there and grab that coon up." Sam said as he walked over to Steven and hit the kill switch on the saw.

Steven looked behind him and then back to Sam who had a crooked grin on his face. He let go of the saw and walked over to where Sam had pointed. Steven was shocked to find a large raccoon,

panting and writhing on the ground. Steven looked back at Sam once more in shock, wondering why he had shot this animal.

133

"Pick him up." Sam said as he waved Steven over.

Steven stood there and watched as the raccoon gave one final shutter. He took in a deep breath and closed his eyes as he reached down and picked up the raccoon by its tail. He walked back over to the tree and climbed over it. He walked back to the truck where Sam was returning his shotgun to its storage spot behind the seat.

"What did you do that for?" Steven asked as Sam took the raccoon from him and set it in the back of the truck.

"You remember that supper I was telling you about?" Sam asked with a smile.

"You mean your going to eat that?" Steven asked in disbelief.

"Oh yeah, we lucked up. Coons are usually out at night, guess we must have stirred him up." Sam said as he put his gloves back on and walked back over to the tree and fired up the chainsaw. Steven took one last look to the raccoon and then walked back to the tree as well.

Sam cut a couple of sections out of the tree and pushed one of them over to Steven with his foot.

"Stand it up." Sam said over the saw's loud buzz. "You see that crack in the middle, take that splitting maul and bust it right in that crack until you get several pieces and start loading them in the truck." Sam further instructed. Steven took the maul and hit the block of wood, nothing happened.

"You gotta put out, son." Sam said as Steven struck the block again, this time busting it into two pieces. Steven smiled at his accomplishment and then stood the two pieces up and busted them as well.

Steven once again fell into a rhythm as Sam would send him a block and he would bust it and load it into the truck. This went on for the better part of an hour until their progress was interrupted when Sam's saw sputtered and died.

"This damned thing." Sam said as he set the saw down and wiped sweat from his brow.

"What is it?" Steven asked.

"Oh this old saw is like me, it's wore out and only works sometimes." Sam replied as he crossed over the tree and walked over to the truck and set the saw in the back.

"Well we got a decent load for today, lets go see if we can get this saw fixed." Sam said as he walked to the driver's door and got into the truck. Steven walked around and climbed in the cab after giving another look to the serene woods and tranquil, open field.

* * *

David Anderson felt a small weight lift from his shoulders as he tightened the final bolt on the carburetor of an old Trans Am that had been in his shop for quite a while. The work was starting to pile up even before Ran quit and since he had been gone the pressure has really getting heavy.

David straightened up from his working position and twisted his back from side to side, trying to loosen up a bit. He looked to the clock that hung above the office door. It was only three-thirty but he decided that he had put in an honest day's work and it was quitting time.

David turned around and began to drop his tools into the tool chest, in their respective drawers. As he did he looked around the shop and felt an aching sense of duty. He noticed on the floor, the old piles of oil dry that had done their jobs and were waiting to be swept up and he also noticed the garbage cans that were overflowing and begging to be emptied.

David threw the last wrench into the drawer with a disgusted air and continued to ignore the eyesores.

He moved over to the sink and began to scrub his hands. As he washed his mind wandered to thoughts of his sister. He was worried about her because of her odd behavior that morning when he returned from Julie's house to get a shower. It was more than just her jealousy of Julie and David's relationship. Something was happening that she wasn't telling him about and it had been eating at him all morning.

David turned the tap off and shook the water from his hands as he pulled some paper towels from the dispenser on the wall. He turned and headed for the breaker box to turn the lights and equipment off when he heard a truck pull up outside the shop. David closed his eyes and shook his head and then looked towards the door to see who it was. He let out a disappointed sigh when he saw that it was Sam Timmons.

As David walked up to the front to meet him he noticed that he had with him a kid whom David had never seen before.

"Mr. Timmons, what can I do for you today?" David asked.

"Aww, this old chainsaw's giving me grief again." Sam said as he looked to the saw that the kid was holding.

"Well I'll be happy to take a look at it for you, but it'll probably be Monday before I can do it. I was just headed out the door." David explained.

"Just set it down over there, Harris." Sam said to Steven as he motioned towards one of the workbenches. "You run all your help off?" Sam continued.

"Yes sir, Ran quit on me." David replied. Steven rejoined Sam and wondered briefly if this guy was talking about the same Ran that Carrie mentioned that morning.

"Well this is the fellow here that you need to hire." Sam said. Steven's comfort level immediately went from mediocre to nonexistent as the focus of the conversation was shifted to him.

"You work on cars?" David asked as he looked at Steven.

"No, Not really." Steven said as he looked to the floor timidly when he really should have said: "No, not at all."

"He'll sure work, though." Sam said on Steven's behalf.

"Well, I'll try to get this saw fixed for you as soon as I can." David said after a short silence, uncomfortably trying to ignore the suggestion.

"That'll be fine, we got a fair load of wood out there now. It ain't no big rush on it." Sam said as he turned to leave. "Have a good one." Sam continued as he exited the shop, followed by Steven.

"Yes sir, you too." David returned as he watched the door close behind them.

* * *

The truck shuttered as Sam slowed down to turn into his driveway. As Sam parked the truck Steven got out and looked around. Sam's house sat right in the middle of town, but around this town that didn't seem to be a bad thing. From what Steven could tell everyone in this community knew each other and had no ill will for anyone and that would be the hardest thing for Steven to get used to.

"Just set the wood out on the porch. After that we got to get the jacket off that coon." Sam said as he walked up onto the porch and went inside the house.

Steven stood there in that moment and took another look around and he could feel the grief that had been weighing him down start to slip away.

As Steven unloaded the wood from the truck he could feel soreness, not only in his knee and shoulder but also throughout his whole body. The day's work was starting to get to him and he felt a subtle shame fall over him when he realized that it had only really been a half-day's work. Over his life, Steven had never done anything more strenuous than cutting the lawn or washing a car.

After carrying the last load of wood onto the porch Steven sat down on the steps to take a break.

No sooner than he did Sam came out of the house and began to inspect Steven's work.

"Looks good to me. Is that gonna be enough?" Sam asked as he handed Steven a twenty-dollar bill.

"Yes sir, that's plenty." Steven replied, although he wasn't sure any amount of money was worth feeling the way that he did at that moment.

"Well I'll be glad to have you if you wanna stick around for supper." Sam offered.

"I appreciate it, that would be nice." Steven said, looking forward to more of Sam's company.

"Alright, lets go skin this coon." Sam said as he grabbed the raccoon out of the back of the truck and headed for a small tool shed that stood behind his house as Steven followed.

Sam slung the raccoon onto a wooden worktable that was in front of the shed and then took a large locking blade knife from his pocket and opened it. He laid the raccoon on its stomach and pulled its tail up.

"See you make that first cut right under his tail and across his ass. Once you cut through his hide you take your knife and cut through that tail like such." Sam said as he broke through the raccoon's tail with a cracking and popping sound.

"Now just pull that hide up and cut his feet off and push his legs through and you can pull his skin off just like a little jacket." Sam directed as he did just as he had explained.

Steven's stomach began to churn and he felt himself breakout in a cold sweat as Sam pulled the raccoon's skin up around its head. Sam cut the raccoon's front feet off and pushed the legs through and then with no warning to Steven he grasped the raccoon's head and twisted it, breaking its neck. Steven gagged and nearly threw up when he saw and heard this.

"You alright?" Sam asked while seeming to enjoy watching Steven squirm.

"Yes sir, I'm Fine." Steven said as he began to regain his composure.

"Well look in there by the door and there's a hatchet hanging on the wall. Get it for me, please sir." Sam said as he pointed inside the shed.

Steven returned with the hatchet and handed it to Sam. Sam gripped the hatchet in one hand and stretched the raccoon out with the other and then slammed the hatchet down through the raccoon's broken neck, lopping its head off.

"I gotta go sit down, Mr. Sam." Steven said as he nearly threw up again.

"Yeah, you are looking a bit peaked." Sam said as Steven returned to the porch and took a seat on the back steps as Sam continued to clean the raccoon.

Steven sat there on the steps watching Sam gut the raccoon and he thought to himself, despite the nausea that he was so glad to be having this experience.

As the afternoon faded away Steven's upset stomach faded with it. Steven and Sam were now inside, relaxing in the living room in front of the fireplace. The smell of the raccoon in the oven was overtaking the house and tempting Steven's hunger.

"Mr. Sam, I wasn't real sure about that raccoon, but if it tastes as good as it smells you won't hear any complaints from me." Steven said as he sat on the couch, enjoying the peaceful silence. Sam only responded with a smile as he stared blankly ahead at a picture over the fireplace.

"Is that your wife?" Steven asked after noticing the picture.

"Yeah, that's my Nancy." Sam said and as he did a smile cracked his stone face.

"She's very beautiful." Steven continued.

"Yeah, she was. That picture was taken right before we got married, about fifty-two years ago. The good lord called her home right before our fiftieth wedding anniversary 'bout two years ago." Sam said as his expression dimmed a bit. Steven felt sympathy for Sam and could relate to how he was feeling.

"She was my angel, I'm lost without her. You know what it's like to lose an angel?" Sam asked.

"Yes sir, I do." Steven said. His eyes welled up as he thought of his mother and sister.

"Hell, I think we could find something a little less depressing to talk about, don't you?" Sam said, trying to change the subject. Steven nodded in agreement.

"Where did you end up staying last night?" Sam asked after a short pause.

"I slept under the bridge, outside of town." Steven said with shame.

"Oh no." Sam said, wishing then that he had asked Steven to help him the day before. "Well your more than welcome to sleep on that couch until you find somewhere to stay." The old man went on.

"Okay, I really appreciate that." Steven said. It was like a weight lifted from his shoulders as he thought about not having to sleep under that bridge again.

"Think nothing of it." Sam said.

"Mr. Sam, would it bother you if I took a shower?" Steven asked.

"Not at all, make yourself at home." Sam said, making Steven feel more at home there than he had anywhere in quite a while.

Steven emerged from the shower with a renewed vigor. The hot water loosened his tense and aching muscles and he felt better than he had in days.

Steven fell into deep thought as he dried his body. He was wondering what his father was thinking. Had he even tried to look for him? Was he worried about him at all? Steven then felt a transient moment of guilt for leaving his father and he missed him for an even more brief moment. As the novelty wore away from his adventure he was starting to wonder if he had done the right thing by leaving his father. Maybe he was being selfish in taking the easy way out; maybe he should have reached out to his father or could it be that the guilt and lonesomeness that he was feeling was in some way attached to the fear he was feeling for himself? Steven had no idea what he was going to do and was suddenly very aware of it and very afraid.

Steven pushed the thoughts back in his mind to be dwelt upon later as he searched through his bag for his toothbrush. He pulled the brush from the bag along with the box of baking soda and then thought suddenly that he could use Sam's toothpaste.

He searched the counter over and found deodorant, mouthwash, cologne and other personal hygiene products but no toothpaste. He then looked over a small shelf along the medicine cabinet under the mirror and found a cup with a toothbrush in it and right beside it sat a box of baking soda.

"What is it with these people and baking soda?" Steven whispered to himself.

Steven took the box of baking soda in his hand and scanned the back of it in search of instructions for use as toothpaste, but found no such instructions. A bit addled, Steven held his toothbrush over the sink and sprinkled the baking soda over it and watched as it all fell to the bottom of the sink. Now slightly agitated he paused for a moment and searched his brain for a solution to his boggle.

Steven decided that he would try the obvious solution, so he tilted his head back and held the box over his mouth and tapped some of the baking soda into his mouth. Almost instantly he was repulsed by the taste. He spat the soda out into the sink and turned the faucet on and began to rinse out his mouth. As he did he noticed the baking soda becoming somewhat thick in his mouth and then he felt a surge of embarrassment mixed with ignorance fall over him.

After his trial and error Steven sprinkled some baking soda in his hand and added some water to it and began stirring it together with his toothbrush. The concoction formed a paste that Steven scooped up with his brush. As Steven put the brush in his mouth and began to scrub his teeth his face involuntarily contorted with disgust and he closed his eyes tightly, however as the taste of the mix remained unfavorable it became somewhat more palatable in this form.

Steven rinsed his toothbrush and stuffed his things back into his bag and got dressed in a pair of shorts and a tee shirt that he had packed and came out of the bathroom feeling like new.

As he made his way down the hallway and into the kitchen he found Sam setting the table around a pan that contained the raccoon and a variety of different vegetables.

"Is sweet tea alright? It's either that or water." Sam asked as he took a pitcher from the refrigerator.

"Tea is fine," Steven said as he sat down at the table. "It looks real good." He continued.

"Well dig in, don't be shy." Sam said as he sat down as well.

Steven prepared his plate and took a reluctant bite of the exotic meat and was pleasantly surprised with its delectable taste. He finished the food on the plate with little time wasted and quickly filled it again.

As he ate, Steven listened to Sam tell the story of the first time he ever went coon hunting with his father. Sam described every detail with great enthusiasm. As Steven listened he imagined that it was himself in those woods with Tim and that his mother and Brooke were waiting back at the house for them to return with a big raccoon and the story of how they got it. Although the fantasy provided Steven with a great comfort he realized that it was a borrowed fantasy and that he and Tim never had that kind of relationship and the harsh truth was that they never would.

After supper Sam set Steven up on the couch with blankets and a pillow and then headed off to bed himself. Sam offered Steven the use of his television set, but the couch was all too inviting to Steven.

As Steven settled into the couch he looked around the living room and could feel the love that had been shared there over the years. He stared at the picture of Sam's wife and imagined how loving she must have been. He then shifted his focus to other pictures on the mantle; pictures of children and next to those were other pictures of the same children as adults. Steven smiled as he imagined what a great childhood they must have had.

Steven fell asleep, warm and with the pleasant thoughts in his mind and he hoped, with his last bit of semi-consciousness, that they would combat the recurring, nagging thoughts of Jake's dead body that he had been ignoring.

Chapter Five

Steven awoke that Monday morning from the most restful sleep that he'd had in a long time. He sat **up** on the couch and rubbed his head while trying to gain his bearings. As he stood up, he stretched his body and then let out a satisfying yawn. He was on his way to the bathroom when Sam appeared from the dark hallway; he was fully dressed and had a cup of coffee in his hand.

"I was wondering if you was going to sleep all day." Sam said with a chuckle breaking his voice as he spoke.

"No, what time is it?" Steven asked, still feeling a little somnolent.

"Seven-thirty," Sam said as he walked by Steven and went into the kitchen. "You want some coffee?"

"Yes sir that might not be a bad idea." Steven said, widening his eyes trying to wake himself up. Sam walked over to an overhead cabinet and took a cup down and began to pour some coffee into it while Steven watched from the hallway.

"We need to get down there and cut the rest of that fire wood. Can you drive?" Sam asked as he handed the cup of black coffee to Steven.

"Yes sir." Steven answered; wondering what Sam had in mind.

"Well if you can remember how to get back to the shop, I'll let you go pick the saw up and come back and get me. I've been stoved up last couple days and I took some medicine, so I gotta see a man about a dog while your doing that." Sam explained with more detail than Steven wanted to hear.

"Okay, I think I can handle that." Steven said, a little shocked at Sam's lack of discretion. Steven took a drink of the coffee and continued on his way to the bathroom.

* * *

Steven felt somewhat liberated as he drove the truck through town; it was the first time in five days that he felt as though he was in control of something. He had little trouble returning to the general area of the shop, but drove right past it before he even realized that he was there.

After turning the truck around Steven returned to the shop. He parked in front of the building and went inside.

The door slammed behind him and the sound reverberated through the shop. Steven looked around at the many projects that were in different stages of completion; it appeared to him as though the resident mechanic was being spread very thin.

"Hello?" Steven called through the shop. The door of a small office in the corner of the shop opened and David appeared to answer Steven's call.

"Can I help you?" David asked, not recognizing Steven at first.

"Yeah, I came to pick up Mr. Sam's saw." Steven said.

"Oh yeah. I haven't had a chance to look at it yet." David said sharply.

"Okay, should I come back later?" Steven asked. David sighed and pondered a moment.

"No, come on." David said as he walked over near the door of the shop and picked the saw up from where Steven had left it a couple of days before.

David carried the saw over to one of the less cluttered workbenches and set it down. After searching the table over he picked up a Phillips head screwdriver and used it to remove a cover from the side of the saw. After removing the cover he then pulled from behind it a green, spongy filter that was filthy with dust and other debris.

David squeezed the filter in his fist as he walked over to a large parts washer, followed closely by a curious Steven. David reached behind the back panel of the washer and flipped a switch, causing a cleaning solution to spew from a nozzle at the end of a long, flexible line.

"It doesn't do any good to tell that man to clean this breather." David said as he rinsed the filter beneath the flow of cleaner. Steven remained silent as David rushed through the cleaning.

David squeezed the excess liquid from the filter and then wiped his hands on a random towel that he picked up from the table. He stuck the rag into his pocket and then returned to the saw and reinstalled the filter. After returning the filter

David unscrewed the fuel cap on the saw and then turned it up and emptied the fuel onto the floor into a pile of oil dry.

"Look under that table over there and bring me that gas can that says: mixed." David directed Steven.

"This one?" Steven asked as he brought the can over.

"Dose it say mixed?" David asked wisely. Steven paused for a second; he was only trying to be sure of what he was getting.

"Well I didn't hear it say anything, but mixed is written on it." Steven said, returning David's dry wit. David seemed at first to be a little annoyed by Steven's retaliation but then cracked a smile over Steven's smug delivery of the remark.

"He always mixes his fuel too heavy," David said as he poured fresh fuel into the saw. "That ought to fix it." David set the saw on the floor and adjusted the choke. He pulled the rope a couple of times and on the second pull the saw fired off. He pulled the throttle a few times and then cut it off.

"There you go." David said as he stood up from the floor.

"What does he owe you?" Steven asked as he searched his pocket for the money that Sam had given him.

"Nothing." David said.

"Okay, thanks." Seven said as he picked the saw up and headed for the door.

David watched Steven for a moment and then turned to move on to his next project, but as he did he knocked over a garbage can. Boxes, old parts and other refuse were scattered over the floor and David let out an aggravated yell.

Steven, who was about to walk out the door turned around to see what had happened. He saw David kneeled over picking the trash up. Without hesitation Steven set the saw on the floor and walked back to David and then proceeded to help him clean up the spill.

"You don't have to do that." David said.

"Well you didn't have to fix the saw for free either." Steven replied.

"It was nothing." David said.

"Well this is nothing." Steven answered.

"I appreciate it." David said as they finished cleaning up.

"No problem." Steven said as he once again started to leave.

"Hey," David said, catching Steven as he was about to walk out the door. "Do you really want a job?"

"I don't know anything about cars." Steven reminded him.

"Do you want a job?" David repeated.

"I definitely wouldn't turn one down." Steven said as he considered his situation.

"I can pay you six dollars an hour to sweep the floor and wash parts." David offered.

"Okay." Steven said, having only to consider it briefly.

"Can you start today?" David asked.

"How 'bout after lunch? I promised Mr. Sam that I would help him cut some more fire wood." Steven suggested.

"Alright, I'll see you at one o' clock." David said. After Steven left David hoped that he hadn't made a mistake by hiring someone whom he knew nothing about, let alone someone who knew nothing about cars.

* * *

The whole morning Steven felt excited and nervous at the same time about his new job. He told Sam about it and felt comfort as Sam seemed to show a certain pride for him. Steven observed the time with eagerness as he split and loaded the wood. Finally eleven-thirty came around and with it came the final load of wood. Steven loaded the saw and splitting maul back into the truck and then he and Sam headed back to the house.

After unloading the truck Steven went inside and found Sam setting out the left over raccoon that he had warmed up. Steven walked over to the kitchen sink and washed his hands and then sat down at the table and graciously accepted the meal.

Steven noticed as Sam walked over to the refrigerator and took down a small tin and opened it up. He took a twenty-dollar bill from it and handed it to Steven.

"Here, put that in your pocket." Sam said.

"No Mr. Sam, really you've helped me enough." Steven said. He already felt bad enough for taking the money before and imposing on the old man.

"Naw, I done worked you hard, here." Sam said as he put the money down on the table and returned the box to the top of the refrigerator. Steven reluctantly stuck the money in his pocket and continued eating.

"You're welcome to ride down to the shop and back this evening in my pick up." Sam said as he began to eat.

"Okay, thank you." Steven said. He continued to look at Sam and wondered what could make someone care so much for someone else whom they barely knew. He didn't think long about it, he was only thankful for it.

Steven finished his meal and set his plate in the sink. He grabbed the keys to the truck from the table and headed for the door.

"I'll see you this evening." Steven said as he left the kitchen.

"Okay." Sam said as he heard the front door shut.

"What am I doing, Nancy?" Sam asked out loud. "I don't even know this boy, yet I feel like I'm supposed to help him. Oh, I miss you."

Sam sat there at the table for a moment wondering why he had made such an uncharacteristic choice by taking Steven in.

"I guess he's helping me too." Sam said as the reason came to him.

* * *

As Steven entered the shop he found David working steadily under the hood of a truck. He walked over to him and made his presence known.

"One o' clock on the dot." David said, slightly impressed by Steven's punctuality.

"That's what you said." Steven replied. David put his ratchet down and began to wipe his hands on the rag that he pulled from his pocket. He walked to the middle of the shop and started an orientation of sorts on how things were to be done.

"The brooms are over there by the bathroom. I want you to keep the floors swept and the garbage emptied; there's a dumpster out back. Anytime you see any oil or water or something on the floor get some oil dry out of that can over there and pour over it. Uh, I'll show you how to use the parts washer later. Any questions?" David asked after feeling that he had made himself clear.

"No, I think I got it." Steven said, feeling a little intimidated by David after noticing, as he spoke, the full sleeve tattoos that covered both of his muscular arms; his shorn head and rugged face also added to the intimidation.

"Good, if you have any questions just ask." David said as he left Steven to his work and returned to his own.

"Well, at least I won't be bored." Steven said to himself as he looked around the shop at the cluttered floor and the brimming trashcans.

Steven spotted a two-wheeled dolly in the corner of the shop. He walked over to it and scooped up the nearest trashcan with it and headed for the door. David noticed this and felt a little relief when Steven took it upon himself to use the dolly instead of having to be told to use it.

"Maybe this one has a little sense." David said to himself.

Steven pushed behind the building, stopping to pick up stray pieces of trash along the way. Trees lined the edge of the large concrete pad that the building sat on which extended well beyond the length of the shop. Naturally the dumpster sat on the farthest corner from where Steven was. With a sigh Steven continued on towards it and then noticed a driveway leading to it from the other side of the building. As he approached the dumpster he looked down the driveway and was surprised to see a certain car sitting at the other end, out of sight from the front of the shop; it was the same car that he had seen Carrie driving Saturday morning. He wondered what the connection was between her and David; what were the chances of there being another car in this town that was identical to that one?

Steven continued working until he had every can empty though half of them were nearly full again when he was done sweeping the floor. After splitting the wood that morning and with the work he had done that afternoon he was very tired and before he knew it, it was five o' clock.

"That's gonna do it for today. I'll see you at seven o' clock in the morning." David said while looking a little tired as well.

"Alright, I'll be here." Steven said as he put his sweatshirt back on; he had to shed it earlier in the afternoon as the work started to keep him warm.

Steven left the shop and drove back to Sam's house slowly. He felt good about where he found himself and the thought of having a steady income seemed to lighten the worry that was on his mind.

Steven walked up the steps of Sam's house and let himself in. Sam was sitting in the living room, watching the news and nursing a cup of coffee. Steven joined him and could tell that he was about half-asleep.

"How did it go?" Sam inquired.

"It went fine, I think its gonna work out." Steven replied.

"Well, David is a fine fellow, he'll do you right." Sam assured him.

"I was gonna wash up a little, is there anything I need to do first?" Steven asked.

"I can't think of a thing." Sam said, fighting his sleepiness.

As Steven made his way to the bathroom, he was stopped by a knock at the front door. He looked back into the living room at Sam, who had nodded off, and then proceeded to answer the door.

Steven opened the door and found himself face to face with a slender, blonde haired woman who appeared to be in her mid thirties. By the looks of the woman Steven could tell that she was Sam's daughter, though he didn't recognize her from any of the pictures he'd seen in the house.

"Who are you?" The woman asked with a confused look about her.

"I'm Steven, I've been helping Mr. Sam." Steven explained.

"Well is Mr. Sam Here?" The woman continued with a suspect tone.

"Yeah, He's asleep in his chair." Steven said as he widened the door, inviting the woman in. The woman hurried in past Steven as if to let him know that she needed no invitation from him.

"Daddy?" The woman called as she made her way into the living room. Steven shut the door and continued on his way to the bathroom; from there he could hear the dampened conversation between Sam and his daughter.

"Daddy, who is that boy?" The daughter asked with a keen tongue.

"Now Susan just calm down, he's just been helping me split some wood." Sam explained.

"Well all I know is that I haven't heard from you in a couple of days and then I get a call from Mrs. Smith saying that you got some strange kid living with you. What's going on?" Susan ranted on a single breath.

"Well what I know is that I'm a damned grown man. This is my house and I'll let whoever I please stay here, Gail Smith needs to mind her own side of the fence. The boy is just having a hard time. I'm helping him and he's helping me." Sam defended. Steven felt guilty for being the cause of this friction between Sam and his daughter, but at the same time it felt good to have someone standing up for him.

"Well what do you know about him, Daddy?" Susan asked as she sat down on the couch.

"Enough." Sam answered.

"I don't like it." Susan said as she shook her head disapprovingly.

"Well it's not for you to like. Did you come down here just to give me the third degree, or do you actually have something to say?" Sam asked after growing tired of the stand off.

"Daddy, tomorrow is Tuesday, remember? I was gonna take you over to Learned tomorrow, to mamma's grave, remember? I've been trying to call, but your phone is still down. What did you do with the money I gave you to get it straightened out?" Susan continued as her anger turned into concern.

"I just haven't gotten around to doing it yet." Sam offered as an excuse. Steven, who was still listening from the bathroom, took the twenty dollars from his pocket and looked at it, realizing that Sam must have been paying him with his bill money.

"Well I guess I'll stay in my old room tonight so we can get an early start in the morning." Susan said as Steven entered the room.

"Steven, this is my youngest daughter, Susan." Sam said. Susan looked away, completely uninterested in the introduction.

"Hey." Steven said modestly.

"I'm sorry if you heard any of that. Susan just gets a little over protective at times." Sam continued.

"Imagine that." Susan said as she got up and went into the kitchen. Steven looked at Sam with a questioned look and he shook his head as if to tell Steven not to worry about it.

"Susan, why don't you get us some supper going?" Sam said as he got up from his chair and went into the bathroom. Susan gave no response; she just got up from the table and began to do as her father had asked.

"Is there anything I can help with?" Steven asked as he joined Susan in the kitchen.

"Look I don't know what your angle is, but my Daddy hasn't got much money, so if that's what you're after you can just move on to your next victim," Susan snapped as she turned around from the counter. "His mind is not what it used to be and it wouldn't be hard for someone to take advantage of him, so yeah I am a little protective."

"Look, I'm not after anything. Your dad was just kind enough to give me somewhere to stay so I didn't have to sleep outside anymore, that's all." Steven said, feeling somewhat angered by the accusations.

"Why were you sleeping outside, are you in some kind of trouble? You know what, on second thought I don't want to know." Susan said as she continued with supper. Steven sat down in a chair at the table still feeling angry, but not knowing quite what to say.

Steven, Sam and Susan sat down at the table over the simple meal of spaghetti. The tension was thick to start with, but as conversation ensued the tension became almost visible.

"Steven," Susan started between bites. "I don't mean to be rude, but my father and I are going on a little trip in the morning and I just don't feel comfortable leaving you in the house alone, so do you think maybe you could find somewhere to go tomorrow?"

"There's no reason for you to feel uncomfortable, besides I have a job, so I'll be there." Steven said, disgusted by Susan's implication.

"Is that right?" Susan asked with a slightly surprised expression.

"That's right, Steven started work with David Anderson today." Sam said in an effort to ease the tension.

"Oh, that should work out nicely, you're in great hands with him." Susan said with a sarcastic laugh.

"What, what's that supposed to mean?" Steven asked as he looked up from his plate.

"Oh nothing, he just committed almost every crime this town and most neighboring towns have laws for, no big deal." Susan said as she took a drink from her glass.

"Oh you're exaggerating, Suzy. People can change." Sam said as he noticed Steven's surprised reaction.

"Yeah, when it suits them." Susan added.

Steven finished his meal in silence thinking of Susan's accusations against David; trying to decide weather or not to lend them any credence. Creditable or not; Steven concluded that David's past really meant nothing to him.

After supper Steven helped Susan clean up the kitchen, despite her repugnant disposition. It wasn't long after that before everyone was in bed for the night.

Steven lay there on the couch under his blanket staring blankly at the ceiling. He couldn't get over the feeling of discord that had filled the house since Susan arrived.

* * *

Steven got up earlier than usual Tuesday morning. He sat up on the couch and listened for, but heard no other commotion in the house. He got up and put his bedding away just as he did every morning. He then went into the bathroom and changed into his work clothes.

Steven checked his pockets over making sure that he had everything that he was supposed to have. As he did he found the twenty-dollar bill in his pocket; he looked it over and felt the ever-growing guilt for having it. Steven looked at himself in the mirror as his wheels of thought begin to grind away.

Steven cut the light off and exited the bathroom with the money clinched tightly in his hand. He looked down the hallway and then proceeded to the kitchen.

Steven entered the kitchen and went straight to the refrigerator. He took the moneybox down, guided only by the dim morning light that was peaking through the window.

Steven gasped as the kitchen light was turned on just as he was returning the money to the box.

"What are you doing?" Steven heard Susan ask from behind him. He bowed his head and turned around slowly, revealing the moneybox. Susan's eyes narrowed and a look of satisfaction fell over her when she realized what she thought Steven was doing.

"I swear I was putting this back." Steven said.

"Yeah right, I'm sure you were. I knew it, you're a damned thief!" Susan said as she walked over to Steven and took the box from him.

"I wasn't stealing anything, really." Steven reaffirmed.

"Oh, really?" Susan repeated as she began to count the money.

"What in the hell is going on in here?" Sam asked as he walked into the kitchen.

"Mr. Sam I wasn't stealing from you." Steven said desperately.

"Here Daddy, count this make sure it's all there." Susan said as she handed the box to her father. Sam took the box and gave a brief look to Steven before counting the money.

"There's twenty dollars more than there should be," Sam said. He then looked at Steven confused. "I gave that money to you cause you earned it."

"You need it more than I do." Steven said, beginning to calm down.

"That's what happened to the money I gave you; you gave it to this homeless kid?" Susan asked in disbelief. Steven looked away, his throat tightened and his eyes began to well up as he fought back tears.

"Susan." Sam began, but was cut off by his daughter.

"Daddy I'm sorry, but I can barely support myself and make sure that you have what you need. I am not going to support some orphan that you drug up too." Susan said, making her point crystal clear.

"Look Mr. Sam, I'm just gonna go. I don't want to cause any problems between you and your daughter. I appreciate everything that you've done for me; I won't forget it." Steven said as he moved into the living room and collected his bags.

"Where are you gonna go?" Sam asked as he turned to face Steven.

"I don't know I'll be okay. I'll come back and check on you," Steven said as he approached the front door.

"You don't have to go." Sam said. Susan remained quiet, but firm in her opinion.

"It's okay, really. Thanks again." Steven said with a shaky voice as he opened the door and walked out of the house. Sam stood there staring at the door. A single tear escaped his eye and rolled down his aged cheek as his new best friend walked out of his life.

* * *

Steven felt a few drops of rain hit his hair as he traveled along the main road through town on his way to work. He looked up at the gray sky and felt a kinship with it, as it seemed to reflect the way that he felt. His thoughts settled on Sam as he walked, staring blankly ahead. He felt sadness and a loss greater than he felt when he left his father and he asked himself the question once more; how could someone care so much for someone else that they barely knew? He chased the thoughts from his mind and increased his pace as the raindrops began to fall more regularly.

As Steven converged upon the shop the rain became steady and he covered the last few feet of the trip in a trot. The door clanged shut behind Steven as he spilled into the shop, shaking the water from his clothes.

"Morning." David greeted as he walked from the office with a cup of coffee in hand.

"Good morning." Steven returned.

"You can set those in the office if you want to." David said after noticing Steven's bags. "After that you can come over here and give me a hand with this car."

"Okay." Steven said as he gave one last shiver caused by the cool rain. Steven went into the office and set his bags in the corner of the room and then hurried back to assist David.

"Tell me what you recognize under here so I can kind of get an idea of what you do know." David said as he pointed under the hood of the car he was working on.

"That's the motor." Steven said, identifying it as one collective piece.

"Yeah, That's the engine." David corrected as he shook his head, slightly discouraged by Steven's lack of knowledge.

"I told you." Steven said.

"It's okay, no big deal. This is the carburetor right here and underneath that is the intake manifold; we're gonna be replacing both of those." David instructed as he pointed to the center of the engine.

"Why, what do they do?" Steven inquired.

"Slow down, I'll explain later." David said, waving his hand at Steven as he picked up a ratchet from his tool chest and began to dismantle the assembly.

"Okay." Steven said as he focused his attention on the carburetor.

"So you're the kid that was sleeping under the bridge, huh?" David asked, hoping not to offend Steven. The question had been on his mind and he simply couldn't resist asking it any longer.

"Yeah," Steven began as he tilted his head, relieved that the subject was out in the open. "What, do they send out a newsletter whenever somebody new shows up around here?"

"Yeah pretty much, besides we don't get many vagrants around here so news travels pretty quick. No offence." David said, continuing to work.

"Well it's a self-imposed vagrancy so I guess I can't get too offended by it." Steven excused.

"So what, you just decided one day to pick up and start walking?" David asked.

"Yeah, that's pretty much how it happened." Steven answered.

"Well it's a life, I guess." David said as he broke the carburetor free from the engine.

"I guess." Steven said.

"So how did you end up with old man Timmons?" David asked, curiously.

"I went into that little restaurant, sat down and he just started talking to me." Steven explained.

"So you're staying with him?" David asked as he began on the manifold.

"I was, but his daughter showed up and had a fit over me being there." Steven said with a bent brow.

"That must have Been Suzy." David guessed.

"Yeah, you know her well?" Steven asked.

"You could say that." David said with a wicked smile.

"Well she had nothing but the nicest things to say about you." Steven said with sarcasm.

"I can imagine." David said as he stood up and switched tools. He caught Steven's curious look and continued. "Me and her had a little thing going at one time and well, a long story short, she took it a little more seriously than I did. We parted on bad terms and ever since then she's never passed up an opportunity to try and make my life difficult."

"Women." Steven said as if he'd had similar problems. David smirked at his apparent naivete. The rain fell heavy on the roof of the shop the whole morning while David and Steven tinkered around on different projects.

Finally, around Eleven-forty five David called for lunch. He and Steven washed up and moved into the office, settling in for a break. Steven took some of his crackers and lunchmeat from his grocery bag, along with one of the hot sodas and set the items out on the desk and prepared to eat.

"There's some cold drinks in that refrigerator." David said as he pointed to the small appliance in the corner of the office.

"Oh, okay." Steven said as he got up and kneeled down beside the icebox and began to look through it.

"I said there were some in there, I didn't say you could have one." David said with a grin. Steven's expression dropped and a look of confusion poured over him.

"I'm kidding, get a drink and get me one too." David continued as he took a sandwich from his lunch bag and turned around at the desk. Steven paused for a moment, remembering what it felt like to joke around with somebody. He took two drinks from the refrigerator and returned to his seat beside the desk.

"So are you married?" Steven asked, awkwardly trying to start a conversation.

"No." David answered simply with a short laugh.

"A bachelor, huh?" Steven concluded.

"I guess. I don't know I live with my sister; she's the one who told me about you. " David said.

"Yeah Carrie, she's your sister, huh? I was wondering about that." Steven said finally connecting the two.

"What made you wonder about that?" David asked.

"Oh the car, she was driving your car. It just made me wonder when I saw it out back yesterday." Steven said. David nodded in acknowledgment. A short silence past, as David seemed to be in thought over something.

"Where are you going to stay tonight?" David asked without looking up from his lunch. Steven paused and then spoke.

"I don't know, I've been thinking about it all day. I guess I'll head back to the bitter creek inn." Steven said dreadfully.

"You can come stay at the house if you want. It's supposed to keep raining and get a lot colder tonight. I got a camper trailer in the back, if things work out maybe you can stay there for a while; its nothing too fancy, but it beats the hell out of freezing to death outside." David offered.

"Yeah, that would be great, thanks." Steven said, wondering how things kept working out for him.

David and Steven finished their lunch and spent the rest of the day goofing off as the rain continued to fall off and on.

"Alright, lets lock up and get the hell out of here." David said as the clock on the wall struck five.

After doing his part in closing Steven stepped outside the shop and waited for David. The rain had now evolved into a mist and everything outside was completely soaked. After a moment David stepped out of the shop, slammed the door shut and then secured the deadbolt with his key.

David and Steven walked around the building, where David's car was parked. Steven stopped at the passenger door as David continued to the driver's side. David unlocked the door and got in the car and then reached over and unlocked Steven's door. Steven opened the door and set his bags in the floorboard before settling into the seat.

"This is nice." Steven said as he looked around the inside of the old Dodge.

"It's my baby." David said as he fired up the engine.

The car roared to life and Steven felt like a little kid getting ready to go on a ride when David jerked the car down into drive. The car inched forward as David released the brake and Steven noticed the antenna whipping back and forth as the engine loped.

David pulled the car out onto the street and punched the accelerator. A smile spread across Steven's face when he felt the car squat to the ground as it sped out of town like an unleashed beast.

David slowed the car down and turned in a driveway, about six miles outside of town. The car crept over the bumpy driveway and came to rest in front of a simple, one level house. The house was old, but had obviously been well kept. David got out of the car and proceeded to the house while Steven followed nervously behind him.

As Steven neared the house he looked the property over in the dwindling daylight. He saw no other house nearby and thought to himself that it must be a very peaceful place to live. As Steven walked onto the porch he could see into the house through the front window. He saw Carrie sitting in a chair talking on the phone. She was wearing a T-shirt and a pair of shorts and with her brown, shoulder length hair surrounding the soft features of her beautiful face she looked quite appealing. Steven's throat tightened with sheepish fear while the perfect words that he would need seemed to elude him as David opened the door and invited him inside.

Steven stepped into the house and shut the door behind him. He stood there at the door and watched as David went over to the table beside Carrie's chair and dropped his keys down and then began to look through the mail that was laid there.

"Okay, yeah I need to go. Alright, I'll see you then." Carrie said and then hung up the phone.

"Hey, you remember Steven, don't you?" David asked as Carrie stood from her chair.

"Yeah, hey." Carrie said, sending a smile to Steven who just smiled and nodded nervously.

"He's gonna stay with us tonight." David said, still looking through the mail. Carrie sighed awkwardly.

"If its alright." Steven added.

"It's alright." David said as he looked up at Steven and then to Carrie.

"Yeah, of course. I just wish you had called first. I could have made more for supper." Carrie said, giving David a look of disapproval for springing such a surprise on her.

"I got something to eat here, if it's a problem." Steven said, feeling like a burden.

"No, your not gonna eat Spam and crackers while we sit in here and dine on," David began as he walked around to the kitchen to see what Carrie had prepared. "Hot dogs?"

"I had a lot of studying to do today and that's all I had time for; unless you want me to quit school and be your maid." Carrie said after sensing David's disappointment over the quick meal.

"No, no hot dogs are fine. You just concentrate on keeping those grades up; you'll need them if you're gonna get that scholarship." David said as he returned to the living room.

"Of course. I'll go put some more hot dogs on." Carrie said as she went into the kitchen.

"She's a little touchy." David whispered to Steven.

"I heard that!" Carrie said from the other room. David cringed and then he and Steven shared a light chuckle.

"Look man, I'm gonna jump in the shower. There's the remote, take your jacket off and make yourself at home." David said as he walked down the hallway to his bedroom.

Steven sat down on the couch and then set his bags on the floor beside him and looked around the room. The house was clean and neat. He looked to the table beside the couch and studied a picture of whom Steven assumed were David and Carrie's parents; it appeared to be quite old. He hadn't heard David say anything about his parents; he simply assumed that they weren't around since David didn't mention them when he said that he lived with his sister.

Steven shifted his attention to the front window when he heard a vehicle approaching the house. After a moment he heard a door shut and short time later the front door opened and a short, slender girl with long blonde hair freely entered the house.

"Who are you?" Lisa asked as she looked down her nose at Steven, knowing full well who he was.

"I'm Steven. I'm working with David." Steven said as he leaned up to the edge of the couch.

"Oh yeah," Lisa said with a dismissive tone. "Where's Carrie?"

"In there." Steven said as he pointed to the kitchen even though Lisa had already started walking that way.

Steven sat on the couch uncomfortably, listening to Carrie and Lisa gab back and forth about different things until David finally returned from his shower.

"We ready to eat?" David asked as he walked back into the living room while putting his watch on.

"Yeah." Carrie said from the kitchen.

"Come on Steven." David said as he walked into the kitchen.

Steven got up from the couch and walked into the kitchen; which was just as clean as the rest of the house. He stood at the end of the table while David sat down and as he did Lisa sat down near him.

"You can sit there." Carrie said softly to Steven as she pointed to the chair in front of him. Steven sat down over a plate that was filled with three hot dogs and a pile of chips and to his left was a glass of sweet tea. His stomach growled as the smell of the food filled his nostrils as he took a bite.

"I'm going over to Julie's tonight." David said as he ate.

"Are you coming back?" Carrie asked as she motioned to Steven, who was obliviously eating his meal.

"Yeah, I'll be back tonight." David assured, to both Carrie and Steven's relief.

"Whatever." Carrie said as her abhor for Julie and her frustration with David began to show through.

"Hey, I appreciate you guys letting me stay here." Steven said in an effort to break the tension.

"Yeah, Sure." Carrie said with a fake smile; David said nothing. Steven made eye contact with Lisa. She gave a smug laugh and rolled her eyes, expressing an unfounded loathing for Steven.

Steven turned his attention back to his meal; slightly embarrassed by his own remark and everyone remained silent.

The silence was broken by a knock at the front door, followed shortly thereafter by Ran's arrogant presence in the house.

"What's up David?" Ran greeted David as he reached over and shook his hand before walking to the other end of the table and taking a seat next to Carrie. "Carrie, Lisa." Ran continued as he settled into his seat.

"Hey, Ran." Lisa said flirtatiously. Carrie didn't say anything; she only seemed to clam up even more.

"So, This is the hobo." Ran said as he stared at Steven with a devilish grin. Steven looked up, surprised that someone would say such a thing.

"Can I call you "ho"?" Ran continued while Lisa encouraged him with a brainless giggle.

"Ran." Carrie said in an effort to stifle him; Ran glanced at her briefly with the same devilish grin.

"Hey, do you have a stick with a handkerchief hanging off of it with all your shit in it?" Ran continued, ignoring Carrie's attempt to shut him up.

"Ran, chill out." David said commandingly. Ran looked at him like a child that was being scolded.

"Aww, I'm just ribbing with you, man." Ran said, daring not to ignore David's word. Steven looked back to his plate, thinking that maybe he would have been better off under the bridge.

"Carrie, I've been trying to call you, are you still mad at me?" Ran asked Carrie quietly.

"Mad about what?" David asked.

"Oh nothing, we just had a little misunderstanding the other night." Ran answered.

"Carrie?" David asked as he looked at his sister.

"It's nothing." Carrie said as she got up and began to clear the table.

Lisa watched Carrie and felt frustration and jealousy towards her. She was of the opinion that Carrie should have given Ran what he wanted; she would have. He was Ran Mitchell and he deserved it. Lisa always thought that deep down Carrie knew that she didn't have to use sex to keep guys interested; they were always falling all over themselves just to be seen with such a beautiful girl, so she never had to use it unless she wanted to.

"Well I'm gonna go then. Carrie, are you sure everything is okay?" David asked as he got up and looked at his watch.

"Go, David." Carrie said without turning around from the sink.

L.B. Kelly

"Alright, I'll see ya'll later. Make yourself at home." David said to Steven as he left the room and then left the house.

"Carrie, can I talk to you in private?" Ran asked as he got up and moved over to the sink beside her.

"I've got nothing to say to you." Carrie said.

"Well I got something to say to you." Ran quickly replied.

"I don't want to hear it." Carrie said sternly.

"Carrie, please." Ran pleaded. Carrie sighed and lowered her shoulders. She dropped the plate and utensils that she was holding into the sink and walked out of the kitchen accompanied by Ran.

The kitchen became silent and even more uncomfortable. Steven looked across the table at Lisa with no idea what to say or do.

"Well I've had enough of the Carrie show, I'm leaving." Lisa said bitterly as she got up and walked out of the room.

"It was nice to meet you." Steven said politely as Lisa past by; she gave no response before slamming the front door as she exited the house.

Steven finished his meal and began to feel homesick for Sam's house while listening to Carrie and Ran bicker at one another. After a moment he got up and walked over to the sink and washed his plate and glass in the soapy water that Carrie had drawn. After washing his own he then proceeded to wash the rest of the dishes and set them neatly to dry in the drain rack beside the sink.

He left the kitchen as neatly as he possibly could and went into the living room and sat down on the couch. He could hear from down the hall, Ran yelling obscenities and occasionally something slamming against the wall.

"I can't get away from it." Steven said to himself, referring to the current situation being parallel to the one that he'd left.

Steven got up and walked out onto the porch and began to breath the cool air deeply into his lungs, hoping it would calm him down, but he could still hear the commotion inside the house and it sickened him. He couldn't help but feel that he should go in and say something, try and break it up.

"It's none of your business, just leave it alone." He said to himself as he leaned over on the handrail that surrounded the house-length porch.

Finally he'd heard enough. Steven went back into the house and walked straight down the hall being led to Carrie's room by the acrimony. Steven put his hand on the doorknob, but then stopped.

"Don't back down, stand up for a change like you did to John. Do it!" Steven said to himself inside his mind. At last he swallowed the lump in his throat and swung the door open. He saw Carrie standing on the opposite side of the room, trembling with her face awash. He then looked to Ran who was seething and he realized that the situation may come to blows and if it did then so be it.

"What the hell are you doing, Hobo? Piss off!" Ran yelled.

"I think it's time for you to leave." Steven said strongly, surprising even himself.

Ran clinched his fists and stared a hole through Steven. He looked at Carrie and snorted out an angry breath before walking to the door.

"You don't want to play this game with me, Hobo." Ran said to Steven as he stopped in front of him on his way out of the room.

Carrie jumped slightly as the front door slammed and she seemed to relax bit when she heard Ran's car tear out of the driveway. She slid down the wall and began to sob. Steven stood there at the door watching her, trying to decide if he should try to comfort her.

He couldn't take it anymore, he decided that comforting her would be a comfort to himself as well so he moved over to her, kneeled down and put his arm around this perfect stranger.

"Thank you." Carrie said with a tremulous voice.

"You don't have to thank me for that, I just wish I had come in sooner." Steven replied with his grip on her remaining steady.

"It's okay." Carrie said as she wiped the tears from her face.

"Are you going to tell David about this?" Steven asked as Carrie got up from the floor and went into her bathroom, leaving the door open.

"No and neither are you." Carrie said emphatically.

"Why?" Steven asked after a moment, slightly puzzled.

"Besides the fact that David would kill him, he really didn't do anything. I mean he didn't touch me or anything; he just gets like that sometimes. I can handle him, his bark is bigger than his bite." Carrie explained as she washed the smudged make-up from her face.

"Well his bark sounded pretty big." Steven said as he stood up from the floor.

"I think I'm just going to become a nun and give up on guys and dating." Carrie jested as she turned the bathroom light off and went back into the bedroom.

"You know, not all guys are like that." Steven said in defense of his gender. Carrie gave a tired smile that sent a chill up Steven's spine and made his heart melt in his chest.

"I better get in here and finish these dishes." Carrie said, breaking an awkward silence.

"I already did it." Steven said. Carrie stopped sharply on her way out of the room and turned around and gave Steven a pleasantly surprised look.

"You washed the dishes?" Carrie asked.

"Yeah." Steven answered.

"Thanks, I don't remember a night that's gone by when I haven't washed dishes." Carrie said with the same tired smile as before.

"It's the least that I could do." Steven said sincerely.

"Okay, well lets go fix you up a place to sleep." Carrie said seeming to appreciate Steven's lack of pretence.

Carrie walked out of her bedroom and stopped at a closet in the hallway as Steven continued on into the living room. Carrie joined him a short time later with a blanket and pillow in hand. She then proceeded to convert the couch into a bed with help from Steven.

"Is that your mom and dad?" Steven asked after once again noticing the picture on the table next to the couch.

"Yeah." Carrie said as she glanced at the photo.

"You look just like your mom." Steven said in compliment to Carrie, trying to build a conversation.

"Yeah, every body always said that. I never knew her; she died after I was born so my daddy was everything to me. He died two years ago.

David had his own thing going, but after daddy died he had to move back here and take care of me. Sometimes I feel kind of like I'm holding him back, you know?" Carrie said as she continued to make the bed, she seemed glad to have someone to talk to.

"I'm sure he doesn't feel that way." Steven assured her.

"Can I ask what your story is?" Carrie asked curiously. Steven smiled in an effort to conceal his reluctance to discuss the subject.

"Yeah, I guess." Steven replied as he searched for a starting point in his mind. "I lost my mother and my sister, Brooke about a year ago in a car wreck; some drunk guy hit them and ran them off the road and." Steven began.

"No, I'm sorry. I shouldn't have asked." Carrie said on second thought, cutting him off.

"No it's okay, really. It's just that I've never really talked to anybody about it." Steven said as he sat down on the made-up bed next to Carrie.

"What about your daddy?" Carrie asked, fully engrossed in the conversation.

"No, Tim likes to talk with his hands. I don't know what happened; after my mother and sister died he just kind of flipped out you know? I guess he just took all his grief and anger out on me cause I never once saw him cry.

When I went back to school after the first time he hit me I could tell people were talking about me and it wasn't long before different rumors started floating around, things got pretty rough." Steven paused for a moment, staring blankly. "It's kind of ironic really, I used to get beat on and talked down to at school because I got beat on and talked down to at home. I just finally got fed up with it all one day and hit the road." Steven summed up with a sigh.

"And here you are." Carrie added.

"Here I am." Steven said.

Carrie stared at Steven while she tried to compute everything that he'd just told her and suddenly her problems seemed to pale in comparison. They spent the rest of the evening talking and getting to know each other. A bond was starting to form between them; neither of them was expecting it and they were both feeling very cautious of it.

* * *

The week wore on and Steven fell into a routine and was becoming settled in the camper trailer. He was also becoming comfortable with his new surroundings and his new role in life.

Strangely, Steven was starting to miss his father and the irony of it angered him. As abusive as his father was the fact remained that Tim was his father, regardless of the fact that Steven couldn't live with him.

Friday morning rolled around and Steven was tired, tired from work, worry and tired from the general discomfort of transition, which was slowly becoming easier.

The shop was cold that morning, but nearly spotless after Steven's week of cleaning and organizing. As Steven entered the shop with David he began turning switches and different equipment on; it hadn't taken him long to catch on to the way David liked for things to be done.

"It's payday." David said as he walked into the office and turned the coffee maker on.

David sat down at the desk and pulled a large checkbook from one of the drawers and began to make out a check.

"Harris, right?" David asked, pausing his writing.

"Yeah." Steven answered with excitement over receiving his first paycheck.

David handed the check to Steven, whose eyes widened when he read the amount: Two hundred Seventy dollars.

"Thanks, thanks a lot." Steven said with gratitude.

"You earned it, the place looks great." David commended.

"What about the trailer; don't I need to give you some kind of rent?" Steven asked.

"We'll work that out later, just get what you need with that." David said.

Steven looked down at his tattered shoes with David's words ringing in his ears; he knew right away that the first thing he was going buy would be the most comfortable shoes that he could find.

"Where's the nearest shoe store?" Steven asked as he looked back up at David.

"Melton, down the highway about twelve miles. I'll tell you what, I'm gonna stay at Julie's house tonight. I'll let Carrie use the car and maybe she'll take you over there and show you around." David said as he got up and walked past Steven and into the shop.

Steven stood there in the office staring at the check in his hand and as he did a pit of anticipation grew in his stomach as he thought about Carrie and he knew then that he would be able to think of nothing else for the rest of the day.

* * *

The whole day Steven counted each minute that passed, looking forward to that night. Finally the day was gone and the night had begun and Steven felt total comfort as he and Carrie walked through the shopping mall. He noticed that guys were casting stares at him along the way. They weren't the loathsome stares that he was accustomed to, but they were envious stares, envy for the beautiful girl that was on his arm. The feeling was strange to him, but it felt good.

Carrie led Steven through all of her favorite stores in the mall from the music store to the girly bath soap store. They stopped at the shoe store where Steven bought the most comfortable pair of shoes that he had ever put on his feet. He wore them out of the store and dropped his old pair in the garbage can along the way. Steven's mind was clear of all other worries in that moment in time.

As they continued through the mall a jacket inside the window of a clothing store caught Steven's attention. He stopped outside and looked at it for a moment and then decided to go in for a closer look.

"What do you think?" Steven asked Carrie as he continued to study the jacket.

"It's nice, you ought to try it on." Carrie encouraged with a smile.

Steven took the jacket down from the rack and pulled it on over his sweatshirt. He turned to the mirror on the wall and looked at himself. The jacket did look good and even better it made him feel less like a bum.

"Well?" Steven asked as he turned to Carrie, holding the jacket out to show it's warm lining. Carrie moved her hand over the outside of the jacket and then moved to the inside to feel the lining; the back of her hand moved gently over Steven's chest as she rubbed back and forth on the fabric. Steven felt goose bumps crawl over the back of his neck and his heart fluttered as he felt her warm touch.

Carrie's heart also fluttered as a result of the inadvertent contact and it surprised her. She would have never thought when she met Steven that he would be the type of guy that she would fall for.

Over the past week Carrie had become aware of Steven's uncommon respect for women and everyone else for that matter. He seemed to have no agenda; he didn't expect anything from anyone that he hadn't earned and he expected no less from everyone else. Carrie's attraction for Steven was growing from mutual respect.

Carrie froze her movement and looked at Steven; she could feel his heart pounding his chest as she slid her hand away slowly.

"I think you should get it." Carrie said softly. Steven swallowed tensely as he snapped himself back to reality.

"Uh, yeah I think I will." Steven said as he awkwardly took the jacket off. Steven paid for the jacket and he and Carrie left the store.

"It looks good on you." Carrie said as they walked, trying to ease the tension that could be felt between them.

"You really think so?" Steven asked as he straightened the jacket out after putting it back on.

"Yeah." Carrie said with a smile.

"So, are you hungry?" Steven asked after spotting the food court.

"Yeah, I could probably use something to eat." Carrie replied.

Steven and Carrie made their way to the food court and stood in front of a small burger stand and began to look the menu over.

"You know what you want?" Steven asked.

"Uh huh." Carrie answered.

"Can I help you?" A young girl asked as Steven approached the counter.

"I want a number six and whatever she wants." Steven said as he stepped to the side while Carrie placed her order.

"Eight sixty-five." The girl said.

Steven paid for the food and in no time it was ready. He picked the tray up and followed Carrie to a small table where they sat down.

"So how are things going at the shop with David?" Carrie asked as she situated her meal.

"Great, David's been real good to me." Steven said.

"Well he'll be that way from now on as long as you're good to him; if you've got David for a friend he'll just about kill himself to try and help you." Carrie explained about her brother. "He really likes you."

"He's got no reason to worry about me." Steven began as he ate. "So him and Julie, are they serious?"

"Yeah, he hasn't said it to me, but I think he wants to marry her." Carrie said.

"So what's the problem?" Steven asked.

"Me." Carrie said bluntly. "I think he feels like he would be abandoning me if he married her. He wants me to go to college and find a job Four years later just like everybody else around here because he thinks that's what daddy would have wanted."

"What do you want?" Steven asked.

"I don't know, but I do know that I don't want my future mapped out for me; I don't even know if I want to stay in Mississippi." Carrie said as she picked at her hamburger.

"Well I've learned that it doesn't do any good; you can follow a plan you're whole life and then one day the ground gets snatched out from under you and none of it means anything anymore." Steven said as he drew upon his own experiences in life. Carrie suddenly felt her connection to Steven deepen as he articulated perfectly the way she had been feeling for the past two years.

Carrie's cell phone rang, interrupting the conversation. She sighed in frustration and then began to dig through her purse in search of it.

"Hello?" Carrie answered.

"Hey, what are you doing? I tried to call earlier; where are you?" Lisa asked from the other end of the line.

"I'm at the mall with Steven." Carrie said as she looked at Steven.

"Oh, well ditch him and come out to the bridge. Ran's here, he said he's real sorry about what happened the other night." Lisa explained for Ran.

"I don't care, I'm sick of even thinking about him." Carrie said.

"Well come on anyway we're having fun, everybody's here." Lisa coaxed.

"Okay I'll see if Steven wants to go, if he does we'll be out there later." Carrie said as she ended the call before Lisa could offer protest over her bringing Steven; Carrie wasn't about to blow him off now.

"Do you feel like making some new friends?" Carrie asked with a smile.

* * *

The engine of the Dodge rumbled low as Carrie slowed the car down and steered it into the narrow driveway that led to the landing by the bridge. As they parked Steven felt sickened by the memory, which still lingered there, of his agonizing first night in Fanning.

Carrie cut the engine and started to get out of the car when she noticed that Steven seemed to be glued into place as he looked out at the small, intimate looking crowd of people under the bridge.

"What is it?" She asked.

"Nothing, I've just never been good with new people." Steven said feeling nervous about being received into the tight circle of friends, not to mention the fact that Ran was there too.

"You've been fine with me." Carrie replied with a smile.

"You've made it easy." Steven said.

"Well this will be easy too, come on." Carrie said as she got out of the car, Steven got out and started walking a few paces behind her.

As they approached the fire-lit area Steven glanced across the creek to his former camp sight, he felt a shock of embarrassment for himself as he thought of how he must have looked to Carrie that night.

Steven shrugged off the disheartening thoughts and continued walking and as he did he found himself alone. He spotted Carrie next to the fire in the company of a short, stocky guy who was seated on a large cooler. As Steven surveyed the rest of the scene he saw another aberrant young man who was sitting on the sandy ground staring impassively into the fire. He then noticed Ran and Lisa off to the side, appearing to be in deep conversation.

"I can't believe she actually brought him. It's so creepy; he's like a real homeless person. He probably escaped from a mental hospital or something." Lisa said to Ran as they stood, watching Steven from the edge of the fire's illumination.

"It's alright. If this freak wants to play with me, I'll play." Ran said as he took a drink from his beer, while staring Steven down. "I've been patient with Carrie for too long, she's not gonna make me look like an idiot now, not with that trash anyway."

"You know Ran, I'd give you what you want if you'd just let me." Lisa said suggestively to Ran who was still watching Steven, who by this time had joined Carrie next to the fire.

"Yeah, me and everybody else." Ran said, totally uninterested in Lisa's proposal as he set his beer down while he lit a cigarette.

Lisa looked at Ran with shock, as though she'd never thought of herself that way. She wasn't a slut, just because she wasn't a prude like miss high and mighty Carrie. Lisa was angered to be put in that category. In her mind she was no different from Ran; because he was a guy it added to his manhood to sleep with as many girls as he could, but since Lisa was a female promiscuity made her a whore.

"Steven, this is Jeff, he's one my oldest friends." Carrie introduced as Steven walked over to them.

"Hey." Steven said as Jeff got up and shook his hand.

"You want a beer?" Jeff asked as he held the lid of the cooler open. Steven's first instinct was to decline, but then after a second thought he reached down and took one. He had never so much as held a beer before although he'd smelt plenty of them thanks to Tim, he only hoped that he wouldn't be as disappointed by the taste as he was by the smell.

Steven cracked the beer open and started to drink it as Carrie took one for herself. Steven's face wrinkled with disgust and he realized that his hopes were in vain as the brew rolled down his throat.

"Are you okay?" Carrie asked with a playful laugh as Steven shuttered with the aftertaste.

"Yeah." He answered through a cough.

"Aww don't worry, the good thing is that the more you drink, the better they start to taste." Jeff said with a slanted smile, Steven just returned the smile and thought that he might as well test the theory as he took another drink.

"So how long have y'all known each other?" Steven asked, still trying to feel Jeff out.

"Since the first grade; me and Jeff got married under the oak tree on the playground the first time we met. Do you remember that?" Carrie asked with her ever-present smile as she hugged a blushing Jeff.

"Yeah, I remember." Jeff reluctantly admitted. Steven smiled as he observed the purity of their friendship and wished briefly to know the feeling himself. Carrie's smile disappeared and her entire demeanor changed as Ran approached followed by Lisa.

"Hey Hobo, did you put in on that?" Ran asked as he gestured to the beer in Steven's hand. Steven said nothing.

"Come on Ran, he ain't hurting nothing." Jeff said as he stood up.

"I didn't ask you anything, Jeff. This beer is for people that were invited." Ran said.

"What do I owe?" Steven asked as he reached for his wallet.

"You don't owe anything, I invited you." Carrie interjected.

"Yeah, I guess your right Carrie. Besides you shouldn't need an invitation to come back to your own house, by the way you don't mind us using your place do you, Hobo?"

Ran asked with an arrogant smile while Ricky and Lisa encouraged him with mindless laughter.

"Ran, shut up." Carrie said.

"Carrie, I'm sorry, but if your going to hang around with a homeless guy your gonna hear things like that." Ran continued with a smile.

"He's not homeless." Carrie said as she looked at Steven, wishing that Ran would just leave him alone.

"Oh, that's right. I heard your were living in my trailer. How do you like my trailer, Hobo?" Ran asked as took another step closer to Steven.

"It's alright. It smells a little funny though; kind of like sweaty ass and idiot." Steven said causing everyone to burst into laughter, including Lisa and Ricky.

Ran clinched his teeth and narrowed his eyes as he glared at Steven. Steven stiffened his stance and prepared himself for anything.

"You know," Ran started as he squatted and picked a handful of sand up from the ground; he let some trickle through his fingers as he stood back up and began to speak again. "If your not comfortable there you could take some of this sand and spread it around, maybe build a campfire in the middle of the floor." Ran then threw the sand in Steven's face, causing him to stumble backward and drop his beer. Jeff stepped in between them as Ran cocked his fist to hit Steven.

"Get off me!" Ran said as he turned his glare towards Jeff. Jeff stepped aside and said nothing.

"Come on Steven, let's go." Carrie said as she walked past Ran on her way to the car.

"You don't have to go, Carrie." Ran said.

"I told you not to bring him." Lisa added. Carrie stopped and then turned to face them.

"If he's not welcome than neither am I.I can't believe you people. How can you be so hateful to someone that you don't even know?" She asked, but received no answer.

Steven took a last look at everyone and then started to walk over to Carrie when Ran stopped him and leaned in close as Carrie looked on.

"You know you're just a puppy to her, a stray dog. Once the novelty wears off of you she'll forget all about you." Ran whispered to Steven, who was staring straight ahead at Carrie. Ran followed Steven's gaze and began to speak again. "She's just having a hard time right now and you're just something to pity, something to make her forget about feeling sorry for herself." Steven just looked Ran in the eye and then looked at Carrie.

"I feel sorry for you." He said before walking away.

Ran stood there wondering what he'd accomplished, other than pushing Carrie further away from him. He just couldn't understand why she didn't want to have anything to do with him and the fact that he couldn't have her and somebody like Steven could burned him up even more.

Lisa sighed and felt a little guilt over her part in instigating the confrontation as she looked at Ran and began to feel the same frustration with him that he was feeling with Carrie.

Carrie took Steven's hand and turned and walked away from her friends with the underlying feeling that things were changing between her and them and that they would never be quite the same again.

* * *

The ride home was spent in silence, with both Carrie and Steven thinking of what had just happened. Steven couldn't help but think that he was still the same old doormat that he'd always been, only with a new set of footprints on him. He was determined to change that, he had a chance to start over and he wasn't going to lie down for anyone anymore.

Carrie parked the car in it's usual spot in front of the house and cut the engine. She and Steven sat in the car; each waiting for the other to say something, anything. Carrie wanted to hear something to make her feel better about leaving her friends the way that she had and Steven wanted to know that Carrie felt good about standing up for him even though there was no reason for her to choose him over her friends.

"Thanks for what you said back there to Lisa about me not being welcome; it made me feel almost human again." Steven said out of the dead silence, while the incandescent shine from the porch light set his face aglow as he stared into it. He'd said exactly what Carrie needed to hear; standing up to Lisa was worth it to her if it made that much of a difference to Steven.

"Well that's how I feel." Carrie said as she put her hand on top of Steven's.

Steven looked at Carrie and memorized every feature of her face in a second, from every curve of her faultless lips to the irreproachable beauty of her hypnotic, crystal-blue eyes. To Steven her beauty was immeasurable.

Carrie took in a deep breath and held it in as she leaned forward, inviting Steven to meet her. Steven moved in also. It was like he was operating on auto pilot; he wasn't nervous or afraid.

Carrie closed her eyes as their lips met softly and she could feel Steven's heart pounding in his chest. She put her hand on his neck and rubbed gently as the kiss intensified.

Steven reached out and placed his hand on the back of her neck, underneath her hair. The moment seemed to last forever as he savored the taste of the kiss and the warmth of her skin upon his face.

Steven touched Carrie's face and slowly pulled away from her. He had never shared a moment of closeness like that with anyone before. He looked at her in amazement through a new set of eyes as the rest of the world faded back in around her. He no longer saw her as the pretty girl that everyone else saw; he was now able to see the beauty inside the girl that no one else could see.

Carrie opened her eyes and reached to her face and took Steven's hand. She saw the look on his face and she knew that there was no other place she'd rather be in that moment. The kiss was like no other she'd ever felt before. It was spontaneous and for once she felt that a kiss was not just the beginning of another five seconds of ecstasy that would be forgotten in a couple of weeks, but this one was sure to be one that she would remember the rest of her life.

"I'd better go in." Carrie said after a moment.

"Yeah, It is getting kind of late." Steven said, still not able to believe what had just happened.

They sat there in the car a while longer, staring at each other before Carrie took the keys from the ignition and got out of the car.

"I did have a good time tonight, certain moments aside." Steven said as he walked around to the front of the car to meet Carrie.

"I did too, I really did." She replied with a smile as they stood there in another shared moment of silence.

"Well goodnight." Carrie said as she slowly walked away. Steven watched as she walked up the front steps and disappeared into the house.

"Goodnight." He said with a smile.

Chapter Six

Nearly three months had past since Steven left his father's house. Though he'd found comfort and shelter in the houses of strangers and the warmth of a loving embrace he still found himself longing for a certain degree of acceptance and the feeling that he belonged.

Over the past few weeks the tension between Steven and Ran had tapered off, however, the conflict was still alive and well. To Steven it had just become commonplace to deal with Ran's ignorance and his unwillingness to accept Steven's relationship with Carrie.

Steven had Ran figured out and was able to handle him, Lisa on the other hand was a different story. She was somewhat of a mystery to Steven, ever since he'd met her she seemed to have a love/hate relationship with Carrie. There would be times when they would act so disgusted with one another and the next day they would be hanging on each other's arms laughing and talking like nothing had ever happened. Steven held little regard for Lisa as a friend and held even less respect for her as a person after seeing the way that she conducted herself around the opposite sex.

David was still a complete enigma to Steven. Even after working with him every day for almost three months he still knew very little about him, however he had come to have more respect for him than he'd ever had for anyone.

Steven lay in his bed, staring out of the narrow window of the camper into the darkness of the night.

"2:17A.M." The alarm clock by his bed displayed.

Steven sighed and then began to visually explore every detail of the trailer in an attempt to take his mind off of the reoccurring dream that had continued to haunt his sleep ever since that night under the bridge. It seemed that every time he had the dream he would feel a new part of Jake's realization and fear in the split second of revelation that engulfed him just before he drew his final breath. There was no change in the dream; it happened each time as it did in reality until Jake's dead body becomes Steven's and Michael takes the form of Steven's father, Tim.

Each time Steven felt terror and an apprehensiveness like no other that he had ever known before as Tim would move closer to him with that sinister grin that was now etched into Steven's mind.

Steven stared at the ceiling for hours, until the sun started to peak over the trees that stood sparsely about the field behind the trailer. Finally six o' clock crept upon him and he reached over to his clock and flipped the alarm switch to the off position as it began to emit its superfluous shriek. He stood up from the bed and proceeded to get dressed even though he felt more weary than he had the night before.

Steven took a soda from the small refrigerator in the kitchen area and began to drink as he looked over the neat and well-kept trailer. He saw Carrie's cell phone lying on the small couch where she had been sitting the night before. He walked over and picked it up. As he looked at it he was reminded of the first time that he met her and how taken he was with her.

Steven took in a cool breath and took a drink from his soda while shutting the door of the camper behind him as he stepped out into the new day. He followed the worn path that led from the camper to the front steps of Carrie's house. He climbed the steps and gave a quick knock to the unlocked door as he entered the house.

The house was quiet and still, no sound could be heard except that of the shower running. Steven walked through living room and stopped at the end of the couch and stared for a moment at the Christmas tree that stood in front of the window on the farthest wall of the house. He studied the needles of the tree and closed his eyes as he took in its bold smell. He and Carrie picked the tree out and cut it down the week before after Carrie found out that Steven had never had a real Christmas tree before. It was always the four-foot, plastic tree at Steven's house since Tim would never take the time to cut a real tree or spend the extra money to buy one.

"Brooke would love this." Steven thought to himself, as he looked the tree over while trying to fight back the lump in his throat. Steven dried his slightly tearing eyes when he heard Carrie's bedroom door open.

"Good morning," Steven greeted as he met her with open arms in the hallway. "How did you sleep?"

"Like a baby." She said as she fell into Steven's arms after a long stretch. Steven kissed her as though he hadn't seen her in a year; it was obvious to him as well as everyone else that they were falling in love. "Did you sleep?"

"No." Steven answered, shaking his head.

"I'm sorry," Carrie began as she hung her arms around his neck and smiled enticingly. "I'll tell you what, how about I come over and stay with you until you fall asleep tonight?"

"I don't know, I may not fall asleep at all then." Steven said, returning the smile.

"Well I think we could find some way to pass the time." Carrie said as she stood on her toes and kissed Steven again.

"Alright, That's enough of that." David said as he emerged from the bathroom, breaking up the kiss.

"Good morning, David." Steven said dryly as he pulled away from Carrie ever so slightly.

"Morning." David returned as he continued on into the kitchen.

"I gotta go get ready." Carrie said as she kissed Steven again before disappearing back into her bedroom. Steven stood there wondering if Carrie was serious about staying with him that night. He felt that old, familiar nervousness as he concluded that she probably was. Although things had become quite heated between the two of them, they hadn't become comfortable enough with each other to take it to the next level. Steven could feel it getting closer and he was terrified. Steven was sure that he loved Carrie and he wasn't at all opposed to the prospect of having sex with her. The fact remained that he had never had sex with anyone and he didn't want to disappoint her. He didn't know how to tell her, or whether he should even tell her at all and he definitely couldn't ask David for his opinion.

Steven shook his head in frustration and went into the kitchen where David was sitting at the table over a bowl of cereal and a car magazine.

"You look like shit." David said as he looked up briefly from his reading. Steven cracked a smile at David's blunt honesty.

"Well I guess that's not too bad since I feel like beat up shit." Steven said as he sat down at the table and took a drink of his soda.

"You still not sleeping?" David asked with genuine concern. Steven shook his head.

"No, I've just been having these really weird dreams, that's all." Steven said.

"You want to talk about it?" David asked.

"To be honest with you, I really don't" Steven answered.

"That's cool, but if you change your mind I'll listen." David said, looking Steven in the eye.

"Thanks." Steven said as he stared at his soda can, wishing that he could tell someone about his dreams.

"Has anybody seen my phone?" Carrie asked as she entered the kitchen. Steven took the phone from his coat pocket and held it up, without saying a word.

"Thank you very much." Carrie said as she took the phone from Steven and leaned against him.

"I'm gonna tie that thing around your neck." David said as he continued eating.

"Yeah, Yeah. You guys must have been talking about me, everybody shut up when I came in." Carrie said, ignoring David's remark.

"Yeah, but it was mostly all good." David joked.

"Your not hungry, Steven?" Carrie asked after noticing that Steven wasn't eating.

"Not really." Steven replied tiredly.

"You will be later, let me fix you something." Carrie said as she walked over to the refrigerator.

"No, you don't have to." Steven said.

"Well hell, I'll take some eggs." David said through a bite of cereal.

"I know you will, I'll make some for both of you." Carrie said while continuing to round everything up.

Everyone sat silently; David was engrossed in his magazine and Carrie was busy with breakfast while Steven sat, watching both of them. He was still thinking of what Carrie said about sleeping over with him that night.

"Will tonight be the night?" Steven asked himself in thought. As Steven pondered the possibility he heard Lisa's car pull up outside, just as she did every morning.

"Good morning everybody." Lisa said cheerfully as she breezed into the kitchen.

"Hey." Carrie said, a little surprised by her peaceful disposition.

"I feel so good today." Lisa said as she sat down at the opposite end of the table from Steven.

"What happened, did you hit a dog or something on your way over?" Steven asked wisely. Lisa cut her eyes at Steven as David snickered at the remark.

"Even you can't ruin my mood today." Lisa said sharply. Steven just rolled his eyes and adjusted his position in the chair.

"Well what's got you feeling so good?" Carrie asked as she set two plates of eggs and toast on the table for David and Steven.

"Well if you must know, Ran came over last night and asked me out for Friday." Lisa answered with a smile.

"What about Ricky?" Carrie asked after a short pause.

"What about him? Its not like we're married or anything." Lisa defended.

"Well are you at least going to tell him?" Carrie asked.

"If it comes up." Lisa said, completely unconcerned about Ricky's feelings. Steven shook his head as he observed her coldness.

"You know who you should go out with?" Carrie asked.

"Who?" Lisa asked curiously.

"Jeff." Carrie said with a smile.

"Yeah, right" Lisa said with a short laugh.

"What? Jeff's a great guy." Carrie said in his favor.

"Uh, he's a fat guy." Lisa said with a disgusted look about her.

"Your such a bitch, Lisa. How can you be so shallow?" Steven asked, having heard enough of Lisa's mouth.

"How can you be such a hobo, ass?" Lisa returned spitefully.

"Okay, Lets go Steven. We're gonna be late." David said in an effort to diffuse the situation as he stood up from the table. Steven sat for a moment, returning Lisa's glare before getting up and leaving the kitchen.

"Just don't let her bother you." Carrie whispered to Steven as she followed him to the front door.

"I don't see how you deal with her all the time." Steven said as David cranked the car.

"She's not that bad. Y'all just got off on the wrong foot is all, she's my friend and I love her so please try to get along with her." Carrie pleaded.

"I can't make any promises." Steven said as he leaned in and kissed her.

"Come on, let's go!" David said as he stepped out of the car.

"You better go." Carrie said, holding Steven's hand as he walked away.

"It's my time to drive, isn't it?" Steven said as he sailed down the steps.

"Think again, lover boy." David said without consideration as he got back into the car.

"I just thought I would try." Steven said, winking at Carrie as he got into the car as well.

"You try every day, why should today be any different?" David asked as he started to back the car out.

"Let me get this straight. You trust me with your sister, but not your car?" Steven asked.

"Weird, huh? Besides who said that I trust you with my sister?" David asked as he pulled the car out on to the road while Steven looked at him confused.

* * *

Steven sat in the office with David at lunchtime. He was ignoring the dull hunger that was trying to remind him that it was time to eat and he was trying to ignore the rattling hum of the air compressor in the shop in hopes that he would be able to catch up on his sleep.

Steven closed his eyes and finally his hunger subsided, the compressor cycled off and the music that was coming from the radio in the shop was starting to fade into the background of his thoughts when the phone rang.

"Anderson's." David answered after the second ring. Steven cracked his eyes open slightly and closed them as David started to speak again.

"Yeah, this is David. Who is this?" David asked with a cocked eyebrow.

"Oh yeah, of course I remember you. What in the hell are you up to?" He continued as his expression lightened a bit.

"Yeah? Yeah? Well that'll be cool; we ought to get together." David said, listening closely as he relaxed in his chair.

"Yeah I got somebody working with me now, but I got more work down here than I know what to do with, so yeah

L.B. Kelly

we could probably use a little help." David said, capturing Steven's attention as he was drifting back to sleep.

"Okay, tomorrow? I'll see you then." David said as he hung the phone up with a somewhat baffled expression.

"What was that all about?" Steven asked while trying to focus in on David.

"That was just an old friend of mine; he said he's coming back to town and he's looking for work. I haven't seen him in a couple of years." David said, still staring at the phone.

"So he's gonna be working with us?" Steven asked, feeling a little threatened by the news.

"Yeah, but don't worry; you're not going anywhere. We just need a little help with some of this work and he's a pretty good mechanic." David said, setting Steven's mind at ease.

"Yeah, I am getting a little tired of carrying you." Steven said with a smirk.

"Oh, you are? Well why don't you carry your ass out there and sweep the floor there hot shot." David said as he stood up from his chair and walked out into the shop. Steven sat there for a minute and as his smile expired he thought of Carrie and the nervous anticipation of the following evening crept upon him once again and embedded itself in the back of his mind.

Steven let out a long, cleansing sigh and then stood up from his chair. He looked out into the shop through the window that was above the desk. He watched David as he hovered around the shop, undecided about which project to start on next. For a brief moment he thought about asking David for his advice on the situation, but then thought better of it as he concluded that he himself wouldn't want to dispense such advise concerning his own sister.

Steven walked out into the shop and found his broom and then began sweeping the floor with the questions burning in his mind: "What am I going to do? How am I going to handle this? What if I disappoint her?" He spent the rest of the day asking himself those questions as he moved back and forth between cleaning and helping David.

"Man, that's enough for a Monday, don't you think?" David said as he looked at the clock, around five-thirty.

"Yeah, I've had plenty." Steven replied, even though it would have relieved him if David had said that they had to work all night.

"Well, let's lock this shit up." David said as he headed over to the sink to wash up.

David finished washing his hands and arms and was drying off when he heard a vehicle pull up outside the shop; from the sound of the engine David recognized it to be Mr. Sam's truck. David lowered and shook his head with his eyes clinched tightly.

"How does he always seem to know when I'm leaving?" David asked aloud. Steven just laughed a bit and waited for Sam to come in.

"How you boys doing?" Sam asked as he slowly moved his skinny frame into the shop while the worn bottoms of his blue jean overalls drug the floor under his heels.

"Can't complain too much, what can I do for you?" David asked.

"Well, I come to see if I could hire Steven to come fetch me some wood. I got it split and loaded I just need some help getting it unloaded. I'm plumb give out." Sam said while adjusting his cap.

"Yes sir I'll help you, just let me wash up first." Steven said as he moved over to the sink.

* * *

Steven tensed up and shivered as the cold wind cut through his jacket as he began to unload the wood from Sam's truck, guided by yellow glow of his porch light.

"Things been going alright for you?" Sam asked, seemingly unaffected by the sharp wind.

"Yes sir, I couldn't have asked for better luck." Steven replied with a smile as he thought of Carrie. "How about you?"

"Oh, I'm making it alright; I'm just starting to feel my age a little more these days." Sam said with a trite tone.

"Yeah, it must be rough getting old." Steven said facetiously.

"Live on son, live on." Sam said wisely, as he thought back to when he was Steven's age. He paused for a second and then shook his head cynically as he realized how long ago it actually had been. Steven considered Sam's words briefly as he unloaded the wood from the truck.

"Hey, can I ask you something?" Steven asked without slowing his pace.

"Well I reckon so." Sam replied.

"Do you remember the first time that you," Steven stammered as he nervously searched his vocabulary for the right words. He stopped and leaned against the truck as his thought deepened.

"Had relations?" Sam asked as he looked at Steven from across the truck with a glaring smile.

"Yes sir." Steven said a little embarrassed, but also relieved that he didn't have to say it.

"Well yeah, I remember it like it was yesterday; it was my wedding night." Sam said, staring into the distance with a smile, as he seemed to be transported back to that night in an instant.

"Were you nervous, were you worried about how you'd do?" Steven asked after seeing that Sam felt comfortable talking to him about it.

"Why hell yeah I was nervous." Sam said as he resumed his work. "I worried about it from the time I set that ring on her finger up to the time the key hit the door that night. I had planned out every step in my head, every word I would say and every move I would make. When the time finally came I was trembling like a puppy, but she was lying there looking up at me with that look, like she trusted me completely and wasn't afraid. Well then everything else just disappeared, it wasn't just sex for the sake of it, it was just her and me in that moment. If somebody had told me that morning that I could have fallen deeper in love with her, I would've called them a liar. I loved her before then, but I'll tell you what, I loved her so much after that night that it hurt." Sam said as he dropped the last stick of wood down on the porch.

"Wow. That's what I want." Steven said, touched by Sam's account.

"Well it's still out there. It's a little harder to find now days, but it's still there; you'll know it when you see it." Sam said as he pulled his gloves off. Steven nodded and felt a weight lift from his chest as he observed his situation in a different light.

* * *

It had become completely dark by the time Sam dropped Steven off at the driveway of the Anderson house. Steven pulled his jacket tightly around his body as he began to walk towards the house. The wind was gusting mildly, but was potent against his face.

As Steven approached the house his nervousness was awakened, regardless of his newly found confidence. He stopped several feet from the house and stood there for a moment. David's car was in the driveway and the living room and kitchen lights were on.

"Carrie is probably cooking supper by now," Steven said to himself. "David's probably going to Julie's later. I'll just go to the camper for a little while before I go in."

Steven continued on down the path to his trailer. He slammed the door shut, closing the wind out and flipped the light on.

"I was about to give up on you."

"Damn!" Steven gasped as he turned around to find Carrie sitting on the small couch in the middle of the trailer.

"I'm sorry, I didn't mean to scare you." Carrie said as she got up and kissed Steven lightly.

"Oh, you didn't. I expected you to be hiding in the dark and yell at me when I came in." Steven said with a pounding heart.

"I was just trying to surprise you." Carrie said.

"Well it worked." Steven said as he began to calm down.

"I got us some pizza and a movie; we can just lie in your bed and be lazy all night." Carrie said with a smile as she held up some goofy horror movie.

"Sounds good, let me wash up a little." Steven said as he pulled his jacket off and began to empty his pockets onto the counter beside his small television set.

"What is this?" Carrie asked of the folded picture that Steven set out with his wallet.

"That's my family." Steven said with a half-hearted smile.

"Why haven't you ever showed this to me before?" Carrie asked as she unfolded the picture.

"I don't know, I barely ever look at it myself." Steven said as he sat on the couch and began to take his shoes off.

"This is your sister, Brooke?" Carrie asked.

"Yeah." Steven answered shortly.

"She's beautiful." Carrie said as she ran her fingers over the folded and worn picture.

"She was." Steven said somberly.

"She looks just like your mom, you look more like your dad I think." Carrie said.

"You think we could talk about something else?" Steven said as he got up and walked down the narrow hallway to the small bathroom. Carrie stood there holding the picture and suddenly realized how uncomfortable Steven was with the conversation.

"I'm sorry, I just know when I talk about my daddy it feels kind of like he's not really gone." Carrie said as she walked to door of the bathroom.

"Well they are gone. Everybody said when Brooke and my mom died that it would get better with time, but it's just gotten worse. My life hasn't been the same since." Steven said as he walked out of the bathroom past Carrie and into the small bedroom.

"It will get better, you just have to surround yourself with people who love you." Carrie said as she sat down on the end of the bed next to Steven.

"The only two people that ever really loved me are gone." Steven said through a sustained sob.

"I love you." Carrie said as she began to kiss Steven tenderly.

Steven began to return the kiss, with his warm breath and his hands on her body saying 'I love you too'. His heart was at a constant beat and his legs had gone weak. The kiss peaked and then faded. Steven pulled away from her slowly and saw that she had begun to cry with him. He also saw the look on her face that he had been looking for and wasn't sure that he would recognize, but there it was as plain as day and it said: "I trust you and I'm not afraid."

Carrie gently pushed Steven back on the bed and laid down on top of him and unbuttoned his pants as she started to kiss him again.

"Carrie, I've never…"

"Shhh." Carrie said, silencing his mouth with a kiss. It didn't matter to Carrie what he had or hadn't done before; to her it was only a matter of here and now.

Carrie sat up and pulled her shirt off and once again to Steven the rest of the world faded away from them, along with his nervousness; which now seemed trivial. He then became closer to her than he ever thought that he could and he honestly knew that he would love her for the rest of his life.

For Steven, the rest of the night was spent in preoccupation as his brain slaved away, reliving every second of the euphoric experience that he had just been a part of. He sat idle, watching the movie with an exultant air about him while he held Carrie warm in his arms, not wanting to let her go for fear of loosing the moment.

Not one word was spoken between them for some time, yet they seemed to be in constant communication. Those few hours seemed to last forever. It was only her and him separate but together, alone within themselves but as one with each other. Their world ended at the edge of the bed and they were unconcerned with anything else.

Carrie listened to Steven's heartbeat and timed her breathing with it. She closed her eyes and basked in the feeling of non-regret as she rested her head softly upon his chest.

Steven's breathing became deeper and heavier and Carrie could tell that he had fallen asleep. She reached over and took the remote control for the TV and VCR from Steven's hand and stopped the movie and cut the power for both of them. She threw the remote to the floor beside the bed and then settled back into Steven's undisturbed embrace and laid there in the dark in thought until she fell asleep with an unburdened heart.

* * *

Steven opened his eyes in shock as he felt the jolting of the rough ride through the floor of the train. He scanned the car quickly and found his own body dead on the floor. He looked elsewhere about the car and found him self again lying dead partially decapitated from gun blast. His pulse quickened, his heart became heavy and he lost his breath.

The environment of the tragedy remained consistent with his previous dreams, however the order of the calamity seemed to be disturbed; in every dream before he'd seen the events unfold and he would try desperately to change the outcome. This dream was different; it seemed to start in the middle and he could hear every sound.

Steven looked to the gunman who was towering in the middle of the car, inspecting the carnage that had been left in his wake. The car was dimly lit, all except for the gunman who wasn't visible at all.

The gunman seemed to be alerted to Steven's presence by his horrified gasps. He set his sights upon Steven and started walking towards him with the gun gripped tightly in his hand. Steven began to squirm and shuffle on the floor with little result. The gunman eased closer, who would it be this time Michael or Tim? The gunman drew the pistol on Steven as he moved even closer.

"No, no!" Steven managed to stutter out in defense. The plea had no effect on the gunman as he converged upon Steven and his face was revealed in the dim light. It wasn't Michael or Tim; it wasn't even a man at all. It was Carrie.

"Why? Why?" Steven screamed feeling betrayed and confused.

"You're just a puppy to me. Once the novelty wears off of you I'll forget all about you." Carrie said with a wicked grin. Steven looked at her in disbelief as she pulled the trigger.

Steven sat up quickly as he awoke from the nightmare sweaty and shaking.

"Steven, what is it?" Carrie asked, awakened by Steven's movement.

"Nothing." Steven answered through hyperventilation.

"Steven, What is it?" she repeated. Steven slowed his breathing and looked at her.

"Another dream." Steven said.

"The same one?" Carrie asked.

"No." Steven replied.

"Well what was different about it?" Carrie asked, eager to understand. Steven looked away, reluctant to explain the details of the horror. "Please, talk to me."

"I always dream that someone is killing me. Sometimes it's my dad and sometimes it's somebody else." Steven began as he looked away again. "This time it was you." He continued as a tear fell from his eye.

"No, baby. Why?" Carrie asked as she moved closer to him and put her arm around him.

"I don't know, I guess I'm afraid of losing you." Steven said as he wiped the tear from his face.

"Well don't be, I'm not going anywhere." Carrie said reassuringly.

"I know, it's just me. Your just too good to be true." Steven said. Carrie gave a short, embarrassed laugh that was followed by a short silence.

"Why do you dream that somebody's killing you? You said it was your dad and somebody else. Who else?" Carrie asked as the thought grew in her mind.

"I don't know." Steven said, avoiding the situation as he looked away again.

"Yes you do. Let me help." Carrie repeated. Steven swallowed hard and tried to decide whether or not he wanted to tell her. "Please."

"Okay, okay." Steven began nervously. "I told you about my dad and how he was and I told you that I got tired of it and just started walking one day, right?"

"Yeah." Carrie said, realizing that he really had something on his mind.

"Well I didn't walk the whole way. I walked around my town for a couple of hours, trying to decide what to do. I crossed over a railroad track so I decided to take it and see where I ended up. I walked and walked and eventually I walked up on a stalled train, so I found an opening and climbed on; I rode it to a freight yard and got off.

I started walking around this freight yard, trying to figure out where I was. It was dark and cold I had no idea where I was, I was scared out of my mind. After a little while this security guard spotted me and started chasing me so I ran all through this place trying to lose him when I saw an open door on one of the trains.

I climbed in the car and waited for the guard, but I lost him. When I got up and looked around I didn't see anything but the barrel of a gun." Steven paused as he recalled the moment and Carrie's eyes widened as he told her this. "There were three other guys in the car with me, they were all acting real nervous and scared. The guy with the gun told me to sit down and he asked me if I had any money, I told him no. The other two sat off to the side and kept quiet. One of them looked to be around my age and he was more nervous than the other two. He kept asking the guy with the gun "Why did you kill him?" over and over again. The guy with the gun just seemed to think it was funny at first, but after a while you could tell that he was getting mad, ya know?

This went on for hours after the train had taken off. Then out of a dead silence the kid Says that he's gonna turn himself in, that he couldn't handle it. The guy with the gun said that he couldn't let him do that and he just stood up and blew the kid's head off." Steven said this with a shutter.

"Oh God." Carrie gasped. "You can't be serious."

"You don't believe me? Why would I make that up?" Steven asked

"It's just not what I expected to hear, of course I believe you." Carrie said as she processed the story.

"Trust me, I wasn't expecting it either." Steven said, looking down at his fidgety hands while fighting tears.

"I know, I'm sorry. So what did you do?" Carrie asked as she took his hands.

"I didn't know what to do, it was like I couldn't move. The other guy tackled the guy with the gun and they started rolling around on the floor. Shots were going everywhere, I think he got the other guy too. Next thing I know I'm lying in the gravel on the side of the track; I don't even remember jumping off. After that I just started walking again until I came to that road that the bridge is on and that's how I ended up here." Steven felt such relief after telling Carrie what had happened that night.

"Well you're here now, it's over so don't worry." Carrie said as she hugged Steven tightly.

"I know, Thank you." He returned.

"For what?" She asked as they rocked softly on the bed.

"For listening." He said.

They laid back on the bed and held each other tight. Steven fell asleep on Carrie's shoulder and slept, undisturbed for the rest of the night.

* * *

Steven moved about the shop with a constant smile the whole morning. It had been so long since he felt such ease with himself. Everything was starting to fall into place for him even though he still felt a certain measure of guilt for completely cutting his father out of his life. As he took stock of his life at this point the thought of killing himself drifted further out of his mind and he thought of a future in this town with Carrie, but as it came into focus he asked himself what kind of future could it be? He had no money, he was working in a shop for peanuts and he had no education to speak of. He thought of his sister and longed to hear the words of encouragement that she always seemed to have readily available; he missed her more and more each time that he thought of her. In spite of the high that he was feeling he still craved complete contentment.

"What are you so happy about this morning?" David asked, almost disgusted by Steven's cheerful demeanor.

"Nothing, I just actually got a little sleep last night." Steven answered with a smile.

"You sure that's all it is?" David asked suspiciously as he handed Steven a pan full of parts to be washed.

"I'm sure." Steven said, still smiling as he took the pan and walked away towards the parts washer. David watched as Steven walked away; he felt like a sheriff that had a criminal, but could prove no crime.

Steven stood over the parts washer for quite sometime scrubbing and cleaning the pistons and connecting rods that David had given him. He wouldn't dare return them to him in any condition less than immaculate.

As he worked he thought of Carrie and his mind began to wander over the events from the night before. He closed his eyes and could still smell the intoxicatingly sweet scent of her hair and could still feel her lips upon his own. He couldn't get her out of his head. He desperately wanted to be with her again at that very moment.

The clanging door of the shop broke Steven's thoughts as it closed.

"Hey, man! You did make it, didn't you?" David greeted the new arrival as he entered the shop.

Steven glanced in the general direction when he heard David shout out his boisterous greeting, but could see nothing past the line of defunct vehicles that adorned the shop. It was then that he remembered that they would be receiving a new addition the workforce. He discounted the reunion and continued to scrub away on the parts.

"Where you been hiding?" David asked.

"I'm coming from Jackson, I've been over there for two or three months now." The new worker said. Steven cocked his ears back and bent his brow as he began to pay attention to the conversation.

"What in the hell were you doing over there?" David asked, slightly surprised to hear the he had gone that far. "Last I heard you were in Hattiesburg."

"I was, but you gotta go where the work is." The new worker answered. Steven sat the parts down in the base of the washer and his perplexity grew, as the voice of the man became hauntingly familiar. He dropped the nozzle and left it running as he slowly started to move to the edge of the obstructing vehicles for a better view. His heart began to pound, his breathing became frantic and his eyes widened as David and the man came into sight.

"Oh God, no." Steven whispered to himself in complete shock and ineffable horror as he saw Michael Rowan, in the flesh, standing in his very presence.

"Steven, come here. I want you to meet an old friend of mine." David said as he waved Steven over, after seeing him standing there.

Steven clamped his trembling jaw shut and tried to calm his breathing. He closed his eyes briefly and then looked again, hoping that Michael would have disappeared, but his dismay was well founded because this time Michael was no dream.

Steven forced his heavy, unwilling feet to take a step forward while his shell-shocked subconscious tried in vain to warn against it. As he eased closer to them, his fists closed tightly in an instinctive defensive action.

Michael's face took on a look of disbelief as Steven moved closer to him and he realized who he was and from where he remembered him. Finally Steven was before him and the two stood eye to eye. They said nothing to each other, but the unequivocal irony glaring in both of their eyes spoke volumes.

"Is there something wrong?" David asked after sensing the odd and sudden tension.

"No, nothing." Michael said after a moment. "I just thought I knew you there for a second. We've never met before, have we?" He asked Steven with a flat tone.

"No." Steven answered.

"Are you sure? You seem awfully familiar." He further questioned.

"Positive." Steven reaffirmed.

"Well then nice to meet you, Steven is it?" Michael said as he held out his hand for a handshake. Steven took his hand and grasped it loosely while he studied Michael's eyes, unable to read his thoughts.

"Okay," David began, dismissing the unusual behavior with a slightly confused, but unconcerned look. "Michael, why don't you come on in the office and we can talk business." He continued as he and Michael began to walk away.

Steven watched until David and Michael disappeared into the office. He bowed his head and stared at the floor while trying to comprehend this seemingly impossible turn of events. His stomach began to churn and his head became dizzy as a result of the confusion. He then quickly ran to the door and burst through it and threw up as soon as he had made it to the side of the building. After giving one final heave he cradled his stomach with one arm, leaned against the outside of the shop and slid to the ground.

"This is not happening." Steven said in a low, trembling voice while tears bled from his eyes uncontrollably. He took the worn family picture from his pocket and unfolded it. He looked at his sister's face, but couldn't feel the usual comfort that normally accompanied it. He felt the emptiness that was left by the lack of comfort and began to sob as he held the picture to his face, wishing that he could dive back into it and the rational world that he remembered from those days.

Steven pulled himself up from the concrete slab and looked at the picture once more. He stared at his mother's face and wished to hear her advice. He looked at Brooke's face again and couldn't help but return the smile that he saw; only his was much weaker. Then he looked at Tim's face, which only reinforced his disgust. He snorted out a short, cynical laugh as a response to his current situation and then stuck the picture back into his pocket. He pulled in a deep breath and walked slowly back to the entrance of the shop and went inside.

As Steven moved through the shop on his way back to the parts washer, he looked over to a car where David was briefing Michael on its malfunction. Michael looked up from the engine and shot Steven a look that cut right through him. It was obvious that he was itching to catch Steven alone.

Throughout the whole day Steven stretched out every job that he was asked to do, he kept his distance from Michael. He worked through lunch and every break until finally, five-thirty arrived.

"Alright boys, let's lock up and get out of here." David said tiredly.

Steven was relieved to hear the call. He dropped what he was doing and proceeded to shut everything down. He walked over to the switchbox and began to cut the power to the different pieces of equipment as David approached.

"Hey Steven, I told Michael that he could stay in the trailer with you until he got on his feet. You don't mind, do you?" Steven's heart sunk after David informed him of this. A stifled look was his only response. "It's just 'til he gets on his feet, he's alright."

"Okay." Steven responded, although he did mind greatly.

* * *

The ride home that evening seemed to last forever. Steven was glad to be separated from Michael, who was in his own car, following closely behind Steven and David, but the anticipation of seeing him again at the house was already sickening him.

Steven desperately wanted to tell David what had happened on the train and let him know what kind of friend that he had. The words were burning his tongue with the will to burst out and make themselves heard.

Steven opened his mouth to break the silence in the car. He was prepared to let David in on everything, but at the last second the thought of actually making things worse dawned on him and the restraint of a self-preserving instinct held his tongue.

"Look, I know what you and Carrie did last night." David said out of the ambient darkness, derailing his train of thought and propelling him into another level of paranoia and nervousness.

"Yeah, we talked for a while." Steven said. His voice sounded weak against the low grumble of the car's engine.

"I'm not stupid, I know what's going on and I've beaten asses for less. Just be honest with me." David continued while keeping a keen focus on the road.

"You're right, I'm not going to lie to you, but…" Steven began.

"No, I don't want to hear any excuses, just know how I feel. She's my sister, but she's grown and I can tell that you respect her that's all that matters to me." Steven watched David as he spoke and he felt as though a huge weight had been lifted from his shoulders. "All I'll ever ask from you is honesty."

Steven checked one burden off of his list as they pulled into the driveway. He got out of the car and rushed into the house while David waited for Michael to join him.

As Steven entered the house he found Carrie sitting on the couch with a beer in her hand listening closely to Lisa, who was sitting in Ran's lap in the chair.

Carrie looked up at Steven and smiled warmly at him. He bent over and kissed her gaining pleasure from both the kiss itself and from knowing that the sight of it infuriated Ran.

Steven settled in next to Carrie on the couch. He placed his hand high on her thigh and glanced at Ran, who was beaming his trademark scowl towards him; Steven no longer found it intimidating, only amusing.

"Hey, baby. How was your day?" Carrie asked as she reached down and rubbed his hand on her leg, but David and Michael walked into the house before Steven could respond with some random lie about how good it was.

"This is Ran and Lisa and you remember Carrie don't you?" David introduced as everyone looked at the newest stranger. "This is Michael, one of the original outlaws around here."

"Yeah, of course I remember Carrie. You sure have changed a lot since I saw you last." Michael said as he moved a step closer to her with a flirtatious smile. Steven put his arm around Carrie in an effort to let Michael know that she was taken and was not to be messed with. Michael shifted his sight to Steven and his smile evolved into one of amusement and unconcern.

"I know I would have remembered you." Michael said to Lisa as he turned to see her and Ran. She smiled playfully and looked at him with a tempting glare. Ran sent him a glare of his own, however it was neither playful nor tempting.

Ran was already feeling threatened by the newcomer, he had a certain air about him that Ran was sensing. The fact that this guy was hitting on Lisa didn't bother him it was the fact that Lisa just happened to be Ran's interest at the moment and no one moved in on his interest.

Ran made eye contact with Michael and narrowed his glare, but his usual brooding intimidation seemed to have no effect as Michael seemed to shrug it off as he continued with his eccentricity.

"You got a beer in this place?" Michael asked, as he looked the house over.

L.B. Kelly

"That's a stupid question, Carrie get Michael a beer." David said as he emptied his pockets onto the table next to the chair. "And get me one too."

"You can still say please even if everybody is around, it'll be okay." Carrie said as she got up from the couch, a little aggravated by David's bluntness.

"You heard what I said." David retaliated playfully as Carrie left the room.

"So Steven, where are you from?" Michael asked, almost seeming uninterested in his answer as he walked aimlessly about the room, still looking it over. David looked up at him briefly; a little confused by the tone of his question.

"What makes you think I'm not from around here?" Steven asked, forced to play the game that Michael wanted to play.

"I just never saw you around before, it's a small town." He returned.

"I'm from the coast." Steven said.

"So how'd you end up here?" Michael asked, hoping to stifle him. He seemed to be enjoying himself greatly.

"It's a long story…."

"Yeah, he's just a hobo; that's the short version." Ran said, cutting Steven off.

"A wittle hobo." Lisa added in a mocking voice. Steven held up a middle finger to her in response.

"Is that the wittiest thing you could come up with?" Lisa asked.

"No, it's just not worth the effort to speak to you." Steven returned.

"Well then shut up." She spat sharply. Steven just shook his head in frustration.

"A hobo?" Michael asked as he turned around from looking at the Christmas tree. David looked up from the mail on the table with a slight grin. He had missed Michael and his tendency to instigate.

"Yeah, he was living under the bridge when he got here." Ran said with a condescending laugh.

Steven turned his head in shame, but felt a bit of comfort as Carrie sat down next to him.

"Well I don't know how many nights I've slept outside, dose that make me a hobo?" Michael asked as he cracked open the beer that Carrie had given him.

"Well?" Michael asked again after Ran stammered and mumbled a bit.

"Naw man, I'm just messing with him." Ran said as a blushing embarrassment warmed his face.

"That's what I thought." Michael began. Satisfied with himself, he turned his attention back to Steven. "Well I hope you had a safe trip, I know how crazy the road can be."

"No, it was pretty boring." Steven said as the whole scenario from the train began to creep back into reality. Carrie also noticed the oddity of the conversation and looked to Steven for some kind of explanation.

"I think I could use a beer too." He said as he got up and went into the kitchen.

"Steven's getting a beer? I guess everybody's drinking tonight." David said as he drank down a good part of his own beer.

Carrie got up and followed Steven into the kitchen as Lisa tried to console Ran's stinging pride with hollow affection.

"Are you okay?" Carrie asked with a concerned tone as Steven stood at the refrigerator and gulped a beer down.

"I'm fine." He said with heavy breath as he paused his drinking. He finished the last part of the beer and threw the empty bottle into the trashcan beside the icebox. He took another beer and began again.

"You don't seem fine." Carrie retorted as she folded her arms in front of her.

"Have I ever since you've known me?" Steven asked as he finished the second beer and started repeating the process yet again.

"What do you mean?" she asked.

"Look at me Carrie, I'm a joke. I'm always gonna be a damned hobo or that strange kid that sweeps the floor down at Anderson's." Steven said as he slammed the refrigerator door shut and flew past Carrie. He walked through the crowded living room and out of the house all but unnoticed by everyone else.

He walked to the edge of the porch and caught the post and lowered himself down as he began to feel the effect of the beer. He sat there on the steps and began to cry.

He made no effort to hide his tears when Carrie walked out onto the porch and sat down beside him.

"Where is this coming from?" She asked as she put her arm around him and laid her head on his shoulder.

"It's been there all along, I just didn't want to see it. This is not a life I'm living; it's just the means to an end." He said dismally.

"Why don't you look at it as a new beginning?" Carrie asked optimistically.

"Well then I guess I'm off to a hell of a start. I'm sweeping floors and I live in a camper; I've got nothing. I'm a joke." He concluded pitifully.

"You got me." Carrie said softly, able to sense his pain.

"But what do you have in me?" He replied as he got up from the steps and walked out to David's car.

"Steven…" Carrie began.

"Just leave me alone!" He mumbled as he left Carrie standing on the porch confused.

He stood there at David's car, facing away from the house. He held his breath until he heard Carrie walk back inside the house and slam the door shut behind her.

The tears started to flow freely as he thought about what he had just done. He was hurting so badly inside. His nerves were shot, his mind was like a kaleidoscope, his spirit was broken and now had he just thrown away the only comfort that he had?

His mind was bombarded with random thoughts, thoughts of his father and of his mother and sister, thoughts of Carrie, thoughts of his haunted sleep and now the thought of having to live and deal with Michael; the source of the madness.

Steven turned around and leaned his back against the door of the car as he took another long swig of his beer.

He turned around to face the car. His equilibrium was jaded and the beer was numbing his senses. He leaned over and rested his forehead on the upper portion of the car door and peered aimlessly inside.

The sight of David's cell phone lying on the seat sparked an idea inside Steven's mind. He opened the door and sat down on the seat, halfway inside the car. He picked the phone up and stared at it for a second while trying to make himself follow thorough on his idea. Finally, after mustering up enough conviction he dialed his father's phone number and listened as it started to ring.

"Hello?" A woman answered, Steven didn't recognize her voice.

"Is Tim there?" He responded after a moment of apprehension.

"Who is this?" The woman asked.

"Steven, his son." He answered. There was a short silence.

"Hold on a minute." The woman said.

Steven heard a bump as the woman set the receiver of her phone down. He tried tuning his hearing in further, but could hear nothing but dampened conversation. After a while he heard another bump and the woman returned to the line. He only heard her breathing at first.

"Hun, are you there?" She finally said.

"Yeah." He answered.

"Uh, he said that he doesn't have a son." The woman said reluctantly. The words hit Steven like a ton of bricks. It was true; his life with his father was over. "I'm sorry."

"Wait!" Steven said hastily, but the next thing that he heard was a dial tone.

Steven sat there, stunned. As he stared at the phone another thought crept into his head, the thought of suicide. If he'd had a gun in his hand at the moment he probably would have ended it all right then and there, but there was no gun; only a half-empty beer.

Steven spent the rest of the evening outside, wallowing in self-pity. He would occasionally make his way back inside the house through the back door in the kitchen for more beer. He found that the world at this moment looked better through clouded eyes.

After a couple of hours had past, his tolerance for the beer had long since met it's limit and time was becoming immeasurable to him.

Steven sat at the edge of the yard in the darkness, unable to concentrate on a single thought for more than a couple of seconds at a time, which was his goal because now he couldn't concentrate on his plight either. His biggest worry at the moment was trying to figure out how he was going to get to his bed.

Around ten-thirty he saw the front door of the house open and David and Michael walked out onto the porch. After Michael paid a visit to his car David led him around to the camper. Steven waited another hour after David went back into the house before he stood uneasily to his feet.

Lisa and Ran had left and the lights were out in the house. Right then the thought of bursting into Carrie's bedroom and begging forgiveness was weighing heavily on his mind, however in his current condition he thought it better to wait for the right moment.

Steven focused his tenuous attention on the camper. He detected no movement inside and could see no lights on.

Steven staggered towards the trailer and as he did it didn't seem to be getting any closer, but he was upon it in no time. He stopped outside the door, pulled in a deep breath and held it as he quietly pulled the handle and opened the door.

He stepped into the dark trailer and looked down the narrow hallway into the second, smaller bedroom area where he saw Michael's dark outline lying in the bed. He made his way to his own bed as quietly as he could, careful not to wake the sleeping murderer.

Steven sat down on the edge of his bed and kicked his shoes off and laid back. As he lay there, the room started to spin and his stomach began to churn. He closed his eyes, but only made it worse by doing so.

He quickly opened his eyes and calmed his breathing and the churning and spinning subsided. He closed his eyes again and his stomach continued to settle. He could feel himself drifting off to sleep almost instantly.

Then out of the dead silence Steven was startled into lucidity by a hand slapping down over his mouth.

"Look you little son-of-a-bitch, I don't know what I did to deserve this, I don't know what I did to piss off the gods of fate, but you're the last person I ever expected to see again!" Michael ranted inches from Steven's terrified face, with his stinking breath blowing hot against it. "I don't know what you've said to who, but I've gotten away with this for this long now and I plan to get away with it forever and I'll do what I have to do to make sure of it."

"I haven't told anybody." Steven said with a trembling voice as Michael took his hand away from his mouth. Michael stared at him intensely for a moment, trying to decide whether or not to believe him.

"I'll do whatever it takes to protect myself. I think you know that you can believe that. I'll do whatever it takes to whoever I have to." Michael warned as he cast a stare out the window of the camper towards the house. Steven sharpened his glare at Michael as he picked up on his insinuation.

"I told you, I didn't tell anybody." Steven said as he moved back against the wall away from Michael.

"You just keep you're mouth shut and we'll get along fine." Michael said as he got up and slowly walked away From Steven.

Steven sat there in the darkness, with his mind reeling from a mixture of intimidation and cheap beer. He was in a state of misery and he wondered how things could possibly get any worse.

He lay there shaking and cold staring down the hallway, daring not to close his eyes for another second.

Chapter Seven

Steven moved around the shop like a zombie Wednesday morning. He was experiencing a hang over for the first time in his life and it didn't take him long to come to the conclusion that the buzz he'd felt the night before wasn't worth the agony that he was feeling now.

His head was pounding, his stomach was sour and his heart was burdened. He felt such guilt for shutting Carrie out, away from his feelings. He wondered if she would forgive his coldness and overlook his ignorance, but the lack of sleep and the distraction that Michael provided prevented him from dwelling upon his guilt for very long.

Steven watched Michael's every action carefully. He kept his distance from him as much as possible by constantly moving around the shop; David didn't seem to notice the odd behavior, or he simply chose to ignore it.

Steven could see a change in David since Michael had arrived; it was as though he'd found something that was missing from him in the form of his old running partner. He seemed to be more carefree and relaxed and Steven was disturbed by the thought that David could've ever been like Michael.

"Here you go, a little job security. I know you love it."
David said to Steven with a smile as he wheeled over a cart-
full of parts to be washed.

Steven looked down at the cart and then back to David with
a disgusted air after seeing the plethora of filthy parts.

"Thanks, I can't wait to get started." Steven replied
sarcastically as he set the broom that he was holding against
the wall and took hold of the cart.

"Be careful with that crank. If you bend it, I'll bend your
ass." David added as he walked away to rejoin Michael
underneath the hood of the truck that they were currently
working on.

"Bend my ass, I'll bend your ass. You might kiss my ass."
Steven mumbled playfully as he pushed the cart over to the
parts washer.

"What?" David yelled from across the shop.

"I said that I'll wash them up nice." Steven yelled back.
David just shook his head and smiled.

Steven parked the cart next to the washer and began to set
the encrusted parts into the basin. He then took a rag from
his pocket and wiped off the empty cart where the parts had
been. He flipped the switch on and started inspecting the
parts.

He picked up the large crankshaft and began to scrub it
lightly with the brush. After a bit of careful cleaning the
shaft was spotless. He picked up the camshaft that was also
there and elevated it to the same condition. After finishing
with the larger pieces he moved on to the smaller, more time
consuming parts and settled into his spot for the tedious

task. He washed push rods, rocker arms, a timing chain and it's filthy cover and he hadn't even made a dent in the job.

As he finished washing a part, he would set it neatly back onto the cart and move on to the next one. After more than an hour Steven put his hand on the last part and started to clean it with the satisfaction of completing the job growing inside him.

Steven tensed up slightly as he saw Michael breeze past him out of the corner of his eye. He turned for a better look and saw Michael disappear into the parts room. He turned his attention back to the piece in his hand and was surprised to hear Michael returning from the parts room so quickly. Steven just ignored him and continued his cleaning.

As Michael approached Steven he quickly looked across the shop at David, who was completely involved in his work. He gave a wicked smirk and as he passed the cart full of clean parts he grabbed its farthest edge and wedged his foot against the wheel on his side and flipped it over, sending the parts clanging to the floor. Steven quickly turned to see what had happened and saw Michael's grin.

"Damn, man! Watch what you're doing!" Michael yelled. David sprung up quickly and looked their way in disbelief.

"Shit, I know you didn't just do that." David said as he walked over and looked at the parts that were strewn across the floor and soiled again with old oil dry and dirt.

Steven sighed and set the part that was in his hand back into the basin. He wanted badly to tell David what really happened, but the fear of making things worse with Michael held his tongue.

.B. Kelly

David squatted down and picked up the crankshaft and started looking it over, while Michael stood back and gave Steven his devilish grin.

"Is it bent?" Steven asked. David looked up at him with a serious scowl.

"I don't know, probably. I'll have to send it to the machine shop to be sure." He began. He set the crankshaft down and then picked up the cam and ran his fingers over the damaged lopes and shook his head. "This cam is screwed though."

"David, I'm sorry. It wasn't…"

"Forget it, just pick the rest of this shit up and wash it again." David interjected as he walked away.

"You really ought to be more careful." Michael said as he too walked away.

Steven lowered his shoulders and looked down at the mess. He took another look towards Michael and wondered how someone could ever become so cruel and hateful. He spent little time contemplating the origin of Michael's iniquity, thinking that he should concentrate on finding a way to get past it rather than trying to figure it out.

With his hangover still thriving, Steven bent over and lifted the cart to its upright position and began to return the parts to the washer for another round of cleaning.

"We'll be back later, try not to wreck the place while we're gone." David yelled to Steven.

Steven looked to the entrance of the shop and saw David walking out with the crankshaft in hand and Michael following after. He could only assume that they were off to the machine shop.

Steven dropped the oil pump that he was holding back into the washer with disgust as he heard David's car fire off and shriek away with a bellow. He looked across the shop to the clock on the wall and shook his head as he observed the time. It was eleven forty five and he knew then that David and Michael would probably be gone for the better part of the afternoon.

As Steven once again finished cleaning the parts he took the rag from his pocket and wiped his hands off and then wiped his brow on his sleeve. His headache was starting to fade and his stomach was becoming more settled. His thoughts settled upon Carrie as he took hold of the cart's handle and started to push it over to David's workbench. He deeply wondered what she was thinking of him and the obscurity was killing him.

Steven heard the door slam shut as he walked back towards the front of the shop, he wondered what curious town's person had come to gawk at the runaway. They were still doing that from time to time and it made Steven feel like some kind of weird celebrity.

"David's not here, he'll be back later." Steven called from the back.

"I came to see you." Carrie replied. A smile grew across Steven's face when he recognized the voice.

"Are you sure that you want to talk to me?" He asked as Carrie came into view from behind the truck that sat in the middle of the shop.

"I think so." She answered. "I think you're worth it."

"Aren't you supposed to be at school?" Steven asked after an awkward silence, trying to ease the tension.

"What, you think I'm above cutting class?" She asked.

"Absolutely not, I think you can be just as sneaky as anyone. That's why I'm keeping my eye on you." He returned with a playful laugh.

"Because I can go back if you want me to." She continued.

"No, I'm glad you're here; I was thinking about you." Steven began, as things became serious. "I'm sorry, There's nothing else that I can say. I was just feeling sorry for myself I guess."

"It's okay, everybody needs to let off some steam every now and then." Carrie said after a short silence. "I just want you to remember that you can talk to me, I'll listen."

"I know, you've helped me more than you'll ever know." Steven said as he took Carrie's hand and pulled her closer to him. "You've given back to me something that I never thought I would have again."

"What?" Carrie asked, looking up with her soft stare.

"Love. I love you." He said freely and without reservation.

"I love you too." She returned with the same freedom. Steven took her even closer and began to kiss her softly. It was then that his fear of being a joke faded and where he lived and what he did for a living made no difference. Carrie was what was important to him now.

* * *

Steven sat quietly on the couch holding Carrie, while everyone else was busy with their own sets of intentions.

Lisa watched, wide-eyed as Michael told stories of his irreverent past. She seemed to be hanging on his every word. Every now and then Michael would look at her and smile or wink and she would blush and giggle like a little schoolgirl.

Carrie caught Lisa's attention and sent her a questioning look after noticing her giddy behavior. Lisa answered with a raised brow and a smile to which Carrie just shook her head.

"So you've been in Jackson this whole time?" David asked of Michael after he finished up another dubious story. "I thought that you went to Hattiesburg to start with."

"Uh, yeah I did. I've only been in Jackson for the last few months, but I started out in Hattiesburg." He answered hastily in his unwillingness to delve into his recent past. Steven picked up on this and recognized the opportunity to turn the tables on him and make him play offence in his own game.

"Hey, didn't you go down there with Jimmy?" David asked after suddenly thinking of their close mutual friend.

"Yeah, but I haven't seen him in a while." Michael seemed to clam up a bit as he answered. He looked quickly in Steven's direction, who was almost smiling. He knew exactly who they were talking about.

"I had forgot about Jimmy. We ought to see if we can get a hold of him and get everybody together again." David suggested.

"Yeah, I think you should." Steven encouraged. Michael looked at him again with a piercing glare.

"I don't know, the last time I saw him he was out of work and strung out. He was dead to the world." Michael began while keeping his focus on Steven. "Isn't funny how that happens to people?"

"Well, it was bound to happen to one of us at the rate we were going." David said as he recounted the close calls and chemical experimentation of his teenage years. Michael stressed his point with his continued stare at Steven. Steven looked away, remembering that he was going to try not to make things worse with Michael.

"Speaking of Jackson," Michael began, in an effort to change the subject. "I've been meaning to ask you if you felt like making a little road trip. I got another car over there that I need to get, but I'm gonna need a wrecker to get it."

"Where is it?" David asked.

"At a friend's house, In the outskirts. All we gotta do is hook to it and haul ass." He explained.

"Sounds good to me." David said after a moments thought. "You wanna make a trip Steve?"

"Oh, uh I don't know. If y'all want to go by yourselves, I understand." Steven said, slightly shocked by the invitation and completely uninterested in going anywhere with Michael.

"I wouldn't have asked if I didn't want you to go. I thought you might have some fun, if you can tear yourself away from the old ball and chain there." David said with a smile as he looked at Carrie.

"Nobody's twisting his arm to make him sit here." Carrie defended.

"Maybe he's scared of you." David suggested.

"Maybe you're scared of me." She retorted.

"Okay, Okay I'll go." Steven said with a crooked smile.

"Your damned right you'll go." David said as he got up from his chair and left the living room.

* * *

That Friday at quitting time David pulled his car into the shop and locked it tight while Steven and Michael hooked the car dolly to the field truck. Everyone piled in and they hit the road, headed to Jackson.

They drove nearly an hour in silence; listening to the radio and watching cars pass by on the dark highway. To his own surprise, Steven was at ease considering the fact that he was sandwiched between his girlfriend's brother and a psychotic killer. He was slightly uncomfortable with knowing that David knew certain things about him and Carrie and now he was going off with him to a strange place where he'd never been before and knew absolutely nothing about. The psychotic killer made him uncomfortable for obvious reasons.

As they rode Steven stared straight ahead, thinking about Carrie and wondering what she was doing, but his thoughts were interrupted and his face wrinkled with disgust as he smelled a foul stench upon the air.

"Did you fart?" Steven asked as he turned to look at David.

"That's right." David said after a moment, with a razor-straight face. Steven nodded his head a bit and then faced ahead again.

"You think you could let your window down?" He asked as he turned David's way once more.

"No." David said after another moment, with the same poker face while Michael began to chuckle slightly. Steven nodded again and slowly turned to look at Michael.

"Hey man, you wanna crack your window?" He asked.

As Steven waited for response Michael began to contort his face. He gave his answer in the form of roaring flatulence. Steven shook his head as David and Michael began to laugh.

"Damn, y'all are grown!" Steven spat in aggravation, which only caused them to laugh harder. "This shit ain't funny."

* * *

"What's wrong with you?" Lisa asked of Carrie as they drove down the road away from the Anderson house.

"Nothing." She answered bleakly.

"C'mon, I've known you too long." Lisa continued.

"If you know me so well, you shouldn't have to ask what's wrong." Carrie stated plainly.

"It's him, isn't it? Carrie, I don't know what you see in him." Lisa said, shaking her head.

"Well you don't have to." Carrie began offensively. "I love him and I miss him."

"Okay, I still don't understand, but okay." Lisa said in closing.

They drove another mile in silence. Lisa still had too many argumentative words dancing on her tongue and she'd held them back for as long as she could.

"I mean, you could've had Ran and you still could, but you would rather have this guy?" She felt relieved as the words spewed from her mouth.

"This guy's name is Steven and it's not about having someone, it's about being with someone. I don't want to be with Ran, I never have and I never will." Carrie said once and for all.

"What about that date y'all went on? Does having sex fall under the category of being with someone?" Lisa asked spitefully.

"What?" Carrie asked with a shocked tone.

"He told me what y'all did. You know, you act like you're so much better than me, but then you go and do the same things that you snub your nose at, at least I'm honest about it." Lisa said, no longer able to stand biting her tongue. Carrie sat in awe at what she had just heard.

"Yeah, we kissed that night, but that was it. He wanted more than that and I thought that he was going to try and take it, but that's where it ended. Nothing else happened." Carrie stared out through the windshield of the car with a hurt expression upon her face and by it Lisa could tell that she was being honest.

"I'm sorry, I shouldn't have said that." She said as she felt remorse bloom inside of her after a moment of awkward silence.

"You can't believe anything that Ran says." Carrie reminded her.

As she gripped the stirring wheel and sharpened her focus on the highway, Lisa could feel her guilt heighten and she was sickened by the things that she'd said to Carrie.

241

"Is that what you really think of me?" Carrie asked without turning to Lisa.

"Carrie I'm sorry, that's not how I really see you. It's just that I feel like the second choice all the time; I'm not as pretty as you, I'm not as smart as you." Lisa began to cry softly as she admitted her envy out loud for the first time.

"Lisa, how can you say that? You are beautiful and every bit as smart as anybody that I know. That's one of the things that drew me to you in the first place. When we first started hanging around each other I could tell that you were smart enough to get people to do what you wanted. I knew that you had a crush on David and were using me to get to him." Carrie said with an understanding laugh. Lisa shared the laugh as she wiped away the mascara that had started to run beneath her eyes.

"You know, you're the best friend that I've ever had. You honestly care so much about everyone else around you. I just wish that I could be that genuinely selfless." She said as she looked over to Carrie.

"I think that you care more about everyone else than you let on." Carrie said.

"Yeah, maybe. Except for Steven." Lisa said with a smile. She and Carrie both felt a thick tension lift from their relationship as they shared a cleansing laughter.

* * *

David applied the right turn signal of the truck as he let it hover into the turn lane to exit I-20 east. He drove up the ramp and cautiously merged with the modest flow of traffic on highway 18. He stopped the truck at a traffic light and took a look around Jackson Mississippi.

"Okay, where to now?" He asked as he began to rub the back of his tense neck for some relief.

"Just keep on straight, I'll tell you where to turn. We still got a little ways to go." Michael said knowingly.

"Well, I hope it's not much longer, my ass is starting to fall asleep." David returned as he squirmed in his seat.

"I hope that this is not all there is to it." Steven said with a disappointed look as he took in the ordinary sights of the capital city.

"Yeah, it's just a Wal-Mart and a red light." Michael said wisely. "What did you expect?"

Steven sneered at his sarcastic remark and then began to survey the area again.

"Yeah this place is huge, but I think we'll save the tour for next time." David said, pressing the truck's accelerator as the light turned green.

Steven watched the unusually quiet city pass by as they drove down the highway. He had always heard about Jackson and the different attractions that would pass through, but the one that stood out in his mind the most was the state fair. Every year Tim would promise to take Steven and Brooke, but something more important always seemed to take its place.

The highway became darker as they drove away from the city. Buildings were starting to be seen farther and farther apart and the flow of traffic was beginning to thin out dramatically.

They had driven about eight miles since leaving the interstate and Steven was beginning to wonder if they would ever stop.

"Hang a left up here." Michael said as he pointed in the direction of the light.

"It's about time." Steven thought to himself as David steered the truck off of the highway and onto an even darker, more desolate-looking road.

David brought the truck to rest at a stop sign where another crossed the road that they were on. Steven looked around a bit anxiously at the shadowy woods that surrounded the intersection and was reminded of the night that he hid in the woods along the train tracks. The night that he'd first met Michael. He remembered then what was sitting beside him; not the wisecracking mechanic that he had now slowly begun to view him as, but he was reminded of the unrepentant innovator of the loathsome revenants that had plagued his sleep for the past few months.

He looked to the left side of the road and saw a very small and very old gas station. It was dimly lit and rather shady looking. Across the road from it sat a tiny bar from which faint music could be heard.

"Damn, a beer sure does sound good right now." David said as he too noticed the bar.

"I don't know, we better go on and get that car loaded." Michael said. "Go straight."

"That ain't gonna take all night." David said with a smile as he proceeded ahead.

They drove less than a mile when Michael navigated them down the first road that they saw on the left.

"Second driveway on the right." Michael said as he scanned the area cautiously.

David drove on a little further and slowly turned in the drive while Michael continued to look around, appearing to be very nervous.

"Is anybody home?" David asked as they crept up the driveway after noticing the dark house.

"It don't look like it." Michael replied seeming somewhat relieved.

"It looks abandoned." Steven said of the shoddy house.

"That brown Nova over there." Michael said, ignoring Steven's remark as he continued to pour over the yard.

David turned the truck around and began to back up to the car feeling slightly ill at ease over Michael's peculiar demeanor since arriving at the house. David positioned the dolly in front of the car.

David stepped out of the truck and took in a detailed observation of the unfamiliar surroundings, while Michael and Steven spilled out of the passenger side of the vehicle. Steven too began to inspect the surroundings as Michael went straight to work, unloading the tire straps and tools that he would need to secure the Nova to the dolly.

"Here Harris, hook the cable up." Michael said hastily to Steven as he handed him the cable to connect the dolly's electric wench to the truck's battery.

David released the hood latch as Steven moved to the front of the truck and raised the hood. Steven connected the positive and negative cable clamps to their respective terminals and then moved back around to the rear of the truck for further instructions.

David took the wenches control in his left hand and began to operate it while he guided the cable out with his free hand.

"Steven, grab that spotlight out of the tool box." David said as he bent down to one knee to find a suitable spot along the front end of the car to connect the cable's hook.

While David and Steven worked, Michael seized the opportunity to check the trunk of the car to be sure that what he really came for was still there.

He searched his pants pocket for the car's keys and quickly recovered them. He slid the trunk key into the lock and popped the lid open. He took a quick look around the yard and then glanced towards the front of the car and heard David clanging around on the bumper.

Guided by the dim cargo light Michael turned his attention back to the trunk's cluttered interior and began to move various items from around the car's spare tire that was also there. He lifted the tire with one hand and reached underneath it with the other and pulled out a burlap sack, which he opened for a hurried inspection. Inside, was ten pounds of marijuana.

Michael had made a deal with the three other people who were living in the house. They were each to put up a quarter of the cost of the marijuana, sell it and split the earnings, but Michael seemed to have a better idea, steal it and split nothing. The deal was made and the marijuana was picked up the weekend before Michael returned to Fanning. After making the pick up he simply disappeared with the keys to the car. He was quite surprised to find the marijuana where he'd left it and was even more surprised to find the property vacant of his moronic, former partners who were probably out looking for him.

He gave a relieved smile and re-tied the bag before stowing it back underneath the tire. He searched the left side of the trunk and retrieved a worn paper bag. He opened it and pulled from it a nickel-plated nine-millimeter handgun. He stuck the gun behind his back, into the waistband of his pants and straightened his jacket and shirt to conceal it before slamming the trunk lid shut.

"I think we're ready to pull her up if you wanna drop it down into neutral." David said as Michael made his way back to driver side door of the car.

Steven stood shivering, watching as David operated the wench and pulled the car on to the dolly with ease while Michael steered.

"Are all the tires up, Steven?" David asked as he disconnected the wench control.

"Yeah." Steven said with a nod.

"Alright, strap her down and we'll be good to go." David directed to Michael over the loud rattle of the truck's still running diesel engine.

As Michael secured the vehicle, David took the magnetic based taillights from the toolbox and connected them to a receptacle on the dolly. He handed one to Steven and took the other himself to the end of the car and set them on top of the trunk.

Steven turned up the heat as everyone crammed back into the work truck. David pushed the manual transmission into first gear and sent the truck creeping slowly down the driveway.

As they drove, Michael reveled in the comfort of knowing that he had beaten his old partners and had avoided them on this trip all together. He was already counting his money and planning out his business strategy for when he returned to Fanning, however his elation was short lived.

Michael's stomach became uneasy and his alert nervousness was re-enlisted when upon leaving the stop sign at the intersection, David proceeded to turn the truck into the small parking lot of the dingy taproom that they had past earlier.

"What are you doing?" Michael asked as David scanned the lot for an empty spot.

"What? I want a beer, remember?" He returned.

"No, not here. I know a better place down the road." Michael said in hopes of detouring David from this particular bar, a known hideaway for his ex-cohorts.

"But we're here now and look, the sign says that they got a pool table. You know about me and pool." David argued while Steven sat and patiently waited while the two came to an understanding or to be said more accurately he waited for Michael's acceptance of David's unrelenting will.

"Okay, but I'm telling you, this place sucks." Michael said with a yielding sigh after looking the parking lot over and finding no evidence of his cohorts.

"Well, beer's beer and pool's pool, let's go." David concluded as he parked the truck awkwardly at the edge of the parking lot.

David exited the truck, followed by Steven while Michael got out on the passenger side. Steven pulled his jacket tight and increased his pace as he trailed David and Michael through the parking lot, feeling like a tag-along younger brother to them on his way into the bar.

They stepped into the bar, unnoticed at first. Steven looked over the room and instantly felt out of place as he studied each of the scruff, uncut patrons through the thick fog of smoke that hung over the place. Even the few women that were there had a look about them as though they were not to be tested.

"You better stick close to me." David whispered to Steven, as he seemed to make the same observation. Steven nodded and followed as David moved deeper into the barroom.

Michael seemed to be drawn to the bar like a magnet; he ordered three beers and joined David and Steven at a pool table in the middle of the room.

"First round's on me." Michael said as he handed the beer out. David turned his beer up and drank nearly half of it in one gulp. Steven looked at his for a moment and thought of the hang over that he'd recently endured. His stomach turned and his body shuttered when the aroma filled his nostrils as he brought the beer to his mouth. He took only a small sip, which he had to choke down.

"You wanna break?" David asked after racking the balls on the table.

"No, go ahead." He answered while keeping a close watch on the door.

David took his stick and sent the cue ball crashing into the tight triangle at the other end of the table; he sunk two solids and then moved on to his next shot which he missed.

"Hey, it's your shot." David said to an oblivious Michael. "You alright?"

"Yeah, sure." Michael said as he set his beer on the side of the table, picked up his pool cue and took aim for an apathetic shot.

Michael missed his shot and instantly reoccupied his position at the end of the table to keep a guarded eye on the door. David stood for a moment, addled by Michael's notable disinterest for the game. He shook his head and continued with his shot.

* * *

Carrie looked down at her watch as she and Lisa exited the Movie Theater; it was nine forty five.

"I'm glad that we did this; it's been so long since I've been to a movie." Carrie said with a sincere smile.

"Me too. You know Ran's idea of a date is sitting in field with the radio on, fogging up the windows." Lisa replied with a smile.

"Speaking of Ran, what's the deal with the two of you?" Carrie asked curiously.

"What do you mean?" Lisa asked.

"I mean, are you guys serious or what? I just wonder because I saw the way you were looking at Michael the other night." Carrie continued.

"Yeah, Michael's nice, huh?" Lisa said with a smile as she searched her purse for the keys to the car.

"He's alright I guess." Carrie said, hiding her true opinion of him, which was as far as she was able to tell he wasn't to be trusted.

"Alright? He's dark and mysterious, not to mention painfully good looking." Lisa said, biting her bottom lip as she thought of Michael.

"I'll take that to mean that you're not serious with Ran." Carrie concluded as she and Lisa got into the car.

"I don't know, I mean I still like him too, but I don't see us growing old together or anything. I'm just having fun not being tied down to anybody, you know? I'm just tasting all the fruits that life has to offer." Lisa said with a smile as she cranked the car.

"Just don't make yourself sick." Carrie said as Lisa backed the car out of the space and started slowly out of the parking lot.

* * *

Steven stood, watching David and Michael play out their fifth game of pool. He was becoming extremely bored and was ready to leave. As time passed, Michael seemed to become more relaxed and more responsive.

David was having the time of his life. He was glad to have someone his own age, other than Julie, whom he could relate to. Before now he was always hanging out with Carrie and her friends, which wasn't terrible, but he often felt like a baby sitter around them instead of a friend.

"I gotta take a leak." David said after nearly two solid hours of playing and drinking. "Hey Steven, you wanna hold my stick while I piss?"

Michael cracked a smile at the remark, as did Steven while briefly staring to the floor, trying to think of a clever retort.

"You know David, I really like you as a friend, but that's about as far as I'm willing to take it." Steven finally responded after a moment.

"Damn, I was hoping for so much more." David said quickly, after only a second's thought.

"Try not to get you're ass whipped while I'm gone." He continued as held his pool cue out to Steven with a sluggish smile.

"Go on before you piss yourself." Steven said, detecting his slight intoxication.

"You ever played pool?" Michael asked as David walked away.

"I think I've played a couple of times." Steven said with a sly smile.

"Well then you wouldn't mind playing for a little cash, would you?" Michael asked with the same sly smile.

"What, five or ten dollars?" Steven asked.

"I was thinking more along the lines of twenty or thirty. Hell, we got paid today, how about fifty?" Michael continued.

"Gee, I don't know." Steven said, detecting Michael's intoxication as well.

"Come on, you can handle it." Michael continued to coax.

"Well okay." Steven said as he dug into his pocket and pulled out two twenty-dollar bills and two five-dollar bills. He slapped the money down on the side of the table and began to chalk up his cue.

"I'll even rack 'em." Michael said with an excited smile as he too put his money down and proceeded to prepare the table.

Steven aligned his sights on the cue ball and then sent it down the table into the tightly set billiards. He sunk a solid on the break and then proceeded to sink his next four shots with ease before missing his fifth with no good shot to take.

Michael looked at him with disgust, feeling as though he'd been hustled when he was trying to do the hustling himself.

"Played a couple of times, huh?" Michael asked, still full of disgust.

"Two or three," Steven began with a smile. "This is one of the few things that I did learn from my dad."

"Well it ain't over yet." Michael said as he lit a cigarette and took his first shot; he sunk it and then moved on to the next one, which he missed.

"I don't know, I smell a skunk." Steven said as he staked out his next shot.

"You know something that I've been thinking a lot about?" Michael asked as he took a draw from his cigarette.

"What?" Steven asked without breaking his concentration.

"I've been thinking about how we managed to meet up again like this, I mean what are the odds?" Michael continued.

"Apparently they're pretty good." Steven answered, pausing for a moment.

"I'm just thinking about what possible reason there could be for me to see you again, but then I think that maybe the reason is for you to see me again and that's what worries me. You think maybe that there's something else that you're supposed to say to me, or maybe try to do to me?" Michael said with a slightly paranoid tone.

"Look, I don't know and I don't care; I could've lived the rest of my life without ever seeing you again. I'm tired of thinking about it, I'm tired of dreaming about it and already I'm tired of talking about it. I haven't ratted you out and I don't see any reason why I would, we'll all pay for the things we've done sooner or later." Steven explained, completely stopping his game and looking Michael straight in the eye. Michael gave a satisfied nod and he and Steven shared a silence.

"Who's winning?" David asked after returning from the bathroom.

"I'm about to." Steven said as he took aim at the eight ball and sunk it with precision. He then stood up and flung his cue onto the table and collected his winnings with a smile.

"Ouch," David said with a short laugh. "Who wants more beer?"

"I'll take one, oh and pay for Michael's out of this." Steven said to David as he handed him a five-dollar bill.

"You wanna go again?" Michael asked as David walked away.

"If you got the money, I got the time." Steven answered as he began to prepare the table once again. Michael pulled only a ten-dollar bill out of his pocket this time and began to straighten it out.

As Steven began to set the balls back onto the table, he noticed a gangly, unkempt young man standing behind Michael, apparently with something to say. Steven also noticed, as he sharpened his observance, two more unsavory and equally unkempt men who took to either side of the table. One stopped at the side of the table while the other continued walking and stopped behind Steven. Michael noticed the two and recognized them immediately. He bowed his head and closed his eyes; he'd been found.

"What's up Michael?" The man asked from behind him. "Haven't seen you around. We've been worried about you."

"Yeah, I'm sure." Michael Replied.

"You know when you disappeared with the keys to the Nova, Gregg and Johnny thought that you were up to something. They thought that you might try to double cross us. They wanted to just tear the trunk right off of that car, but I said no. I was gonna give you the benefit of the doubt and wait to hear from you. I said to myself "Hey this is Michael, He'd never do that." The man moved closer to Michael and began to speak again, almost directly into his ear. Steven became more nervous with every second that passed and he started scanning the barroom for David. "But then two days passed and then a week and still no Michael. I was prepared to tear my car apart tomorrow to get to what was inside, I was even gonna save you're cut because I trusted you so much. Then I get a call on my cell phone from somebody saying that my car is down at the bar on a wrecker. I gotta say Michael, I'm a little pissed."

"Well you know what they say Tony; it's better to be pissed off than pissed on." Michael said with a laugh. Tony grabbed Michael's shoulder and turned him around and got in his face.

L.B. Kelly

"I'm not playing with you Michael, I know you don't think that you and you're little bitch are walking out of here, do you?" Tony hissed through clinched teeth.

"Yeah, right over you're ass if we have to." Michael answered confidently. Tony shook his head and began to laugh at the prospect.

Steven was shaking and had begun to sweat. He clinched the eight ball tightly in his hand, waiting for something, anything to happen. Then, through the thick tension Tony threw a punch at Michael that sent him sprawling onto the pool table. Steven turned around and hit Gregg, who was standing behind him, with the eight ball. As he made contact with the side of his nose, he heard bones crack and saw blood spurt. He was reminded of the day when he'd put John Larson in his place with the History book, but he also felt that somehow he wouldn't get out of this one as easily.

As quickly as the thought had entered his mind Steven felt a blow to the back of his head and he fell to the floor, seeing stars; after hitting the floor he felt repeated kicks to his legs and stomach.

Michael had managed to get his hands around Tony's neck as he came in for another attack; he pulled himself up from the table while Tony continued to wield punches to his stomach. While keeping a tight grip on Tony's throat with one hand he began to smash his face with the other.

Steven began to wonder how much more he could take as the kicks continued unrelentingly. Finally the kicks slowed and he peered out from behind his hands, which he was using to protect his face and saw one of the guys hit the floor with impressive force. When the kicking stopped all together, he looked above him and saw David pounding on the other guy's face.

"Get up!" David yelled to Steven between punches.

Steven pulled his sore and beaten frame up from the floor and tried to figure out just what he should do. By this time Gregg, the one whom David had first disposed of, made it back to his feet and had begun hitting David in the ribs. Steven looked around and quickly grabbed one of the pool cues from the table; he gripped it tightly and swung it, hitting Gregg in the back of the head.

Finally the bar was silenced by a gunshot. David and Steven looked to see Michael holding a smoking pistol.

"The next one's not going into ceiling, Tony!" Michael yelled through heavy breath.

Tony pulled himself up from the floor, wiping blood from his nose. Steven stood at guard with the pool cue cocked while David released Johnny, who fell limp against the pool table.

"Come on boys, I think we'd better get down the road." Michael said, still holding the gun on an enraged Tony.

David moved towards the door, shaking the pain from his bloodied knuckles. Steven stood in shock, still trying to comprehend what was happening.

"Steven, come on." David said, waking him from his disbelief.

Steven finally dropped the pool cue; he could hear it's distinct clacking sound clearly as it hit the floor in the hushed bar. He quickly joined David behind Michael, who appeared to be perfectly calm behind the gun. Steven looked around the bar at all the patrons as he and David and Michael slowly walked out of the bar. Some of them looked to be slightly shocked and some seemed to be relieved to have a break in the norm while others seemed not to be bothered by it either way.

After walking the twenty feet to the door, which seemed like twenty miles at the time, Michael and David both broke out running while Steven stood beneath the awning of the tiny building in the dim porch light, blown away by what was happening.

"Steven, come on!" David yelled without breaking stride.

Steven was snapped out of his daze once again and kicked up dust as he too ran away from the bar. He had no trouble catching up to David and Michael; in fact he beat them both to the truck. Steven opened the driver side door and was pushed into the truck by David. Michael quickly got in on the passenger side while David fished the keys from his pocket; finally he found the key and got into the truck.

"David, they parked in the way." Steven said dismally after noticing an older model, mid-size truck parked in front of theirs with the front end in the way. David stuck the key into the ignition and switched it on to allow the diesel's glow plugs to heat the fuel.

"Oh shit," David said after seeing, in the side view mirror, Tony standing outside the bar with a gun of his own aimed at the truck. "Come on you diesel ass son of a bitch!"

David spun the engine over several times before it finally came to life. As it did Tony fired a shot from his gun, shattering the side view mirror on the door of the truck, just inches from David's face.

"Shit, their shooting at us!" Steven yelled, looking around franticly.

"Yeah they are," Michael began while slumping down in the seat. He grabbed Steven's collar and pulled him down also. "That means that you duck."

David jammed the truck into gear and fed the massive diesel its fuel. The truck's tires dug into the gravel and it's body shuttered and shook as it pushed the obstructing truck out of the way. The shriek of metal on metal could be heard and felt as the trucks scrubbed together as they pulled away.

Steven jumped after hearing two more gunshots as they pulled out of the parking lot of the bar; one of which shattered the back window of the Nova that was riding piggy back on the truck.

"What the hell was that all about?" David yelled as he worked the gears in the truck like a racecar driver.

"Whoa!" Michael yelled with a nervous laugh. "What a rush, damn! No, I don't know. He lost this car to me in a poker game, I guess he didn't really think I was gonna take it."

David looked over at Michael, trying to decide if he should accept his excuse. Of course Michael gave his patented jive talker's smile and shrugged his shoulders; David just smiled and shook his head as they sped down the road.

"You alright, Steven? You got kind of quiet. You ain't got any new holes do you?" David asked as they blew through the intersection at the main highway.

"No, I'm alright." Steven said, looking a bit rattled.

"You know, you were supposed to turn back there." Michael said, pointing back towards the intersection.

"Well, I'll be damned if I'm going back." David said, looking up into the rearview mirror. " We'll just find another way."

* * *

Steven lay in his bed, wide-awake at daybreak Saturday morning. After the beating that he had taken the night before he was finding it difficult to even breath. His ribs were searing with pain and his face was tender from the few shots that he had taken in it.

He held his breath and moved very slowly as he sat up and lifted the covers from his side to inspect his ribs. He was in shocked when he took in the sight of the dark purple and black bruise that extended from his hip to just underneath his arm on his left side.

He flopped back down on the bed, letting out a moan of agony as he came to rest. He could feel anger grow inside him as he stared at the ceiling, listening to Michael snoring from the other end of the trailer; the way he saw it Michael should be awake and as miserable as he was since it was all his fault in the first place.

As the dawn's first light began to peek through the blinded window above Steven's bed, he could hear the footsteps of someone who was approaching the trailer. He then heard the latch of the camper's unlocked door begin to rattle.

The door opened and Steven saw Carrie Standing outside, still wearing her nightclothes, which included a thin T-shirt, a pair of panties and nothing else.

Chill bumps popped up all over Steven's body as the cool winter air gushed into the room. Carrie quickly hopped up the steps and closed the door behind her as she ran over to get into the bed with Steven.

Steven held the blanket up, inviting her in, but her coy smile turned into a look of perplexed concern when she saw the bruise that covered Steven's side.

"Oh baby, what happened?" She asked, stopping to inspect his ribs more closely. She lightly touched the bruise and then looked to Steven's face for an answer.

"Oh you know, just a night out with the guys." He answered with a forced smile as he moved over to make room for Carrie on the bed.

"What happened?" She repeated more sternly.

"I don't know, really. We stopped for a couple of beers last night and Michael ran into some of his old friends." Steven began to explain.

"Some friends." Carrie interjected.

"Yeah, apparently they had a misunderstanding!" Steven yelled through the trailer, in hopes of disturbing Michael's sleep, but he never missed a beat, he just kept snoring.

"I really don't know, he was acting funny all night and when those guys came in they started asking him about something in that car. I don't know and I don't want to know." Steven continued.

"You don't think that you should go to the hospital?" Carrie asked with concern.

"No, I'll be alright." He assured her.

"Are you sure?" She asked. Steven nodded his head in agreement.

"Anybody else get hurt?" Carrie further inquired as she settled gently into the bed next to Steven.

"No, Michael took a couple shots to the face, but it wasn't too bad and David didn't get hurt at all, he did the hurting." Steven explained.

"I'm not surprised," Carrie said while propping up on her elbow to face Steven. "Now what can I do for you?" Steven smiled devilishly and looked at Carrie's body desirously.

"I don't think I can take what I want right now." He said disappointedly.

"You just relax and let me worry about it." Carrie said with the same devilish smile as she began to kiss his body and rub him gently, careful not to disturb his soreness.

Steven folded his arms behind his head and closed his eyes. His pain seemed to fade as Carrie began to indulge him.

Chapter Eight

Over the three weeks since Michael had arrived, Steven found himself forming an odd and uncomfortable friendship with him. He was no longer reliving the nightmarish scenes from the train in his sleep and was no longer intimidated by him, however his natural, subconscious fear of him was still very much alive and well founded.

Steven's relationship with Carrie was becoming stronger than ever and more genuine as well. It was becoming common for them to be seen together and people were starting to accept the relationship, everyone except for Ran.

Although Ran's not so subtle brand of annoyance was starting to ebb, it had become apparent to Steven that he would remain an ever-present thorn in his side. Ran always seemed to be readily available with his constant brow beatings, to which Steven had become accustomed and quite adept at retaliating against.

Steven also noticed Lisa's interest in Ran start to wane as her adoration for Michael began to bloom and Steven was concerned over this; regardless of his rocky relationship with Lisa, he was starting to recognize her qualities as

Carrie saw them. He knew what kind of person Michael really was and he knew that even Lisa didn't deserve the kind of torment that he could, most certainly dish out.

Christmas had come and gone during the past few weeks as well. This one was like no other Steven had ever experienced before; he actually felt the way that he did when he was younger, when he and Brooke couldn't sleep on Christmas eve and would sneak through the house in search of Santa, careful not to scare him away.

He felt the excitement of Christmas morning again, the way that he used to. He also felt the love in the Anderson house when he sat down and exchanged gifts with Carrie and David and Julie while Michael slept in out in the camper.

Now with New Year's eve coming up, Steven had spent the past few days trying to think of a proper resolution to institute, but the only one that he could think of was enroll in a local GED program that Carrie had been hounding him about.

"Later you'll be glad you did it." She would say.

"I will, I will." Steven would promise with luke-warm interest. Steven was unconcerned with his future, for once in his life he was living for the moment.

Steven walked into the house that Monday evening after work to find it warm and clean and clear of the Christmas tree. He continued through the living room and down the hallway to Carrie's bedroom. He walked in and stopped at her closed bathroom door. He stood there for a moment, listening. He could hear Carrie singing softly to herself as she lay, relaxed in the bathtub. He opened the door slowly and peeked around to see her smiling face.

"Hey." She said through her smile as Steven walked into the room.

"Hey, how was you're day." Steven asked as he leaned over and kissed her. He sat down on the edge of the tub and took in the sight of her naked body, as she lay unabashed by his presence in the room.

"Long and boring, I'm gonna need a vacation from my Christmas vacation if I don't find something to do." She answered while swirling the water around in the tub.

"Well I saw that you cleaned up today and took the tree down." Steven said.

"Yeah, Daddy used to keep it up for weeks after Christmas, but it's just not the same anymore. Now I just get tired of looking at it." She said with a cynical tone.

"I'm sorry." Steven said sympathetically.

"It's alright." She said, sliding down slightly in the tub.

"Hey, subject change. Lisa called earlier and she said that Eddie's gonna have a New Year's party out at his place this weekend. She said everybody's coming." Carrie said with an excited expression.

"Eddie, have I met him?" Steven asked while trying to find his profile in his mind among the many others of people who he'd met over the past few months.

"Yeah, I think so; him and Jeff are good friends. Anyway, you'll have a good time, he's crazy." Carrie assured him.

"Well it can't get much worse than getting beat up and shot at in a bar fight." Steven said while adjusting his perch on the tub.

"Oh, it can always get worse." Carrie said with a devious laugh. Steven just shook his head with a smile as he stood up.

"You leaving?" Carrie asked with a disappointed frown.

"Yeah, I'm gonna go get a shower, besides you know how funny David get when I come in the bathroom with you. I don't want have to kick his ass." Steven said boldly with a crooked smile.

"Yeah, right." Carrie said, dismissing the idea quickly.

As he entered the living room, Steven noticed David emptying his pocket on to the table beside his chair, just like every day.

"Where's Carrie?" David asked tiredly as he looked up from the table.

"She in the bathtub." Steven answered sheepishly. David narrowed his eyes and held his finger up, while trying to find his words.

Steven could notice the contour of the muscle underneath the ink in David's lean fore arm as he pointed at him. He also noticed the grave and tired look in his eye and he knew that it would be tricky business to rib with David when he was in this mood.

"You're walking a thin line there; it's one thing what y'all do when I'm not around and don't know it, but it's something different in my house." David said in total seriousness.

Steven waited for a moment before saying anything. He knew that saying the right thing would either piss David off or pull him out of his sour mood.

"She forced me." Steven said shortly and sincerely, in a way that only he could. David looked at him a little longer before letting a smile spread across his face.

"Let me catch you again and I'll force my foot up you're ass." He said, finally.

"Only if you catch me, right?" Steven asked with a smile, pushing his luck.

"Keep it up." David warned, still smiling.

"Keep what up?" Carrie asked as she entered the room. David and Steven continued to look at each other, keeping the joke to themselves.

"What?" Carrie repeated.

"Nothing." David said with his smile still present before returning to his routine.

"I'll be back." Steven said, winking at Carrie as he headed to the door.

"Thanks for the warning." David said as Steven stepped on to the porch.

Steven began to unbutton his jacket as he walked around the house to the trailer, while the mild winter wind blew against him.

He could hear two voices inside the camper as he approached. He looked back to the front of the house and saw Ran's car in the driveway. He shook his head in disappointment and wondered what he and Michael could possibly be talking about.

Steven set one foot on to the step and then grabbed the door handle and was surprised to find it locked.

"Open the door!" Steven yelled as he bang his fist against it, slightly agitated.

He could hear a slight commotion before Michael opened the door, while sticking a wad of cash into his pocket.

"Don't get you're panties in a bind." Michael said as he walked back over to the living area where Ran was seated.

"Hey, Hobo." Ran said with an arrogant smirk as Steven closed the door and walked into the trailer.

"Hey, bitch." Steven returned quickly.

The two stared each other down for a minute, while Michael looked on, entertained by the unavoidable face-off.

"I'm gonna take off." Ran said as he stood up from his seat. "I think I'll stop and talk to Carrie for a while first, though."

"Tell her that I'll be back over there in a little while, in case she gets bored talking to you." Steven said as he stopped on his way to the small bathroom, completely unaffected by Ran's attempt to get under his skin.

Ran was silenced by Steven's retort and was generally dumfounded by recent unwillingness to accept any more of his mindless harassment.

Steven stood in place for another moment and then continued to the bathroom, after giving Ran ample opportunity to reply to his comment.

"So, you think you're gonna make an appearance Friday night?" Ran asked of Michael as he walked to the door.

"Great, that's all I need, those two teaming up." Steven said to himself after hearing Ran's question.

"Yeah, I might come through." Michael said nonchalantly.

"Hey!" He continued in haste, as Ran was about to walk through the door.

"Yeah?" He answered.

"That little split-tail you're fooling with, Lisa." Michael began.

"Yeah." Ran acknowledged.

"Yeah, I was thinking of hooking up with her." Michael continued.

"Oh yeah, That's cool; it's getting old. Go ahead." Ran said after a second, giving his blessing. "Besides, Carrie's mine."

"It don't look like it from where I'm standing." Michael pointed out as he looked towards the bathroom to where Steven was.

"She'll get it out of her system." Ran said, as he too looked Steven's way.

"Whatever man. Oh and by the way, about Lisa; I wasn't asking you, I was telling you." Michael informed him.

Ran gave Michael a cold, yet innocuous glare as he left the trailer. Michael simply responded to it with a short, breathy and unconcerned laugh. He continued to watch Ran walk away from the trailer through the window, thinking of what an idiot he was for letting someone like Steven take his woman from him and then for just rolling over when he told him that he was taking the one that he had then.

Michael, once again looked towards the bathroom, thinking about Steven and his reoccurring doubts that he had concerning his reliability to keep his mouth shut about what he already knew and also about what he might think that he saw when he entered the trailer.

* * *

Steven endured the day of nervous torture that lead him to the evening on which Eddie's New Year's party was to be held. Although he'd gained a great deal of confidence since leaving his old life and former self behind him, he was still a bit gun-shy over the idea of trying to fit in with people who considered themselves to be more than a few classes above a runaway. Deep down, in some ways he felt that they were right, especially when it came to popular opinion concerning his relationship with Carrie.

Steven and David left work together that Friday, while Michael took his own direction as always.

"So, are you and Julie coming with us to the party tonight?" Steven asked, hoping that they would for the sake of his own comfort.

"I don't know, I don't know if I want to hang out with a bunch of punk-ass kids." David responded with a sincere tone, but Steven had known him long enough now to tell that he was joking and would, more than likely join them at the party.

David locked the dead bolt on the door of the shop and then proceeded on his way to the car accompanied by Steven. As he searched through the key ring for his car keys, he and Steven both were alerted to attention by the shrill honking of a car's horn approaching from behind them. They looked back to see Julie's car headed towards the shop.

She slowed the car and steered it into the small parking lot of the shop. She lowered the passenger side window as she stopped next to David and Steven.

"Hey, what are you doing off so early?" David asked, pleasantly surprised.

"I don't know, I guess Simmons grew a heart. He let everybody off early for New Year's." Julie said with a smile.

"Yeah, that would've been nice." Steven interjected with a half-hearted smile to David.

"You just got it so bad, don't you?" David asked.

"Yeah, a nice long, paid vacation would be good." Steven went on.

"How about a permanent vacation?" David suggested.

"You'd be begging me back." Steven said confidently.

"Don't count on it." He was warned. Steven's smile died slowly as he tried to pick the truth from the levity in that last statement.

"Don't worry Steven, I got you're back." Julie said, with a wink. Steven had noticed, the few times that he'd met Julie, that she seemed to be immune to David's rough and often intimidating demeanor.

"So, what's up?" David asked as he placed his forearms on the roof of the car and leaned in for Julie's answer.

"I wanted to go to the liquor store before I went home and I want you to take me." She more or less told him, instead of asking him.

"Okay, I'll be over later to take you." David said.

"But, I want to go now." Julie said firmly.

"Baby, I gotta take Steven home." He reminded her.

"Steven, you can't drive?" She asked, leaning over a bit in the seat.

"Oh yeah." Steven said with an uncontainable smile.

David closed his eyes as if he'd just realized defeat. He stood up and looked at Steven and then to his car. He looked back down to the car keys in his hand and pondered for a moment, as if he were making a life altering decision.

"It's just a car." Julie said shortly. David cut his eyes at her sharply.

"I'll pretend that I didn't hear that." He said.

"Pretend what you wa…"

"No, no, I didn't hear it." David interrupted.

"If you damage my car in any way, you might as well just keep going, because not even Carrie would be able to save you." David said as he dangled the keys to his Dodge Charger in front of Steven. Steven's smile grew even larger as he reached out to take the keys, giddy with excitement.

"There'll be nowhere to hide." David said before dropping the keys into Steven's hand.

"Don't you worry, I got it under control." Steven said, with his smile reaching its limit.

David walked around Julie's car and got into the driver seat while Julie moved over to the passenger side.

"Straight home." David said as he reluctantly got into the car. Steven turned back with his smile as he walked over to the car.

"Let's go." Julie said, while rubbing David's leg to ease his worry.

He pulled the car into drive and eased away from the shop as Steven waved at him from beside the Charger.

Steven watched until David and Julie drove out of sight. He then looked down at the keys in his hand and then at the massive, powerhouse of a car that sat before him. He opened the driver's door and sat down in the seat. The excitement that he felt sent a chill up his spine and nearly caused him to laugh out loud.

He slid the key into the ignition and turned the engine over. After a few rounds the car awakened with a roar. Steven sat there for a moment, intimidated by the car as it shook him slightly. He looked out through the windshield and saw the antenna of the car whipping back and forth with the growling of the engine.

Steven pressed the brake firmly and then gripped the shifter on the floor of the car with his right hand. The car jerked and slowed its growl slightly as he pulled the transmission into drive. He released the brake and the car pulled itself towards the road. Steven checked for traffic on both sides and then double-checked, deciding it best to heed David's warnings.

He released the brake once again and fed the beast it's fuel as he took to the road, feeling as though he owned it.

The car was even more powerful than Steven had expected and it was so responsive in every way that it was almost frightening. Even though the car was more than capable of reaching impressive speeds, Steven drove it slower than he'd ever driven anything; the rush and excitement was worth savoring.

Steven pulled up to the house and cut the engine. He sat behind the wheel for a moment, sorry that the ride was over. He gripped the steering wheel once more before getting out of the car.

As Steven approached the house Carrie opened the door and stood there for a minute, amazed by what she'd witnessed; someone other than David or herself driving the Charger. Not even Ran had driven it when he was working in the shop.

"What happened to David?" Carrie asked curiously.

"Nothing, what do you mean?" Steven responded with a soft confusion.

"What did you do to get him to hand the keys to the car over?" She continued. Steven smiled as he made his way up the steps.

"I didn't do anything, Julie was behind that." He answered.

"Julie?" Carrie asked, cocking her brow.

"Yeah, she showed up as we were leaving and wanted David to take her somewhere." Steven began to explain.

"She said jump and David asked how high?" Carrie finished with a disgusted tone.

"Yeah, I guess." He agreed. Carrie shook her head and turned and stormed into the house, aggravated by the under lying feeling that her brother was slipping away from her.

"She's not that bad." Steven said as he walked into the house, closing the door behind him. Carrie stopped short and shot him a burning look.

"For a bitch, I mean." Steven added. Carrie retracted her look and continued on her way to the kitchen. Steven shook his head and smiled, unable to notice how much her brother's increasing interest in Julie was bothering her.

* * *

A couple of hours had past, during which Steven showered and had gotten dressed for the party and now found himself waiting in the living room for Carrie to finish getting ready herself.

As Steven whittled the moments away, he found himself contemplating the possible reasons for a woman's exorbitant use of time in preparing to leave the house. It seemed rational to him that they should become more efficient at the task with as much time as they take to carry it out each time. Then the thought dawned upon him; perhaps they derived as much enjoyment for getting ready to go somewhere as they do from actually going.

Just as he felt that he was on the verge of answering a timeless question, his thoughts were interrupted by the sound of Lisa's car approaching the house.

Steven adjusted his position on the couch to better his view of the yard. He was then able to see Michael's car pull up to the house behind Lisa.

Steven got up from the couch and moved to the window beside the front door. He saw Michael step out of his car and motion, with his poisonous smile, for Lisa to join him. He watched as Lisa sauntered over to him, smiling flirtatiously.

L.B. Kelly

They began to talk, but from inside the house it was like watching a muted television. By the reaction from both Lisa and Michael, it was obvious that a mutual agreement had been reached and both of them were pleased.

Michael slid back into his car and drove to the camper. Steven heard the car park and continue running with an increased idle.

As Lisa hurried up the front steps of the house Steven also hurried, back to the couch where he sat, nonchalantly trying to seem as though he hadn't been eve's dropping.

"Hey, where's Carrie?" Lisa asked as she opened the door and stopped there.

"She's still getting ready." Steven said as he motioned to the back of the house. Lisa tilted her head in brief thought.

"Well is David going tonight?" She asked quickly.

"I think so." Steven answered a little confused.

"Y'all catch a ride with him, I'm gonna ride with Michael." She spat out hurriedly as Michael's car crept back to the front of the house.

"But David's not…" Steven began to inform her.

"Tell her that I'll talk to her later." Lisa continued as she pulled the door shut and scurried off to Michael's car, deaf to Steven's words.

"Here." Steven finished, only for his self to hear.

Steven waited for a few minutes more, less than thrilled to inform Carrie of the recent change of plan. He knew that she would be quite unpleasant because of it on top of her already foul mood.

276

"Did I hear Lisa's car pull up." Carrie asked after finally appearing from her bedroom.

"Yeah." Steven said truthfully.

"Well, where is she?" Carrie continued with a dropped tone, sensing that something was wrong.

"She left With Michael." Steven answered reluctantly. Carrie sighed deeply and closed her eyes.

"Did she leave her car keys?" She asked calmly. Steven shook his head in response.

"I'm gonna kill her." She said after a second as Steven looked at her as though she was a bomb that was about to explode. "How does she expect us to get there."

"I think she assumed that David was here." Steven said, considering the presence of the charger in the front yard.

"Why didn't you tell her that he wasn't?" Carrie tried to understand.

"I tried, she was in a hurry." Steven defended against her sharp tone. Carrie began to pace a bit while weighing her options.

"Well, we'll just take David's car then." Carrie said as she headed to the door.

"You think that's a good idea?" Steven asked, remembering David's words from earlier in the evening.

"What are you scared of him?" Carrie asked as she stopped sharply at the bottom of the steps.

"Yeah, as a matter of fact I am, a little bit. When it comes to this car anyway." Steven admitted.

"Well I'm not." Carrie said as she continued on to the car. Steven stood there at the steps, questioning the idea.

"Are you coming?" She asked as she opened the driver's door of the car.

"You're driving, he can't get mad at me." Steven said as he walked over and got into the passenger side.

Carrie cranked the car and pressed the accelerator to the floor, causing the engine to howl fiercely, expressing her frustration. Steven shook his head and gripped the armrest on the door and hoped for the best.

* * *

Steven and Carrie arrived at Eddie's place around seven forty five. They drove past his vacant house and into the field in the back where the parties were usually held. As they converged upon the location, Carrie noticed that there were quite a few more people there than usual. She hoped that there wouldn't be any fights tonight and that everyone could get along for once.

While Carrie searched for a spot to park the car, Steven nervously scanned the place over in search of David and Julie. He saw them nowhere and was able to relax for the moment.

Steven stepped out of the car and began to absorb the scene; it was still a strange feeling for him to be included in something like this, it never would've happened back home. Carrie walked around the car and smiled as she noticed Steven's reaction to everything.

"Are you okay? You seem a little overwhelmed." Carrie said as she took his hand, letting her mood lighten a bit.

"Oh yeah, I used to do stuff like this all the time." Steven said, thinly disguising his excitement. Carrie just widened her smile and led him towards the crowd of people.

Eddie made his way to Carrie after spotting her through the jumble of bodies. He had two unopened beers in his hand and an intoxicated smile upon his face.

"Hey, Eddie." Carrie said after noticing him.

"Hey, glad you made it, girl." He greeted as he gave Carrie an unexpected hug. Steven was certain that he hadn't met Eddie before. He definitely would've remembered him. Eddie handed Carrie one of the beers.

"You must be Steve." He said as he handed Steven the second beer.

"Yeah." Steven responded quietly, still looking around. Eddie stood, awkwardly silent for a moment nodding, wondering if he'd said enough to Steven to be considered polite.

"Y'all are riding in style tonight, huh? Got the 'Cuda out." Eddie said to Carrie with his dumb grin as he noticed David's car.

"Charger." Steven corrected, still looking around as he walked a little further into the party, followed by Carrie.

"Yeah, right." Eddie said, not quite sure what Steven was talking about, but feeling a little out done none the less.

As Carrie and Steven navigated their way through the crowd, Carrie spotted Lisa and Michael sitting on the ground close to the large fire that was there. They seemed to be very cozy with each other. They were surrounded by a small group of people, who were unknowingly falling victim to Michael's dangerous charm. Michael was beginning to reestablish his reputation around town and his recent business endeavor had jump-started his popularity with the younger crowd.

"Hey." Lisa said to Carrie as she noticed her walking up. She got up from the ground and met her with an apologetic look.

Steven continued towards Michael and his captivated audience as Carrie and Lisa scurried off to talk.

"Hey, Steve-o!" Michael slurred. "Get my man a beer." He said to one of the kids that were there.

"I got one." Steven said as he held up his unopened beer.

"There's always room for one more." Michael continued.

"No, I'm good." Steven reiterated as Carrie and Lisa rejoined the group.

"Okay, it's here when you want it." Michael relented.

"You know him?" One of the kids asked. They had known of Steven's presence in town and had heard the rumors, but now with Michael's validation, he would surely become a popular mystery to be unraveled.

"Yeah, we know each other, don't we?" Michael began sloppily. "We go way back."

Steven raised his brow and focused his attention on what Michael was saying, wondering where he was going with it. Carrie grew slightly interested in the remark and she began to listen more intently as well.

"I don't know how much good he'll do you in a bar fight, but he's a hell of a guy to have on a train ride." Michael continued, shocking Steven with the remark.

Steven's eyes widened and he briefly glanced at Carrie to see if she'd caught the point of the statement. She looked back at him with an unsure expression and Steven quickly looked away.

"What do you mean?" The kid asked.

"I think you caught some knots in that bar fight too." Steven said, trying to cover up Michael's slip as he opened his beer. Michael looked at him with a drop in his expression as he realized what he'd said. As the confusion lingered, David and Julie's presence interrupted the situation.

"Y'all started without us, huh?" David said as he opened the nearest cooler and took a couple of beers from it.

"We're just getting warmed up, man." Michael said as he stood up and took a cigarette from his pocket and lit it.

"Hey, Carrie." Julie said warmly, still trying to win her over. Carrie's mood headed south again, along with her interest in the comment made by Michael.

"Hey." She said shortly.

"Did I see my car up there?" David asked as he looked to Steven for an answer.

"Talk to her." Steven said, pointing to Carrie.

"Yeah, we needed a ride, if you'd been there we could've come with you." Carrie said without hesitation.

"Oh, it'll be alright." Julie said in an attempt to diffuse the growing tension.

David gave a yielding sigh as he took a drink from his beer. Carrie shook her head and then walked away from the group. David sent a chilling look to Steven that he'd never seen from him before and he quickly followed Carrie to remove himself from the thick position that he was in.

As Steven caught up to Carrie, he saw that she had bumped into Ran and Ricky. Ran gave Steven his customary dirty look as he approached them.

Steven put his arm around Carrie's waist and responded to Ran's dirty look with a victorious smirk that cut right through him and fueled his jealousy.

"Is Lisa here?" Ran asked of Carrie after a second.

"Yeah, she's over there." She answered.

"With Michael." Steven added with his smirk still present.

Ran reinforced his dirty look and then turned to begin his search for Lisa, followed by his drone, Ricky.

Carrie found a comfortable place to settle in, away from the crowd. She began to drink her beer without restraint as her attitude sank further.

Steven sat down on the ground next to Carrie and moved close to her to share her warmth. He looked out over the crowd and could see David and Julie standing with Michael, but Lisa was nowhere to be found. He continued to look over the small sea of people and he finally spotted Lisa and Ran on the outer edge of the circle, talking.

"I figured I would find y'all sooner or later, this is some party ain't it?" Jeff said as he suddenly appeared and knelt down next to Carrie. Jeff took a drink from his beer and as he did, Carrie finished hers and took another from Jeff that he was carrying for a spare.

"Yeah, what's going on, Jeff?" Steven greeted as he shook his hand. Jeff gave Steven a look as to inquire about Carrie's disposition and Steven only responded by shaking his head unknowingly.

"Hey, is Lisa here?" Jeff asked.

"Boy, she's popular tonight." Carrie said bitterly, causing Jeff some perplexity.

"Yeah, it's some party." Steven said as he too began to drink his beer down in hopes that it would numb him to the quickly descending festivities.

"I'm sorry, Jeff. Yeah, she's here somewhere with Michael or Ran or somebody." Carrie continued.

"It's alright; I guess I ought to just give up on her anyway." Jeff said as he lit a cigarette.

"Decided not to quit, huh?" Carrie asked after seeing the cigarette.

"I gave up on that too." He said with a vague smile. Carrie shared his smile and then drank the rest of her beer down.

"Baby, will you get me another one?" She said to Steven as she ran her hand along the inside of his thigh as an incentive. He looked at her a little doubtful. He'd never seen her drink that way before.

"Yeah." He finally said as he got up and finished his own beer. "Jeff, you ready for another one?"

"Naw." He answered.

Steven walked back over to Michael's dwindling circle, where the cooler was and took from it two of the last three beers that were there. As he shook the ice from the cans Ran and Lisa joined the circle.

283

"David, Julie." Ran acknowledged as he walked up, completely ignoring Steven and Michael.

"What's up Ran? Ain't seen you in a while." David said as Ran made his way to the cooler.

"You know how it is." Ran replied with little thought; David just shook his head disappointedly. Ran reached into the cooler and took the last beer.

"Thanks." Michael said, taking the beer from Ran as he closed the lid of the cooler.

Ran stared Michael down intensely with keen eyes.

"What's you're problem?" He spat.

"I can't let you have my last beer." Michael said as he adjusted his wobbly footing.

"If you don't want anybody to drink your beer then you need to put your cooler back in your car." Ran told him boldly.

"I don't mind anybody else, I just don't want you drinking it." Michael continued with an arrogant smile. Steven couldn't help but laugh at Ran as Michael made a fool of him.

"You got something to say to me, hobo?" Ran said as he got in Steven's face, unwilling to take the same treatment from him.

Steven stood intimidated by Ran, reliving memories of intimidation by John Larson. He clinched his fist, willing to make a stand if he had to, if that's what it would take to settle things between him and Ran once and for all. By this time, Carrie had taken notice of the confrontation and was coming over to find out what was happening.

Steven's breathing was becoming heavy and he was obviously nervous. Ran found pleasure in this and was gaining confidence in the weakness that he sensed. It was then that Ran noticed Carrie and Jeff headed their way and this only enraged him further.

"Don't worry, here comes your little whore to save you again." Ran said in his anger, forgetting that he was in the presence of David.

David was instantly infuriated, he handed his beer, hastily, to Julie, but before he could react, either physically or verbally Steven launched a punch that connected firmly with Ran's nose. The impact seemed to be felt by everyone.

Steven dropped the beers from his left hand and prepared for the worst. Ran shook the punch off and lunged at Steven. They both hit the ground and Ran gained the upper hand quickly, landing blows to Steven's nearly healed ribs. Steven grunted in pain with each shot and knew that this fight was lost.

"Stop it!" Carrie screamed as she began to hit Ran across the back, with no effect at all.

David stepped across the tangled mess that was Ran and Steven. He grabbed Carrie, pulling her away from harm while Jeff looked on in dismay.

Michael was next to react. He took a step forward and kicked Ran in the side of the head, knocking him off of Steven. Then, without a second thought, he pulled a pistol from his inside jacket pocket. He cocked the gun and pointed it at Ran, who after seeing it, froze instantly.

"You want to fight, fight this." Michael said as he looked at Ran's stunned face through vertigo.

Everyone took a collective gasp and Steven waited for Michael to pull the trigger, knowing that he was fully capable of doing so.

"Michael," David began calmly, as he moved over to him and slowly pushed his arm down. "Think about it. It ain't that bad." Michael stood, silently breathing and not at all shaken.

"I guess it's your lucky day." He said after a second, feeling that he had embarrassed Ran sufficiently. He smiled as he sensed a pure and genuine fear in Ran's eyes. It was the same fear that had filled Jake's eyes just seconds before his death.

Some of the younger teenagers that were there were frightened nearly to tears, while most everyone else was still frozen with shock.

Ran took in a shaky breath as he pulled himself up. He looked at everyone and then walked away quickly, wanting not to shed even one of the impending tears that were pushing at his eyes in front of a single person.

Steven grabbed David's out-stretched hand and allowed him to hoist his damaged body from the ground.

"You'll be alright." David said as he playfully punched Steven, lightly in his ribs. He only winced a bit, not wanting to draw any further attention to himself.

"Are you okay?" Carrie asked as she pushed Steven's hair away from his eyes. He nodded and with a still expression made eye contact with Michael as he walked away, wondering why in hell he'd done what he did. Michael stared back at him with a hollow look, offering no answer, only reinforcing Steven's fear of him and reminding him of why it was there in the first place.

Carrie picked up the beers from the ground and followed Steven back to their spot. She sat down on the ground next to him and laid her head on his shoulder and shared in his silent pain.

Lisa saw Michael in a different light as he went on with his mingling as if nothing out of the ordinary had happened. She began to have fleeting doubts about her intentions with him. He looked at her and smiled, she returned it half-heartedly, wondering what she was getting herself into by starting a relationship with him.

Steven could feel the pain in his ribs start to fade as he downed another beer. Carrie could feel her pain start to dwindle as well, but her pain wasn't physical, it was the pain of frustration and aggravation towards Ran and her brother that she was feeling.

Carrie spotted Ran sitting on the hood of his car, in a self-imposed exile, looking pitiful while trying to soothe the sting of his marred pride. He was also watching her, with an undecided look, as though he felt justified in calling her a whore, but also wanting to walk over and take her from Steven and claim her for his own. The frustration that he felt was equal to what Carrie was feeling.

Carrie threaded her arm under Steven's and took another drink from her beer. By now she'd lost count of how many that she'd had, but it didn't matter. As far she was concerned at the moment, too much wouldn't be enough.

"Hey, we're gonna go, but I'm probably gonna come back and stay at your house tonight, if it's okay with you." Lisa said to Carrie, surprising Steven, who hadn't seen her come up through his impaired perception.

"Yeah, sure. Your not gonna stay with Michael?" Carrie asked, trying to re-align her perception also.

"No, I don't know. He kind of freaked me out earlier." Lisa said.

"You can ride back with us if you want." Carrie offered after sensing Lisa's worry.

"No, I'll be over later. I already told him that I would ride back with him." She said.

"Okay, be careful." Carrie said as Lisa walked away.

As Steven watched the crowd of people swirling together, he was able to focus on David and Julie walking towards him and Carrie.

"We're gonna cut out too." David said as he stood, trying to measure Carrie's inebriation. Carrie's body language changed instantly and she clamed up even more. "Are you okay to drive?" He asked.

"Yeah." Carrie said without looking at him.

"Carrie." He began again.

"David, I'm fine." She said.

"Okay." He said after a moment of doubt as he began to slowly walk away. He looked at Steven, who gave him a goofy, drunken wave that only clouded his doubt further.

"Hell, I guess we'll go too." Carrie said as she prepared to get up from the ground.

"Yeah, we got some love making to do." Steven said with a smile.

Carrie straightened her stance and then began to sway, her complexion turned pale and she quickly ran a few feet away and began to throw up.

"That's no good." Steven said as he too struggled to his feet. "Are you okay, baby?" He asked as he staggered over to Carrie, who was now headed back his way.

"No." She answered as she wiped her mouth.

"Ooo, I think you better let me drive; I'm not as drunk as I am." Steven said, letting the nonsense spill from his mouth.

"I think you are." Carrie said, feeling her intoxication evolve into an early hang over.

"You sure?" Steven asked, unable to discern for himself.

"Yeah." She answered, a little shocked by his intolerance for the alcohol.

"Okay, you be the driver." Steven said as Carrie took his arm and began to guide him through the crowd, towards the car. "Whoa, slow down, Driver!" He said as he followed with his eyes and balance useless to him.

Carrie let go of Steven's arm as they reached the car. He seemed to float forward like a tiny boat being pushed out into a pond. He stopped, sharply in place after hearing several loud pops and crackles. His first instinct was to run for cover, thinking that perhaps Michael had come back to follow through on his thwarted actions towards Ran. His caution turned to enchantment when a shower of colorful sparks that illuminated the night sky followed the pops.

"Oh shit." He said as he stood, mystified by the sight of the New Year's celebration.

"Get in the car, Steven." Carrie said from the driver's seat as she cranked the Dodge's enormous engine.

Steven staggered around the side of the car and pulled his door open, after finding the handle with blazing imprecision. He fell into the seat and slammed the door shut.

"Let's go, Driver!" He commanded with a smile as if he were the captain of a grand ship. Carrie just shook her head and pounded the car's accelerator, letting it tear the grass up as she left with sparkling light show reflecting in the immaculate deep-purple paint of the car.

Carrie pulled the car out on to the road and swerved a bit as she struggled with her impaired mind to gain complete control of the car.

"You are so drunk, maybe I should drive." Steven said as he reached over and grabbed the steering wheel.

"Shut up and quit grabbing stuff." Carrie said, pushing him back into his seat.

"What's wrong with you?" He asked, honestly surprised by her tone.

"Nothing." She answered.

"Not nothing, what?" He continued. Carrie looked at him and then took his hand.

"I'm sorry, I'm just aggravated with Lisa leaving us at the house to start with and then David always acts like an ass when he's with Julie. It's just stupid stuff." She explained.

"It's not stupid, it's the way you feel. You ought to cut Julie some slack though; it's not her fault. She's really trying." Steven said in a moment of clarity.

Carrie took in a breath to lash out against Steven's suggestion, but instead she exhaled it and actually considered the validity of the statement. She looked at him and smiled, finding comfort in his goofy smile.

* * *

Steven was awakened the next morning by the sound of Carrie's voice. He couldn't tell with whom she was talking or what about. He opened his eyes and his vision was bombarded by the bright sunlight that poured through her bedroom window. He looked to the nightstand beside her bed for her clock, while rubbing his eyes. His depth perception was non-existent, he felt as if he were looking through the viewfinder of a camera.

It was eleven-forty am. He shook his head in disbelief. He hated sleeping so late, it made him feel like he'd missed something.

"Did you hear me?" Carrie said, nudging Steven's butt.

"Am I still drunk?" He asked out loud, he didn't know a hang over could get any worse than his last one.

"She didn't come in last night and I can't get her on her cell phone. Go over to the trailer and see if she's with Michael." Carrie said with a hopeful expression.

"Who?" Steven asked, unable to follow the one-sided conversation.

"Lisa." She said with an agitated tone.

"Maybe she's at home, sleeping, like I was." He said as he rolled over and buried his head in the pillows on the bed.

"Her car is still outside, just do it." She said as she slapped him, again, a little harder on the butt.

Steven looked back at her with a submissive look and began to roll out of the bed while letting out a useless, disapproving growl.

He stood up from the bed and discovered that he was still wearing his blue jeans. It was then that he realized that his hopes of making love the night before must have been in vain.

"So, how was it for you?" He asked. Carrie knew immediately what he was referring to.

"Don't make me laugh." She said, causing Steven's already weak smile to straighten. "Go."

He turned and walked to the bathroom door and flipped the light on.

"You want me to make you something to eat?" She asked with a smile, already knowing his response. He waved his hand at her and cradled his sour stomach before slamming the bathroom door behind him.

* * *

Steven stepped out onto the porch and walked down the steps. He noticed that it had rained quite a bit the night before as he made his first, flimsy step onto the soggy ground. He walked around the house and found that the trail leading to the camper was now nothing but mud.

He noticed Michael's car was parked dangerously close to the trailer, obviously parked by someone who shouldn't have been driving in the first place. He opened the camper's door and knocked as much mud from his shoes as he could before going inside.

The trailer was dark with all the blinds closed and deadly quiet. Steven looked to his own bed and found it just as he'd left it. He continued through the small living area and down the cramped hall to Michael's crypt-like bedroom where he saw him fast asleep, fully clothed and alone.

He looked to the floor below Michael's bed and saw an overflowing astray and a toppled beer can lying on a spot where it's spilled contents had dried. Steven raked the layer of dirty clothes away with his foot to make a path to the bed. He saw that the gun that Michael had brandished the night before was nestled beside him on top of the covers. He thought for a moment and then picked the gun up. He looked at it with a nervous awe, wondering if it was the gun that he'd used that night on the train. He shook the thoughts from his head, not wanting to think about it any further. He set the gun on the floor and then shook Michael's shoulder in a fruitless effort to wake him.

Steven shook him again, harder this time and got a vague sign of life from him as he rolled over to his back.

"Michael." Steven said with another shake. Michael moved his legs around and groaned a bit.

"Michael, do you know where Lisa is?" Steven asked in a voice that was almost a whisper.

"Piss off!" Michael yelled. He simply rolled over and went back to sleep.

Steven stood up straight and sighed, wondering what his next move should be. After a bout of random thought in his aching mind he decided to give up on Michael and report back to Carrie with no more information than he'd left with.

"Well?" Carrie asked as Steven returned to the house and closed the front door behind him.

"She wasn't over there and I couldn't get anything out of Michael." Carrie turned away, now quite worried about her friend and wondering what she should do next. She sat down on the couch and stared blankly at the cordless phone that was in her hands.

"I'm sure she's alright, maybe Jeff finally lucked up with her." Steven said as he sat down next to her. Carrie looked at him, completely missing the humor in his statement.

"She would've called me by now. She definitely would have come back for her car. I'm worried about her. I'm calling Ran, maybe he's seen her." Carrie said as she began to dial Ran's cell phone number. Steven snarled his nose in disapproval of the idea of Carrie saying anything to Ran, but he could sense her unsettled worry and he kept his disapproval to himself.

Steven buried his fingers in Carrie's hair and gripped the back of her neck gently. He gave her a comforting kiss on the cheek and she returned his comfort with a short smile. She rubbed his leg as he got up and walked down the hall to the bathroom.

Steven shut the bathroom door. His thoughts were becoming plagued as his own worry for Lisa was aroused. His head was pounding and a subtle ringing shadowed everything that he was hearing. He walked over to the sink and drew some water and then leaned over, submerging his face in it. As he stood up he wiped his hand over his eyes and wondered what the end of the day would bring. A pounding on the bathroom door briefly covered the ringing in his ears.

"Ran hasn't seen her. I called Jeff and Eddie and I even called Ricky. Nobody has seen her. I think we should go look for her." Carrie said as she entered the bathroom.

"Okay." Steven said as he pulled the plug in the bottom of the sink.

* * *

Carrie and Steven had covered what seemed to be every inch of the small town. They had gone back to Eddie's to see if Lisa had been over-looked among the few passed out casualties that still remained from the night before, they'd scoured every nook and cranny of any place that Lisa could possibly be, but their efforts turned up nothing.

They were now in route to the under belly of the bridge, he only place that they had left to look. As they slowed down and turned off the road onto the narrow trail, the Charger's tires slid and the car rocked back and forth, trying to gain traction in the mud that the previous night's rain had created.

Carrie parked the car and Steven got out and began to look around. No matter how many times he visited the bridge, he would always be reminded of the cold and fearful night that he'd spent there where suicide still seemed to be his last best hope. He had to smile when he thought of how far he'd come since that night.

Carrie seemed to be somewhat disappointed when she walked under the bridge and found nothing. Deep down she was hoping to find Lisa there in one of her depressed, self-loathing states that she'd been known for, induced by the meaningless break-up of a meaningless relationship, but there was no one there and from the looks of the place there hadn't been anyone there in weeks.

L.B. Kelly

"Maybe you should just call her house." Steven said, thinking that that would have been the first place that he would've looked to start with.

"Yeah, and get her in trouble with her parents? They think she's at my house. Besides, she wouldn't have gone home without her car." Carrie said, sitting down on the sandy ground.

"Michael didn't tell you anything?" She asked after a minute.

"Just to piss off." He answered as he sat down beside her.

"What did he mean last night when he said that you were a hell of a guy to have on a train ride?" Carrie asked after another minute of silence. Steven looked at her and shook his head.

"What?" She asked, feeling that she was on the verge of pulling it out of him. "If you think that he could have done something to her, tell me."

"He was the guy on the train that night, he shot those guys." Steven said, feeling that he'd just turned his life upside down in one fell swoop. "I know it's hard to believe, I couldn't believe it when he came in the shop that day, but that doesn't mean anything. That doesn't mean that he did anything to Lisa, we'll find her and we'll all laugh about this later."

Carrie looked at him with her suspicions confirmed. She stood up from the ground and walked away.

"Steven, you're gonna have to tell somebody about this, no matter what happens." She said as she turned to look at him. "If you don't then I will."

"Just forget about it, I'm trying to. Let's go and find Lisa. Is there anywhere else to look?" Steven asked as he walked closer to her. She shook her head and prepared to say no when an idea dawned upon her.

"Yeah, there is one more place, the cotton fields out by the train tracks." Carrie said as she hurried off to the car.

"More train tracks." Steven said to himself as he shook his head and followed Carrie to the car.

* * *

As Carrie drove, sweat started to separate her hand from the steering wheel. She hoped that this would be the last place to look. She also hoped, on a certain level, that she wouldn't find Lisa there either.

Carrie turned onto the old gravel driveway and drove slowly, steering the car around the water-filled potholes. She began to think of the last time that she was down there with Ran, when he exhibited his brief and seemingly uncomfortable affectionate side. She suddenly felt pity for him, hoping for a moment that he would be able to find some one who was compatible with him, because deep down she knew that he had a good heart.

"We all used to come down here. One night a bunch of us were here and we had a fire going and somehow it got out of hand and ended up burning half the cotton up. Since then they've kept a closer watch on it, but some of us still sneak out here." Carrie said as Steven stared out the window into the woods.

As they emerged from the tree-covered section of the driveway, Steven's heart dropped in his chest when he saw the ocean of flat land as far as the eye could see. As they drove further he saw a large oak tree in the distance,

297

surrounded by a thin patch of smaller ones. Beyond it, the land made a sharp, almost ninety-degree turn at the tree line, which continued on. Through the trees he could see a familiar sight, the train tracks. He shook his head as he considered the irony that he had probably passed by this very field on his way into town.

Carrie stopped the car at the old oak and got out and looked around, slightly relieved that she saw nothing.

"Where could she be?" She said as Steven got out of the car.

Steven looked around the huge tree at the scattered beer cans and burnt wood. The surrounding trees were very thin, but provided some cover and a vague sense of protection from on-lookers. He looked back at the gravel road and then over the endless field. He felt so small in the presence of it. He then took another look back through the woods at the train tracks that were about fifty yards away, it seemed like a lifetime had passed since he had walked them.

"I don't know, maybe we should just go back to the house and wait for her. Maybe call David and see what he thinks." Steven said as he reached the end of his list of ideas.

"I'm gonna try her cell phone again." Carrie said as she dialed the number. Steven nodded and then began to look around again.

Carrie pressed the send button on her phone and listened for a ring. Her eyes met Steven's and her stomach knotted with sickening realization when she heard the phone ring, not from the other end of the line, but from the surrounding trees.

Carrie dropped her phone to the ground and began to look around, in shock, for the source of the ringing. Her chin began to quiver and she began to breathe erratically. Everything seemed to be happening in slow motion.

Steven stepped in front of Carrie and began to walk, guided by the ringing. He had only walked to the other side of the tree when he saw an extended arm. As he continued to walk, his legs became weak and a chill swept over him when Lisa's body came into full view, pale-faced with her eyes wide open.

"Oh God." Steven said as he knelt down beside her. He was instantly sorry for every cross word that he'd ever said to her. He was sorry for every cold look and for every rude comment that he'd made about her.

"Lisa?" Carrie said softly as she calmly knelt down beside Steven. She slowly reached out and touched Lisa's face. It was cold and stiff, she'd been dead for quite sometime.

Carrie leaned over and hugged Lisa's rigid body and began to cry loudly, as if she were in physical pain as well as emotional. Steven placed his hand on Carrie's back and began to cry silently as he pulled Lisa's ringing phone from her nearby purse with his free hand and ended the call.

Chapter Nine

The Sheriff's office was cold and dim. The pungent scent of stale pipe tobacco and whisky hung thick in the air. Steven sat alone in the room, staring at the water-stained ceiling, waiting for Sheriff Grisby to come in and hear his account of what had happened earlier that afternoon, when he and Carrie found Lisa's body.

Carrie had already had her time alone with the old buzzard and was shown to the waiting area. Steven was brought from a separate waiting room and shown into the office just as David was arriving.

Steven sat, fidgeting nervously in his chair when the sheriff finally made his entrance into the room. Grisby threw the door shut behind him and as he did, the old, nicotine-stained blinds clanged rhythmically against the window.

The old Sheriff waddled across the floor and settled into a large, well broken in chair behind a cluttered desk. He took off his cowboy hat and dropped it down onto the desk.

"I already told, like three guys what happened." Steven said as if he already knew what Grisby was going to ask.

"Just hold your horses, I don't want you to tell me what happened I don't think I'd believe you if you did." Grisby said as he searched through his desk drawer and pulled out a faded and worn deck of cards. "You know how to play poker?" Steven settled back in his chair, completely caught off guard by the Sheriff's inquiry.

"Poker? Yeah, I know how to play poker. I know how to play checkers too. What's that got to do with anything?" Steven asked.

"Don't be a wise ass, I got a place for wise asses." The sheriff said as he shuffled the cards and began to deal them. "I just want to talk to you, Harris is it?"

"Yes sir." Steven answered.

"I don't know you and that bothers me; I know all these kids around here, I've watched them all grow up just like the little girl y'all found out there this evening." Grisby began as he picked his five cards up and motioned for Steven to do the same. Steven sighed and took the cards and wondered where the old man was going with all of this. "Some of them I've had more dealings with than others, like your friend David Anderson." He broke his train of thought as he stopped to throw back three of his cards; Steven took one. "His daddy was good as gold and his sister, well she ain't never even thought about acting out of the way, but David he just ain't worth a shit. In my opinion, until you show me different, just because you keep with him that means to me that you ain't worth a shit either." Sheriff Grisby looked Steven in the eye, without a bit of restraint as he spoke. "What you got?" He asked as he threw his cards down on the desk, revealing his pairs of kings and nines.

"Flush." Steven said with a smile as he dropped his cards on top of Grisby's.

"You know, poker's a game of luck. No matter how many times you win, sooner or later your luck's gonna run out." The Sheriff began as he dealt the cards again. "But it's also a game of bluffing and feeling out you're opponent, lying some folks might say, either way I'm pretty good at it." Steven smiled again when he took two cards off of the draw this time. He looked the old man in the eye with a victorious glare when he threw his full house down on the desk.

"Aces and eights," Grisby said as he inspected Steven's cards. "That's a dead man's hand." He continued as he dropped his four tens and a king down on top of them. Steven frowned and his victorious air disappeared instantly. "Like I said, I don't know you and honestly I don't care to know you, but as long as you're in my town you stay in line and keep your nose clean. You do that and we'll get along fine, maybe be friends even. Just remember what I said, we got a place for wise asses around here." Grisby leaned back in his chair and dismissed Steven with a light gesture towards the door. Steven sat confused for a moment, wanting to say something, but not knowing what. He got up and walked to the door and opened it.

"Oh Harris, don't plan any trips, I'll most likely be calling on you again." Grisby said as he began to pack the bowl of his pipe with tobacco.

* * *

David said his good byes to Julie and then got into his car, where Steven and Carrie were already waiting. He said nothing. He just cranked the car, backed out of the parking space and left the parking lot of the Sheriff's office.

He looked over to Carrie, who was sitting in the passenger seat. She was staring, aimlessly out the window at the light rain that had started to fall. The early evening sky was dark with rain clouds and everything was covered with a yellow tint. He didn't know what to say to Carrie to ease her obvious pain, if there was anything at all that he could have said. He touched her shoulder and let out a disappointed sigh when she pulled away.

David slowly pulled his hand back and then looked up, into the rearview mirror at Steven who was in the back seat. He appeared to be anxiously awaiting the end of the ride, if for nothing else than to be anxious and nervous in a more open and less-confining space. David said nothing to Steven either, he just gripped the steering wheel and drove, and the mood in the car was sickening.

As they pulled up to the house, Carrie saw Lisa's car still in the driveway. For a split second she thought of her being there, waiting for her. She wiped away a tear from her eye and then looked away, unable to bear the sight of it any longer.

David parked the car in his usual spot and looked over to the side of the house and saw Ran's car and Jeff's truck parked there. As he stepped out of the Charger, he saw Jeff sitting in the porch swing and Ran sitting on the rail that surrounded the porch. Michael, who was sitting on the front steps got up and met David as he approached the house.

"What happened?" He asked with a genuine tone of concern. David shook his head, tired and unknowingly.

Carrie walked past Michael and up the steps. As she passed him, she gave him a burning look of accusation that would have made anyone else cower. She walked past a teary-eyed Ran and over to Jeff, who she draped her arms around as she began to sob into his chest. He held her tight and let his own tears flow as they both mourned the loss of their friend together.

Steven walked past Michael on his way up the steps and gave him the same look that Carrie had given him, only in a more tamed and less intimidating manner.

"What did you say to them?" Michael asked as Steven continued by him.

"Nothing." Steven said. Michael grabbed his arm and turned him around to see his eyes, as if he were trying to look through a lie for the truth. Steven snatched his arm away and walked onto the porch past Ran, skipping the customary staring match as he looked into his oddly mournful eyes.

"What did you do to her, you bastard!" Carrie screamed as she dove at Michael with her fists swinging wildly. Michael took a step back while Ran restrained her.

"Nothing, I didn't do anything. This is bullshit. I dropped her off last night!" Michael defended.

"Where?" Carrie asked, already discounting his excuse.

"I don't remember where. That store over on Main Street I think." He said.

"Yeah right, or maybe in the field out by the tracks, huh?" Carrie said as she pulled herself from Ran's grip.

"Prove it." He said through his building anger.

"Don't worry, the Sheriff's gonna talk to you, I'm sure. You can tell him how you dumped her off." Carrie said as she turned and entered the house, slamming the door behind her.

David walked by everyone and into the house without a word. Ran stood still for a moment and then walked off the porch and to his car, followed shortly there after by

L.B. Kelly

Jeff. Steven stood there on the porch in a silent stare with Michael.

"What, is this just a thing with you?" He asked, half-expecting to hear the truth. Michael shook his head and walked up to meet Steven on the porch.

"I hope, for your sake, that you didn't say anything to that old bastard about shit that's between me and you." He said with a flat and unrevealing tone. Steven stared into Michael's dark soul that seemed to be shrouded by an unbreakable veil of mystery that he just couldn't see through.

Michael broke his gaze and stepped off the porch and made his way back to the trailer while Steven sat down in the porch swing and held his aching head in his hands, with too much running through his head to concentrate on any one thing.

* * *

Carrie's eyes were puffy and tired from crying by the end of Lisa's funeral. Lisa's parents were there consoling Carrie from a distance, unable to decide if she was partially to blame for Lisa's recent rebellion and ultimately her death. Carrie recognized, and on some level understood that it was somehow easier to cope with things that we can't understand or control if we have someone or something to blame for it.

Carrie reached down and took Steven's hand as they walked away from the gravesite.

"I guess this is somewhere that we've both been before, huh?" She said, referring to their respective losses that was their first common connection.

"Yeah." Steven said with a short laugh. He shook his head in disbelief when he stopped and thought about how long it had actually been since his mother and sister were killed. It seemed like only yesterday and he still missed them both so much.

"It doesn't make it any easier though." She added as they reached David's car. Since David and Julie rode together she and Steven took the Charger.

Steven opened the passenger door for Carrie and knelt down next to her as she sat down in the seat. He placed his hand on her leg, just below her skirt before kissing her passionately, letting every ounce of love that he felt for her flow into her lips.

"I'm sorry for my part in this, if Michael had anything to do with this, maybe I could have stopped it by telling somebody what I know." Steven said remorsefully.

"I have no doubt in my mind that Michael did this, but its not your fault; he's crazy." Carrie said as she stroked the side of Steven's face. "You don't think that he did it?"

"I don't know." Steven said with his brow bent as he looked away. "Yeah, I guess I know he did. It's just that he seemed more concerned about what I said to the Sheriff the other day rather than you calling him a murderer. I don't know, it's just making me crazy thinking about it."

"Well don't, just don't even think about it. Sooner or later he'll slip up and hang himself." Carrie said.

"I was hoping he would just leave." Steven replied.

"No he's not gonna do that, they'll be on him for sure then." Carrie pointed out. "You can move into my room and just keep your distance from him."

L.B. Kelly

"Yeah, me and David's just gonna have to rumble, cause I ain't sleeping in the same room with him any more." Steven agreed.

"Don't worry about David; I can handle him, besides he's been with Julie so much lately that I don't even think he would notice." Steven didn't argue with her this time, he knew that she was probably right. "Let's get out of here."

* * *

"You wanna talk about it?" Steven asked as he drove, casually through town. Carrie sat quietly in the passenger seat and hadn't said a word since leaving the cemetery.

"What?" She asked, as though she'd been awakened from a deep sleep.

"You just looked like you were thinking about something. Were you thinking about Lisa?" He asked, further defining his question.

"Not really, I was just thinking about everything." She said with a tired smile. Steven considered pushing a little further, wishing that she would confide in him, but he didn't want to upset her anymore than she already was.

"Stop at the grocery store before we go home." Carrie said as they converged upon the store on their way out of Melton, Mississippi.

Steven found a parking space right in front of the store. He put the transmission in park and cut the engine.

"I'll be right back, it'll just take a second." Carrie said as Steven prepared to get out of the car.

"Okay." He said, thinking that maybe she just wanted to be alone for a while.

Steven sat there in the car and waited and waited. He began to consider going into the store, in search of Carrie when she finally came walking out the door. She sat down in the seat and slammed the heavy door of the car shut.

"What took so long?" Steven asked.

"It was a long line." She said.

"What'd you get." Her further asked.

"Nothing." She said. Steven looked down at the plastic bag that she was clutching.

"The bag's not invisible." He said.

"It's nothing, just girl stuff." She said modestly.

"Oh, that's all you had to say, just something for your monthly visitor or crimson curse or whatever you call it." Steven said, dismissing one subject that he really didn't care to delve into.

"Yeah, it's something for that." She said. "Or something for the lack there of." She continued in thought with a nervous pit aching away inside her stomach.

Steven steered the car into the driveway. He felt his stomach knot up and an instinctive defense took over his actions when he saw the Sheriff's car parked in front of the house. Steven continued on and parked the car beside the Sheriff's.

Steven got out and walked around the car and opened Carrie's door and watched as she hurried into the house.

Steven made his way around to the camper, wondering what was going on. As the trailer came into view, he saw Sheriff Grisby exiting the small dwelling.

"Whats going on?" Steven asked as he met the old Sheriff half way in the muddy path.

"Oh, I'm making my rounds. I just stopped by to talk to an old friend of mine." The Sheriff said as he tapped out the burnt tobacco from his pipe and began to repack it.

"You're not taking him with you?" Steven asked in a tone that was halfway sincere.

"Well no. Do you know of a reason why I should?" Grisby asked, letting his aged experience suppress his aroused curiosity in the statement.

"No, it was just a joke; you got a sense of humor, don't you?" Steven said after a second of consideration. Grisby looked Steven in the eye and then stuck his pipe in his mouth.

"Well just in case you think of anything, you just give me a call." Grisby continued as he dug around in his coat pocket and pulled out a business card. Steven took the card and studied it as the Sheriff walked away.

"Harris." Grisby began as he stopped and turned around. Steven looked up met the old man's eyes. "I lost my sense of humor a long time ago."

Steven watched as Sheriff Grisby walked away. He took another look down at the business card and began to consider turning Michael in as a realistic option.

He jammed the card into his pocket and looked up to the window of the camper after sensing that he was being watched. He saw Michael peering out through the blinds, watching him with a stale look upon his face. After a moment, Michael let go of the blinds and disappeared into the darkness of the camper. Steven just stood there for another moment and then turned and made his way back to the house with a heavy and uncertain sense of duty weighing him down.

* * *

The first morning back at work after Lisa's funeral was slow and dull. David seemed to be alone in his thoughts; thoughts that Steven couldn't discern with just a moment's study the way he normally could. He could, however sense a certain suspicion in David and everyone else for that matter. Everyone seemed to be sure of Michael's guilt in Lisa's murder, yet no one besides Carrie was willing to point the finger of blame at him publicly; they only tip-toed on egg shells around him, waiting for the next person to make the ultimate accusation.

Steven felt a gnawing responsibility to make that accusation and finally relieve himself of the torturous burden that he'd been carrying in his heart this whole time.

He had spent the morning tinkering around on an old carburetor that David had given him the week before to rebuild as practice. He turned each screw and replaced each linkage with an unconcerned hand while his conscience continued to keep the idea of handing Michael over to the Sheriff fresh in his mind.

Steven tightened the final screw on the old carburetor. He looked at it briefly with a skeptical glare, unable to decide whether or not he had done it any good. He dropped it down on the workbench in front of him and let out a frustrated sigh as he leaned over it with his thoughts still plagued.

"How could I not turn him in?" He said to himself in thought. "It would get it off my mind and get him out of my life."

311

He wiped his hands on the rag that was on the bench beside him and then took his wallet from his back pocket. He opened it and found the Sheriff's card quickly.

He refolded his wallet and stuck it back into his pocket as he looked around the shop for David. He saw him standing on the far side of the shop, engrossed partially in his current project, but largely preoccupied by whatever it was that was on his mind.

Steven moved upon light steps as he made his way to the office. He stood at the desk and took another look behind him as he picked up the phone. He read the number off of the card and then pressed the buttons on the phone accordingly with a nervously shaking finger. He stood up straight and took in a deep breath as he waited for an answer on the other end of the line.

"Fanning County Sheriff's office." A scratchy-voiced, female deputy answered. Steven opened his mouth to speak, but found no words. "Hello?"

"Uh, Sheriff Grisby, please." Steven finally stammered.

"May I tell him who is calling?" The deputy asked.

"Steven Harris." He said, feeling as though he had crossed the point of no return.

"Hold please." The deputy said quickly. While Steven waited for Grisby to take the call, his stomach began to roil and knot up as he anxiously considered the possible outcomes of what he was doing.

"Mr. Harris." The Sheriff began with a jolly tone. "I was expecting to hear from you, just not quite so soon, what's on your mind?"

"I think we need to talk." Steven said, ignoring the increasingly uneasy pit in his stomach.

"What about?" Grisby asked, playing along with Steven as though he really thought that it could have been a social call.

"What do you think?" Steven asked, aggravated by Grisby's nonchalant approach.

"Are you trying to tell me that you have information to report about a crime?" He asked in his unrelenting, nonchalant tone.

"Yeah, that's what I'm saying." Steven said in the loudest voice that could still be considered a whisper. "It's about Michael Rowan, I know about something that he's done. I think…"

"Stop right there." Grisby interjected. "Just come on down here to the office and you can make a statement."

"Now?" Steven asked.

"Yeah, now." The Sheriff said plainly.

"I don't know if I can get away right now." Steven said.

"Find a way, I'm waiting on you." Grisby said before hanging up.

Steven hung up the phone and automatically began running down excuses that he could give David as to why he needed to leave in such a hurry.

"What about Michael Rowan?" David asked from behind Steven, causing him to jump. Steven turned around to see David standing in the doorway, waiting for an answer, but Steven remained silent.

David looked down to Steven's right hand that still held the business card. He deepened his scowl and then moved over to Steven and snatched the card from his hand.

"Grisby?" David said as he held the card up. "What were you talking to him about Michael for, what in the hell is going on?" Steven started to deny David's suspicions, but before he could speak a word, David emphasized the uselessness of any excuses with his determination to get to the truth as he began to speak again. "Steven, there's something between you and Michael, I've noticed it since he's been here, now what is it? What are you talking to the Sheriff about?"

Steven stood, cornered with no other alternative than to finally tell David the truth. He swallowed the lump in his throat and began to choose his words carefully, uncertain of David's reaction.

"I think that Michael had something to do with what happened to Lisa." Steven said.

"Something to do with it? What do you think that he killed her?" David asked in an almost defensive tone against the accusation made towards his old friend.

"Yeah, I think maybe he did." Steven replied. David stared at him for a moment, wondering where all of this was coming from.

"You don't know what in the hell you are talking about. I've known Michael for a long time, he's rough, but there's no way that he could do anything like that. He's all talk." David said.

"He's not. David, I've seen it for myself." Steven said as he began to once again conjure up his well-kept memories from the train.

"What, you saw him kill her?"

"Not her," He began. "Your friend Jimmy."

David shook his head and his confusion flew off of the chart as he tried to find the logic in what Steven was telling him, how could this be true.

"Jimmy? What do you know about Jimmy?" David was confused and doubtful, but very interested in what Steven was going to say next.

"A lot more than you think." Steven said as he sat down on the edge of the desk and took a moment to prepare his thoughts. "I know a lot more about Michael too, more than you know. The first time that I met him wasn't in here; it was on a freight train somewhere between here and the coast. Michael was there; Jimmy and his brother Jake were there too. They were all real nervous acting, like they had done something. Michael had a gun and was waving it around. Jake kept asking him why he had to kill some guy, I don't know who. Then I guess Michael just got tired of hearing Jake ramble on, the guy was freaked out bad. He said that he was gonna go to the cops when they got to where they were going. They went back and forth for a while and then Michael got up and just shot him in the head." Steven's expression went blank as he saw it all happen again in his mind. "Michael and Jimmy started fighting over the gun and it started going off. I think that he killed Jimmy too." David shook his head again, overcome by skepticism.

"You expect me to believe that load of bullshit? You're crazy, I knew that taking you in would be a mistake. I knew that sooner or later some crazy shit would happen, I just never thought it would be something like this." David said, as he looked Steven in the eye.

315

"Why would I make something like that up?" Steven defended.

"I don't know why you would, but I've known Michael my whole life and I've only known you for a few months, a few of the strangest months that I can remember now that I think about it, so what do you think I'm going to believe? You know I think that this would be a good time for you to get your shit and get out of my house and leave my sister alone." David said as he moved even closer and whipped the Sheriff's card in Steven's face. Steven watched as the card floated to the floor. He then looked David in the eye and could feel every connection that they had fray and break. It felt like he was losing his family all over again. After a moment Steven turned and left the office, without another word to David. As he walked through the shop on his way out Steven took one last look around and wondered where he would end up next.

David stood alone in the office. He closed his eyes and bowed his head when he heard the main door of the shop slam shut. He sat down at the desk and felt worse with each second that passed. He wondered what Carrie was going to say, but he didn't have to wonder; he knew what her reaction would be. But the thought that struck him most oddly was considering that what Steven told him could be true.

David thought of Jimmy as he sat at the desk meticulously recounting every word that Steven said.

"He heard me ask Michael about Jimmy that night; that's how he knew about him." David thought to himself in an effort to rationalize the situation. "But how did he know about Jake. I barely remember him and why would Michael mention him to Steven?" None of it made any sense to him, unless it could actually be true.

David fidgeted with a pen on the desk while he bounced his knee nervously. Then all at once, he pulled the bottom, left-hand drawer open and pulled out a phone book. He opened it and flipped to the "D" section and quickly found the name and number of Jim Dent Sr., Jimmy's and Jake's father, who still lived in Fanning, Ms., with his wife. David picked up the phone and then put it down quickly.

"Just do it." He said out loud as he picked the phone receiver up again.

David dialed the number and waited. The call was answered after one ring.

"Hello?" Jimmy's mother, Sandra Dent answered.

"Mrs. Dent, this David Anderson. I don't know if you remember me or not; it's been a while."

"Sure David, I remember you. What can I do for you?"

"Well, I was just thinking about Jimmy. I was wondering if you had a number for him, we just kind of lost touch and I was wanting to talk to him." There was a long silence, the only noise that could be heard was the dull buzz in the phone connection and the sound of Sandra Dent trying to hold back her unexpected tears.

"Jimmy's dead, his brother too. They were found on a train near Meridian, shot to death." Mrs. Dent began to cry softly as she spoke. Shock poured over David as he arrived at the conclusion that he hoped was a lie.

"I'm sorry, I hadn't heard." David said after a minute.

"I begged Jimmy to come back home and leave the kind of life that he was living behind him, but he wouldn't listen. He just dragged his brother down there with him." She was now sobbing without restraint as she continued. "David, for God's sakes, I hope you have changed. You all used to be just alike."

"Yes mam, things have definitely changed." David said somberly, considering how things had changed and how they would certainly continue to change.

"Come by to see us sometime." Mrs. Dent said after another silence.

"Yes mam, I will." He said as he hung up the phone with the question weighing upon his mind of what he would do next.

David opened the desk drawer again and dropped the heavy phone book into it. He sighed heavily as he settled back into his chair with his thoughts running wild. He'd barely had a chance to put everything together in his mind, to even consider the truth in what Steven was saying when he heard the shop door slam shut again. He jumped to attention, still seated in the chair and heard footsteps, becoming louder as they drew closer to the office.

He expected that Steven had come back to the shop to talk, which David was prepared to do after calming down a bit, but David was surprised to see Michael appear in the doorway.

"Hey man, sorry I didn't call in this morning; I had a long night last night." Michael presented the excuse with little sincerity.

"Ain't no big deal; it's been slow today anyway." David said, unconcerned at this point with Michael's absence for the day.

"So what's up, where's dip shit?" Michael asked, referring to Steven.

"I don't know, let him off early; there wasn't anything going on." David said, wondering how he was ever gonna find him now that his anger had subsided and was replaced with guilt.

David stared at Michael intensely, trying to peer into his thoughts. He was wondering how to get inside his head.

"Hey, I talked to Sandra Dent today." David said suddenly. He studied Michael's face carefully, to gauge his reaction.

"Oh, really?" There was a short, but revealing delay in Michael's response that spoke volumes in favor of David's suspicion. "What did she have to say?"

"She told me that Jimmy was dead, Jake too." David replied bluntly.

"No shit?" Michael said with hollow concern as he walked past David and plopped down in the chair at the end of the desk.

"Yeah."

"Man, that's crazy." Michael continued.

"Yeah, it is."

There was a silence, it was the most uncomfortable silence that David had ever experienced. It was so difficult for him to picture Michael putting a bullet in anyone, least of all one of his best friends. However the lack surprise in his voice and his unconcern with the details of Jimmy's death seemed to offer some support to Steven's accusation.

Michael's brain was grinding away at full speed trying to figure out why David was talking to Jimmy's mother. There was a layer of suspicion that had marked David's words as he spoke. It was undeniable.

Without a word, David got up and walked out of the office. Michael leaned forward in his chair and began to consider the oddity of the conversation that had just taken place. He lifted his hand to his chest and found the pack of cigarettes that was in his jacket pocket. He took one out and lit it; he closed his eyes and listened to the soothing crackle of the burning tobacco as he sucked the smoke into his mouth. He opened his eyes and searched his mind for a fresh take on the situation and that was when he saw Sheriff Grisby's business card lying on the floor just under the edge of the desk. He knew then that the inevitable had happened.

Michael picked the card up and studied it for a moment. He could feel the anger build inside him, the anger for not having dealt with Steven when he had the chance.

David took his cell phone from his pants pocket and found Carrie's number in the contact list. After finding the number, he pressed the send button and waited for an answer. He let it ring several times and was about to end the call when Carrie finally answered.

"Hey, are you at home?" David asked in a whispered voice.

"No, I'm at the cemetery. Why, what's wrong?" She said in a weak and raspy tone. It was obvious that she had been crying.

"I need you to help me find Steven." He said with worry.

"Why, what happened?" She asked.

"I messed up." David jumped when Michael hurried out of the office and blew past him.

"Man I got to run, I got to take care of something." Michael said in his hasty passing.

David watched as Michael left the shop. His heart sank in his chest and a chill crawled up his back as he heard Michael's car tear away.

"David, what's going on? David?"

"Just start looking around town, I'm sure he's left the house by now." He said to Carrie as he ended the call.

Michael steadied his hand and sharpened his focus as he approached the Anderson house. He slowed his car and prepared to turn into the driveway, but then a grin parted his lips when he saw Steven walking down the long, straight stretch of road, away from the house with a large bag draped over his shoulder. Michael pressed the accelerator and continued down the road towards Steven.

Steven turned to look when he heard Michael's car approaching from behind him. He knew instantly that something wasn't right when he saw who it was. Michael rolled his window down as he slowed the car to a steady crawl.

"What are you doing, man? Moving?" Michael asked. Right away, he could sense Steven's apprehension.

"Yeah, I'm taking off." Steven said as he continued to walk. His answer was short; he was eager to get as much distance between him and Michael as possible.

"Why, what's up?" Michael asked, hoping to get some clue as to what really was going on.

"Nothing." Steven replied, keeping his eyes straight ahead.

"Problems with the little woman, huh?" He asked.

"Yeah." Steven said with a fake laugh; he was willing to let Michael believe anything, he just wanted him to go.

"Yeah, she's a pistol." He said as he took a quick look to the rearview mirror. "Well come on and get in, I'll give you a ride into town."

"No, that's alright." Steven refused quickly.

"Man, get in the car. You don't have to walk." Michael insisted. Steven stopped and looked into Michael's eyes. He knew if he refused any further it would seem suspicious, against his better judgement he relented.

"Okay." He said. As he walked around the front of the car, Steven could feel every sense of reason that he had telling him not to get in, but he didn't know what else to do. He put his hand on the handle of the door and then gazed down the open road into the fading sunset. He thought of Carrie and wished for her strength.

He took in a deep breath and forced himself to open the door. He pushed the front seat forward and dropped his bag into the back. He flopped the seat back and then climbed in.

David pushed the Charger harder and harder as he sped down the road towards his house. He rounded the curve as he approached his driveway in just enough time to see Michael's car disappear into the distance ahead of him. He pressed the accelerator even harder and knew that it would be no problem for the Dodge to catch up with Michael's car, even though he still hadn't thought about what he was going to say or do when he did catch up to him. He only wished now that Carrie would be able to catch Steven.

Michael reached up to the car's blaring radio and turned it off and then looked at Steven.

"Anything you want to talk about?" He finally asked.

"No." Steven answered. His heart started to pound and his palms became sweaty.

"What did you say to David?" Michael then asked straight out.

"Nothing, what are you talking about?" Steven muttered through his tight throat. Michael looked at him with disgust, the least that he could have done after all of this was to be honest with him.

"Do you remember what I said to you?" Michael asked as he stared straight ahead. "I told you that if you kept you're mouth shut we'd be fine, we wouldn't have any problems. I told you that I would hate to see anything happen to you or to somebody that you care about, but I guess you thought that I was just bullshit'n you." Michael broke his speech to take a quick look at Steven, who was on the edge of crying.

"Why did you kill Lisa?" Steven asked as his face became flushed due to the effort that it took to hold back his tears. "I was trying to forget everything and then you did it again, I should have said something sooner."

"I can see how it would be easy for you to think that and I can see how it would be easy for anybody else that you told to think that too. If David is the only one that you told, I'll be fine; David will listen to reason, but for some reason you won't. Now I gotta make sure that you don't say anything to anybody else and there's only one sure fire way that I know to do that, but I don't think that you're gonna like it. You can't say that I didn't give you a chance, Steven." Michael reached inside his jacket and pulled out his pistol and laid it in his lap and then looked at Steven once again. He began to breathe heavily as tears escaped from his eyes. "Oh come on now, don't be afraid of it; we all got to go sometime. You gotta take it like a man. It'll all be over soon."

Steven sat, stunned and overcome by what was happening. Was this how it was all supposed to end? Had he pushed through the deaths of his mother and sister and endured his father's mental and physical torture just to get to this? Not to mention his recent suicidal tendencies and everything that had happened over the past few months. Without thinking, he reached down to the door handle and jerked at it franticly, but nothing happened. He pressed the button on the door panel to lower the window and again, nothing happened.

"I've been meaning to fix all that." Michael said with a bent grin. "I bet you're wishing that I had."

Steven continued his instinctive reactions and drew his elbow back and slammed it against the window as hard as he could. Pains shot up his arm, but he ignored the pain and just kept pounding away at the glass. Michael picked the gun up and hit Steven in the back of his head with its heel.

"Come on Steven, don't make me do it in here!" He yelled as he blindly accelerated the car.

Michael drew back and hit Steven in the head again. This time Steven was able to grab the gun and push it away from himself. At the same time, he made the tightest fist with his free hand that he'd ever made in his life. He slung it wildly at Michael and hit him in the jaw, causing him to let the car dart over the road as bullets from the gun fired aimlessly into the windshield.

David was now following undetected, about eight or ten car-lengths behind them. He realized suddenly that he'd found Steven as he watched the taillights of Michael's car dart back and forth in the thickening darkness of the early evening.

Steven threw another punch at Michael that sent his head crashing into the driver side window. He felt the car sway sharply to the right. He looked ahead through the cracked windshield just in time to see the car veer off of the road and plow up the steep embankment that edged the road on either side.

The car barreled across the hill, mowing down road signs and small trees along the way. Finally the car met resistance in the form of a towering pine tree that deflected it and sent it rolling down the hill and back into the road.

David slammed the brake pedal of his car into the floor. He was awe-struck by what he had just witnessed. In his mind there was no way that anyone could have survived what he had seen. He was preparing himself for the worst.

As the car slammed down onto the asphalt, Steven saw visions of his mother and sister and a lingering image of Carrie filled his mind as the car finally settled on its roof.

Steven could feel Michael's hand around his throat, gripping it weakly. He tried lifting his right arm to move it, but it was useless to him, the pain that he felt in it kept him from trying to lift it any further. He didn't know if it was hurt when he was slamming it into the window or during the wreck that was still sinking into his mind, none the less he knew that it was injured badly.

Steven threaded his left arm through the mangled wreckage and pulled Michael's hand from his throat quite easily; he wasn't sure of whether or not he was even conscious and he had no idea what had happened to the gun.

Steven could feel blood trickling down his face from a gaping gash just above his hairline. As he tried to inch his way to an upright position he could feel the blood flow increase and as it did his strength was fading fast.

Steven's vision became jittery as he collapsed into a semi-conscious heap on the inverted ceiling of the car. His mind went into full panic mode, however his broken body offered little reaction when he realized that the interior of the vehicle was filling with smoke and the sickening stench of burning rubber and plastic. He began to fade away and could hear, but wasn't alarmed by Michael's desperate pleas for help.

Although he was diminished greatly, both physically and mentally and was teetering on the brink of death, he managed to find the strength to smile a satisfied smile.

"Not what you had in mind, huh?" He asked, Michael's only answers were more agony-ridden cries.

The car was becoming hotter and hotter. Steven closed his eyes and prepared to meet death, but it didn't feel the way that he always thought that it would, it was a cold and lonesome feeling. He thought about how ironic his life had become in just a few short minutes. After all of the times that he thought that he wanted to die and all of the times that he had threatened to do it, now it was the last thing that he wanted, now he wanted to live.

Steven jumped when he heard a crashing thud above his head. He opened his eyes and could see nothing through the thick smoke. He heard the noise again and then felt pieces of the car's windshield fall upon him. Then all at once he could feel his limp body being dragged from the car.

"Steven? Steven, can you hear me?" David asked franticly as he freed Steven from the car. Steven moaned and muttered incoherent words.

"David?" Michael murmured faintly from inside the car.

David hauled Steven away from the burning car, several feet away to the Charger that was parked crossways in the road with the engine still running. He flopped him up against the front, passenger side tire. Steven was jarred back into awareness. It felt to him as though a boulder had been lifted from his chest as he greedily sucked in a breath of fresh air.

"Steven, I'm sorry! I'm sorry I didn't believe you!" David said through heavy breaths as he knelt down in front of Steven, almost able to feel his pain just by looking at him. Steven answered him in the form of a forgiving look.

"David!" Michael screamed painfully from the car with the last bit of strength that he could muster.

David stood up and turned around. He saw that the car was now blazing.

He took a step forward and the car was revealed to Steven. Then with a squealing hiss, the fire ignited the vehicle's fuel tank and the car exploded violently, killing Michael instantly. David was knocked against the car and to the ground next to Steven, the heat that swept over them from the blast was incredible. Steven felt instant relief and a sense that justice had been done for Lisa, Jimmy and Jake. The nightmare was finally over.

* * *

Hours after the wreck, Steven was being released from the hospital in Melton with a dozen stitches in his head and with his right-arm in a cast that extended to just above his elbow. Carrie hadn't left his side since she arrived at the hospital. She wouldn't allow him to lift a finger for himself.

Steven walked out of the treatment area of the emergency room and into the waiting area. He saw that everyone had come to see the results of the harrowing story that had quickly spread across the small town like a wild fire. Julie had come to console David. Ran and Jeff were there to get the facts straight and even Ricky had shown up just to gawk. Sheriff Grisby was there also, but not out of concern for Steven's well being, but to get to the bottom of the recent contravention that had befallen his quiet town.

Steven stood in the middle of the room with his hand held tightly by Carrie. Julie was the first to greet him. She stood up from her chair and gave him a short and friendly hug. For once, Carrie looked upon her with a neutral and inoffensive smile.

"How are you?" Julie asked as she pulled away from Steven.

"I don't know yet." He answered with a broken down smile. His head was clouded and reeling with a mixture of pain medication and pain itself.

"You'll be fine." Carrie said lovingly as she rubbed his chest to comfort him.

"Yeah." Julie agreed with a smile.

David stood up from his seat and looked at Steven with an indescribable look of regret for the things that he had said to him earlier that day. He knew that no matter how many times he apologized, it would be impossible to take them back completely.

"I'm sorry, I guess I just didn't want to believe it." David said.

"It's alright; don't worry about it." Steven said. David looked away, too ashamed to look him in the eye. He couldn't understand how someone could be so forgiving over something like that, he was sure that he wouldn't if the situation was reversed.

"Harris, I'm sorry to interrupt, but I still got a lot of work to do tonight." Grisby said as he waddled over. "Anderson here tells me that you saw Michael Rowan kill them two Dent boys down in Hattiesburg. Is that right?"

"Yes sir, that's right."

"You willing to sign your name to it?" Gribsy further asked.

"Yes sir."

"And you say that Rowan admitted to killing the Carter girl to you too?" Steven looked away briefly, unable to remember in his jaded mind what Michael actually did say to him, but in his heart he was clear of doubt.

"Yes sir."

"I suppose you'll put your name to that too?" Grisby asked, narrowing his eyes slightly as he looked at Steven. Grisby felt as though his years of experience had turned him into a human lie detector and to a certain extent, they had. Steven nodded in agreement and then closed his eyes as a sharp pain ran through his head.

L.B. Kelly

"Is that enough? He needs to go home." Carrie said to the Sheriff.

"Yeah, for now. I'll be talking to you." He said, continuing his detection even as he walked away.

"Come on, let's get you home." Carrie said as she gently took Steven by the arm.

"Let's all go home." David agreed, taking Julie by the hand.

"Hey, y'all up for some company?" Jeff asked as David passed.

"Steven, you up for it?" David asked.

"Yeah man, come on." He said weakly with another broken down smile. Jeff followed as they continued to leave the hospital.

"I'm taking off." Ricky said to Ran as he too left the waiting room, seeming somewhat disappointed by the lack of drama.

Ran said nothing to Ricky as he left. He seemed anxious and unsure of what to do with himself. He took another look towards the entrance, to make sure that everyone was gone and walked over to the nurse's station.

"Yes sir?" A young nurse asked from behind the desk.

"Yeah, they said that Michael Rowan died in that accident earlier, is that true?" Ran asked nervously.

"Yes sir, he was DOA, I'm sorry." She said sympathetically before continuing with her work.

"Thanks." Ran said automatically as he walked away from the counter.

Ran smiled faintly as he stood in the middle of the room. He shook his head in disbelief and could feel the knot inside his stomach untie itself.

"I don't believe it; it worked itself out. Who would've thought that that little hobo would save my ass?" He said softly to himself as his smile continued to grow. "Now nobody will ever know what I did."

Chapter Ten

"Hey, we're gonna go, but I'm probably gonna come back and stay at you're house tonight, if it's okay with you." Lisa said to Carrie, surprising Steven, who hadn't seen her come up through his impaired perception.

"Yeah, sure. You're not gonna stay with Michael?" Carrie asked, trying to re-align her perception also.

"No, I don't know; he kind of freaked me out earlier." Lisa said.

"You can ride back with us if you want." Carrie offered after sensing Lisa's worry.

"No, I'll be over later. I already told him that I would ride back with him." She said.

"Okay, be careful." Carrie said as Lisa walked away.

Lisa made her way back to Michael, who was still entertaining a small group of eager listeners. He looked at her as she arrived and smiled.

"You ready?" He asked. Lisa nodded and then took another look back at Carrie, partly wishing that she had taken her up on her offer of a ride. "Well let's go."

Lisa followed as Michael led her by the hand to the car. He swallowed down the rest of the beer that he was drinking and then dropped the bottle on the ground without a thought. As they approached the car, Michael continued to guide her to the passenger side where he opened her door and politely showed her to her seat. She smiled a genuine smile and her tension eased a bit when she realized that this was the first time that she had ever been shown even the slightest gentlemanly respect.

"Maybe he's not so bad after all." She whispered after he shut the door and walked towards the rear of the car.

After waiting a moment for Michael to get into the car, she turned in the seat to see what was taking him so long. She saw him through the back window of the car standing freely, relieving himself for everyone to see. She flung herself back around and shook her head.

"Maybe so." She continued to herself disappointedly.

After another moment Michael opened the driver's door and climbed in. With a smile and without a word, he cranked the engine and pulled the car into drive and hit the accelerator.

"So what do you want to do now?" Lisa asked suggestively as Michael drove down the dark and narrow road, somewhat less than perfectly. Michael smiled again.

"I don't know, but I'm sure that we can think of something." He said as he looked at her devilishly, placing his hand high on her thigh.

"I think so too." She agreed.

They drove another five or six miles and they were just inside the small town of Fanning, when Michael's phone rang. Michael dug around inside his pocket and pulled out his phone.

"What's up?" He answered loosely, having recognized the number displayed on the caller ID.

"Yeah, I still got some. How much you want?" Lisa shook her head as she listened, sensing the impending change of plan.

"I'm in Fanning right now." Michael said as he looked down at his watch. "Yeah, I can probably be there in about fifteen minutes. Okay, cool."

Michael ended the call and quickly scanned the area for somewhere to pull the car over. He spotted the barbershop up the street a little ways and thought that the benches out front would make a good place for Lisa to wait while he attended to a little business.

"A little change of plans, baby." He said as he whipped the car over to the side of the street in the dead-quiet town.

"What?" Lisa asked with an agitated tone.

"Yeah, just wait here for me and I'll come back to get you in a little while." Michael said, unable to see a reason for her to be angry.

"Are you serious?"

"Yeah, I'll be right back." He reassured her as if it made a difference. Lisa sat, fuming as she grabbed her purse and pulled at the door handle.

"You wanna let me out?" She asked after finding that it was broken.

L.B. Kelly

"Damn, yeah I need to fix that." Michael said as he hurried out of the car and trotted over to her side and opened the door. "I'll be right back." He said as he ran back to the driver side and got back into the car. He slammed his door shut and took off quickly.

"Asshole!" Lisa screamed at him out of frustration as she watched him disappear into the darkness.

She turned around and sat down on the bench outside of the barbershop. A tear rolled down her face as she pulled her phone from her purse. She looked at it for a moment and prepared to call Carrie for a ride, but embarrassment for what had happened kept her from doing so.

She stood up, stuck the phone back into her purse and started walking. With every step that she took, her anger grew even more. As she walked, Lisa cursed Michael in every way that she could think of, but her thoughts were broken when she saw a vehicle approaching ahead of her.

The car passed and then stopped suddenly behind her. She turned around and saw that it was Ran's car. Ran pulled the car into reverse and then backed up to meet Lisa.

"You window shopping?" Ran asked as he leaned across the passenger seat to lower the window. Lisa shook her head and smiled as she wiped away another tear from her cheek. "You want a ride?" Lisa didn't say anything; she just stepped off of the sidewalk and got into the car.

"You're car's at Carrie's house?" Ran asked after a minute.

"Yeah, but I don't want to go back yet." Lisa said as she stared out the window. "Unless you have something else to do."

"No, Where do you want to go?" Ran asked.

"I don't care." She said.

* * *

Ran turned the car off onto the long, gravel driveway and drove away from the main road. He and Lisa both knew what was likely to happen out there. They were both quite familiar with this place.

Ran continued to drive until he converged upon the old oak that stood close to the gravel road. He parked close to the oak and cut the car's engine.

They both sat silently, thinking of the first time that they were there together just a few weeks earlier.

"Do you remember?" She asked as she stared out at the hood of the car.

"Yeah, of course I remember." Ran said with a smile. "Right out there, just about in this same place."

"Yeah, it felt right, didn't it? I mean it felt different than with anybody else." Lisa said, leading them into an awkward silence. "For me, it did anyway."

"Yeah, sure." He agreed, not knowing for sure what she wanted to hear, or to be more exact, not feeling the same way about it as she did.

Lisa got out of the car and walked around and slid up onto the hood. Ran got out and followed.

"Do you think that it could feel like that again?" She asked, leaning back on her elbows and looking at him invitingly.

"Yeah, I do." Ran answered with an excited smile.

Ran walked over to her. She spread legs apart and pulled him into her with them. They began to kiss softly to start with, but the intensity increased as they began to give in to each other.

Ran's mind became excited and jumbled with thoughts of Carrie. He felt surges of anger towards her when he thought of her and Steven together. She should be with him, he thought.

"I can always count on you." He said as his excitement increased further.

"What?" Lisa asked as she pulled away, a little confused by the statement.

"Nothing." Ran said, continuing to touch and kiss her.

"No, what does that mean?" She asked, wanting an answer. Ran stopped, breathing heavily.

"I was just thinking about Carrie. You know about how she keeps playing with me, not like you."

"Yeah, not like me." Lisa said with a hurt tone, pushing Ran aside. She slid down off of the car and straightened her ruffled clothes.

"Come on, that's not a bad thing." Ran said as he took Lisa by the arm.

"I don't want to be the one you can always count on, you're second choice." She said, snatching away from his grip. "Take me home."

"No, you're not going home. Come on and finish what you started." Ran said, grabbing her arm again, harder this time.

"No, I want to go home. Ran, you're hurting me!" She screamed and tried in vain to pull away from him again. He stared deep into her with the most wickedly awful look that she had ever seen from anyone.

"You're not leaving until we do what we came out here to do." He said with rage pouring from his eyes.

"Ran, you're scaring me." She said when she realized how unstable he had become so quickly.

Ran grabbed her other arm and slung her back onto the hood of the car and crawled on top of her. He slid his hand underneath her shirt and under her bra and began to grope her. She began to cry when she realized what was happening.

"Ran, stop it!" She screamed in terror. Ran silenced her by jamming his tongue into her mouth. The only defense that she could think of was to bite his tongue as hard as she could. As she did, she could taste his blood as it poured into her mouth.

This stunned and deterred him enough for Lisa to slip out from underneath him as he stepped back to cradle his bleeding mouth.

She rolled off of the car and fell to the ground. She clawed and scratched her way to a crawling position and was finally able get to her feet. As she started to run towards the rear of the car, Ran lunged forward and grabbed her by the ankle, pulling her off of her feet again. Her face hit the ground and the taste of the bitter dirt turned her stomach as it found it's way into her mouth. She then started kicking at him franticly until he let go.

She continued to run towards the back of the car when she felt Ran's hand come down hard in the middle of her back.

"Get back over here, you bitch!" He yelled as he jerked her back to him by the shirt, with more force than he ever thought that he could fathom. Ran was blind with rage and could hear and feel, but not see the impact of Lisa's head slamming into the bumper of the car.

The most intense pain that she had ever felt in her life overcame Lisa. She could hear and feel her skull crack as it crashed into the steel bumper.

Her eyes became clouded, but were still functional and her breathing became faint quickly, but was still present. She tried to move to continue the fight, but she couldn't, she tried to scream for help, but she couldn't. All that she could do was die.

"Oh, God. Oh God, no!" Lisa could hear Ran scream hysterically through the warm blood that was slowly starting to fill her ears.

She could hear Ran pacing and ranting to himself incoherently. She heard nothing but silence for a moment and then could feel her limp body being drug across the ground to the other side of the oak tree.

She heard Ran's footsteps fading as he ran away. She heard the car door slam and then the engine crank. After a moment she heard footsteps again and then saw her purse hit the ground just in front of her face. She heard Ran run away once again and then a short time later she heard his car roaring as he raced away.

Lisa could feel raindrops hit her face as it started to lightly rain. She could also feel a dull vibration in the ground, caused by a train approaching in the distance on the nearby tracks. She felt a slight comfort from the rain as it cooled her face and then she thought of Carrie and wished that she had stayed with her.

She felt a tear roll down her cheek and blend with the rain and she knew then as her body went numb and her vision faded into a sparkling blur that she would never move from where she laid.

Chapter Eleven

Carrie paced back and forth, nervously in front of the bathroom cabinet where a home pregnancy test sat, waiting to be read. She'd had the test for a while, but couldn't find the nerve to take it until now. She was terrified to read it; even though she already knew what the results would be, she was still terrified for it to become reality.

She stood with her back against the wall, biting at her fingernails anxiously. Then all at once, she stepped forward, picked the stick up and looked. It was positive. Her heart dropped into her stomach and her eyes began to tear up. She stood for a minute looking around the bathroom, not knowing what to do next.

Finally, she squatted down and began to search underneath the cabinet in the wastebasket for the package that the test had come in. She picked it up and began to carefully read the instructions from the back of it to be sure that she was reading the test correctly. As she read, her shoulders dropped and she exhaled an overwhelmed sigh. She was so afraid and didn't know where to turn. She stood up and looked at herself in the mirror.

L.B. Kelly

"Mamma?" She said to herself, just to see how it sounded. She burst into tears and her overwhelmed feeling grew.

She thought of Lisa and wiped her bare hands across her face as she sobbed. She suddenly felt the absence of her friend solidify itself as she so desperately longed for her advice and company.

Carrie took the roll of toilet tissue from the cabinet and wrapped the used test and it's packaging with it and then buried them deep inside the wastebasket. She took another look in the mirror and could barely stand the sight of herself. She shook her head and could feel all of her dreams of leaving Fanning Mississippi and making something out of herself fade away. She had always wanted to be something, anything other than what was expected of her. Ironically, what was expected of her and every other young woman in Fanning was to marry young and start a family.

She flipped the light switch off and slowly opened the door and walked out of the bathroom, feeling defeated and ruined. She felt as if she were floating as she walked through the house, with no particular destination in mind. She was simply looking for anything that would take her mind off of her pregnancy.

Almost without realization, Carrie found herself standing on the front porch. The day was unusually warm and pleasant for this particular time of year, yet she was unable to see or feel the beauty in any of it. All that she could look at was Lisa's car that still sat in the same spot, untouched since she left it. Lisa's father told Carrie to keep the car, that it would only rust away if he picked it up. He said that it would only serve as a reminder of the pain and that he would never be able to bear even looking at it again. Carrie couldn't see how having the car would be any easier on her. She promised herself though, that she would try to look it as a reminder of Lisa's life as opposed to seeing it as a symbol of her death, even though it may have still been hard to do that at the moment.

As Carrie stood, she found that her legs were becoming weak due to the worry over her pregnancy. She looked behind her and found her way to the porch swing and sat down. Her chin began to quiver and her throat tightened up as a number of questions cluttered her brain. How was she going to tell Steven, what would he say? How was she ever going to be able to look David in the eye again? She had done what she said she would never do and now her life was ruined. How was she ever going to finish school and go to college while trying to raise a baby? She could already feel her brother's disappointment and she could almost feel her father's as well from beyond the grave.

* * *

Steven sat, uneasily in the passenger seat of the county deputy's patrol car that had been enlisted to return him to the Anderson house. He had been at the Sheriff's office for the better part of the day, making his official statement that would serve as the proof of Michael Rowan's guilt in the murders of Jimmy and Jake Dent and Lisa Carter.

He was already enjoying the absence of the burden that he had been carrying. Since the very night that Michael was killed, Steven's nightmares began to dwindle and at this point were almost non-existent. Now that he felt just in the eyes of the law, he felt that he might finally be able to find a normal life among the insanity that had saturated his existence for the past several months.

"Long drive, huh?" Steven said nervously as he looked over at the female deputy that had driven the whole way stone-faced and silent. She responded with only a vague nod. Steven turned straight ahead and began to fidget and scratch at the synthetic stock of the twelve-gauge shotgun that stood against the car's dashboard, secured by a strap.

"Don't touch that." The deputy said sternly, causing Steven to jump. He pulled his hand away and sat, a little embarrassed. He hadn't realized that he had done anything wrong. The silence continued.

"You ever shot anybody with that?" Steven asked after a minute.

"Not yet." She answered suggestively. Steven nodded and turned ahead in his seat again with a smile.

The remainder of the trip lagged on until they finally arrived at the Anderson home. The deputy steered onto the driveway and proceeded to the house. Steven grabbed the door handle and could hardly wait for the car to stop to let him out.

"Okay, thanks for the ride." Steven said as the car came to a stop. He exited quickly and received only another short nod as acceptance of his gratitude.

Steven slammed the door of the patrol car and watched as the deputy drove away. He hoped, as he watched her leave, that he would never have any reason to step foot in the Sheriff's office again.

Steven turned and began to walk to the house. As he strolled across the yard, he couldn't help but glance at the camper in the back. He didn't want to look at it or think about or even be reminded of it in any way. To him it represented Michael and everything that he stood for. His presence could still be felt there. Steven shivered as he looked away from the camper. He was beginning to put his life back together and he was so happy to have his dreams back, free of any traces of Michael Rowan and what had happened that night on the train. As far as he was concerned, if the memories and nightmares of his recent past could be contained in that camper, he would gladly give it up.

Steven noticed Carrie sitting in the porch swing as he began to climb the front steps. He gave her a smile, as she looked at him weakly.

"It's over." He began as he took a seat next to her on the swing. "I hope I never have to see that fat man again." He continued, referring to the Sheriff.

"I'm glad." Carrie said, taking his hand. She studied him for a moment, wondering how he might receive what she had to tell him that was weighing so heavily on her mind.

"Is everything okay?" He asked, able to tell that it wasn't.

"Yeah." Carrie said with a nod. Steven studied back at her as he scratched at his arm underneath his cast.

"Well I'm just ready to relax, I don't know if I could take anything else." He said after a moment. Carrie found the answer to her question in that statement. She knew that he was right. He had been through a lot and he didn't deserve to be burdened again, not then anyway.

Steven leaned in and began to kiss Carrie, but was surprised when she pulled away from him.

"Carrie, what's wrong?" He asked.

"Nothing. Come inside, we need to clean your cut." She said as she got up from the swing and walked away. Steven was wrapped in confusion and frustration, frustration for not being able to read Carrie's mind and for not being able to scratch his arm underneath that damned cast.

He looked out at the yard where Lisa's car sat and thought that Carrie must have been thinking of Lisa and that was why she was acting so strangely.

Steven got up and walked into the house from the front porch. He stood in the middle of the living room and could hear Carrie in the bathroom, collecting the alcohol and swabs that she would need to clean the wound on Steven's head.

Carrie walked back into the living room and met Steven as he sat down on the edge of the couch. She sat down on the coffee table in front of him and pulled his head to her to inspect his cut.

"It's looking better, don't you think?" He asked. He put his left hand underneath her shirt and began to stroke her bare side affectionately. She closed her eyes and savored the moment, wishing that things didn't have to change. She then wondered how things would be when they did change.

"Do you love me?" She asked suddenly.

"Ah." He grunted, yielding to the sting of the alcohol as Carrie applied it. "What?"

"Do you love me? I mean really love me." She said.

"Of course I do, don't you know that?" He answered with a bit of shock.

"I know you say it all the time, but if it came down to it and everything that we are is not just about sex and drinking parties any more, would you stick with me? Could you see yourself with me forever?" There was a thick sincerity in her voice that grabbed Steven's attention.

"Well yeah." He answered truthfully. "What are you saying? Do you want to get married or something?" Carrie remained silent as she dabbed the laceration on his scalp with the alcohol-soaked cotton swab.

"Carrie?" He asked. She dropped her hands to her side and drew a deep breath.

"I…" She began, but her thought was interrupted by the sound of David's car approaching the house. She expelled her breath, aggravated by the interruption. She quickly gathered the things from the bathroom and disappeared down the hallway, leaving Steven confused on the couch.

After a minute or two, Steven saw the front door open and David and Julie entered the house, holding hands and looking more in love with each other than ever. Steven looked down to their interlocked hands and noticed, right away that Julie was wearing a new piece of jewelry, an engagement ring.

"What's up? Grisby finally let you go, huh?" David asked as he closed the door behind him and Julie.

"Yeah, I'm done with that. What's up with y'all? Y'all seem a little more sappy than usual." Steven asked. David blushed a bit, to Steven's surprise.

"Where's Carrie? We need to talk to her." David asked. Steven motioned towards the back of the house as David started walking in that same direction. Steven looked at Julie and she smiled back at him with a beaming glow. Steven knew then, judging from her blissful air, that they really must have gotten engaged.

"Carrie, come in here. We got something to tell you." David called from the end of the hallway.

David returned to Julie's side in the living room and waited anxiously for Carrie to join them. Steven looked behind him as he heard Carrie walk up behind the couch. She placed her hand on Steven's shoulder and looked at David, curiously wondering what he had to tell her.

"What's going on? You're grinning like a mule eating briars." She asked. David looked as though he were about to burst with the news.

"I asked Julie to marry me and she said yes. Y'all think we can make room for her?" He said with the biggest smile imaginable.

"Yeah, that's great." Steven said with a smile. He got up and shook David's hand and congratulated Julie with a hug; her smile was even bigger than David's was.

Carrie lacked Steven's enthusiasm over the news and was in fact bothered by it. She knew that it was bound to happen sooner or later. She knew that one day Julie would take her brother from her. She never knew her mother, she had lost her father and now she was losing her brother too. Now with Lisa gone and her uncertainty of Steven's reaction to her pregnancy, she had never felt so alone.

David stood expressionless and Julie's smile faded as Carrie's silence expressed her reaction to the news. Steven pulled in an uneasy breath and waited for Carrie to say something, the way that he knew that she would.

"Well, how does it feel?" She said to Julie. She could feel her face getting hotter with each second that passed. "You finally got what you wanted. You got you're hooks into David, your getting the house, how long do you think that it'll take for you to get rid of me?"

"Carrie, what are you doing? I thought we were passed all this." David said, hurt by his sister's unwillingness to accept Julie into their family.

"Carrie, I'm not trying to take you're brother away from you, I'm not trying to hurt you. You're opinion means a lot to me." Julie said to her sincerely. Steven remained silent.

"No it doesn't, you don't even know me." Carrie snapped.

"I'm willing to get to know you, if you'll let me." She pleaded.

"Don't bother." She said as she hurried around the couch towards the door, grabbing the keys to Lisa's car from the table by David's chair along the way.

"Carrie, stop." David said.

"Just leave me alone!" She said without slowing her stride.

Carrie slung the front door open and stormed out. David started to follow when Steven grabbed his arm.

"Let me talk to her." He said. David gritted his teeth in frustration and reluctantly allowed Steven to go after his sister.

Steven bounced down the front steps and ran to the passenger side of the car and got inside just as Carrie was backing out of the yard.

"Carrie, stop. Let's go in and talk." Steven said, putting his hand on her shoulder in an effort to calm her.

"Steven, don't even say anything. I'm not going back in there. There's nothing to talk about." She said as she said as she pulled the car into drive and pressed the accelerator.

"Okay, fine. Slow down at least." Steven said, trying to brace himself as Carrie whipped the car onto the road from the driveway. "Where are you going anyway."

"I don't know." She answered, gripping the steering wheel as she intended to drive out her anger.

* * *

Carrie drove blindly, thinking about everything that had changed in her life so suddenly. She was beginning to calm down somewhat and it was then that she realized that she was on the same road that led to the cotton field where she and Steven had found Lisa's body.

Her stomach twisted and her eyes narrowed when she spotted the gravel road ahead in the fading daylight. She hit the brakes and then headed the car down the long driveway.

"Why do you want to come out here?" Steven asked after having said nothing since leaving the house.

"I don't know." She said, fighting back tears.

"What's wrong? It's more than just David and Julie." He asked as they continued down the gravel road.

"It's everything. It's like I don't know who I am anymore." She made no effort to hold her tears back any longer. Steven shook his head. He didn't know what to say to her; her pain was hurting him.

Carrie stopped the car at the oak tree. She got out and walked around the car and stood, looking at the crime scene that was still partially draped in police tape. She felt her head become dizzy and her stomach turn. She staggered back and leaned against the hood of the car and watched as the police tape fluttered in the light breeze that was blowing. Steven got out of the car and slowly approached her.

"Are you okay?" He asked, leaning against the car beside her.

"No."

"What can I do?" He asked.

"Bring Lisa back, give me my brother back, bring my daddy back. Can you do that?" She asked through her tears. Steven looked away with no answer to give her.

"I didn't think so." She said after a moment.

Steven heard a train whistle blow down the nearby tracks. Every sickening thought from the last few months came flooding back to him and he wondered if the misery would ever end. He had finally come to a place in his life where he was actually content with himself and now the one person that had helped to get him there seemed to be taking his place in the torment that he had left behind.

"It feels like I'm losing everything. My daddy, my best friend, my brother and I'm afraid that I'm gonna lose you too." She said as she stared up into the darkening sky.

"You'll never lose me, why do you think that?" He asked. He began to feel the train rumbling the ground as it approached. Carrie shook her head, not wanting to change another single thing by telling Steven what she knew that she had to.

"Sometimes I think that I would be better off dead." She said angrily, reminding Steven of himself just a few short months earlier.

"Don't say that, we'll get through this." He assured her as he took her hand.

"Steven, I'm pregnant." She said, freezing time for a second.

Steven sat in shock, he didn't know what to say or do. The train broke up his already aching thoughts as it roared up the tracks. Carrie looked at his still face and felt that she had gotten the reaction that she had feared. She pulled her hand from Steven and then stood up from the car. She began to cry and knew of nothing else to do but run away.

Steven snapped himself from his daze and watched as Carrie ran away from him towards the train tracks. He felt a thunder roll across the open cotton field that shook his body along with the rumbling of the train.

"No." He said to himself, fearing that Carrie was about to do the unthinkable.

Steven ran after her as she hurried towards the brush-shrouded train tracks. He could feel a few ice-cold raindrops hit his face as he pumped his legs as hard as he could. He was determined to catch her before she reached the tracks. He wasn't going to let it end this way. The darkness of the night seemed to fall upon them all at once, but neither Carrie or Steven slowed down a bit.

He saw Carrie disappear into the brush a few yards ahead of him. He was breathing heavily and could feel his head begin to throb at the cut on his scalp. The rain increased and Steven could hear the fat drops of water hit the leaves on the small trees around him as he too entered the brush that lined the tracks. The roaring of the train became more intense and the shaking in the ground was unreal. He could now see the train's bright head light as it poured though the thicket. He had lost sight of Carrie and wasn't able to tell how close he was to the tracks, but he continued to run with tree limbs and briars tearing at his body and face. Then all at once the thick trees and brush came to an end and he stood just a few yards from the tracks. He saw Carrie standing, in the middle of the rails with the most hurt and unreachable look on her face; she was illuminated clearly by the train's light.

"No!" Steven yelled as he ran to her franticly.

"Why did you stop?" He said to himself, noticing now that the train was so close.

He gave all that he could as he ran up the loose and rocky bank that supported the tracks. He looked to his left and could see nothing but the brightest light that he had ever seen as he wiped the rain away from his face.

Steven stopped running and saw Carrie standing just on the other side of the tracks. He then looked down to his own feet and saw that he stood in the middle of the rails; they looked so familiar to him and oddly comforting.

He looked back to Carrie and in a second and without a word, the love that they had shared and the time that they had spent together was relived between them. The train's roar was now deafening. Steven looked back into the light and was lost in it and then just as quickly, it was gone. There was nothing but darkness.

* * *

Steven lay on the ground with his eyes shut tightly and with his head pounding with unbelievable pain. He shifted around on the ground involuntarily, trying to regain his awareness. He was once again blinded by the light and couldn't understand what had just happened. He looked ahead; his eyes were useless against the bright light.

L.B. Kelly

"Why is the train still here? Did it stop?" He thought as he pulled himself to his knees. He held his hand up and peeked from behind it and saw someone moving towards him.

"Carrie, what happened?" He asked through his disorientation. She gave no response as she continued to move towards him.

"Brooke?" He said with shocked revelation as his sister stood just inches in front of him. She looked completely different than he remembered, yet at the same time she hadn't changed at all; she was so beautiful.

"How?" He asked as the tears began to flow free. She still said nothing; she only looked past him.

Steven turned to look and as he did, his shock was deepened when he saw Carrie kneeling on the ground, holding his limp and broken body in her arms. She was crying hysterically.

"Carrie." He said, desperately and hurt. He took in a deep breath and then turned back to Brooke, confused. She touched his face and gave him the most comforting look that he had ever seen.

"I missed you." He closed his eyes and melted into her embrace when he felt her fingers on his skin. She knelt down to meet him eye to eye.

"Come on, Mamma's waiting for us." She said softly.

"I missed her too." Steven said with a heavy sob breaking his voice.

"So have I." Brooke said. Steven looked at her and his perplexity grew.

"How could you miss her? Haven't you been with her this whole time?" He asked.

356

"No Steven, I've been waiting for you." She said as a tear rolled down her smooth and flawless cheek.

"I don't understand." He said. Brooke looked away and calmed herself with a short and cleansing sigh before she spoke.

"I held your hand that night behind the house, I pushed you off of that train car and I led David to you the night that Michael was killed." Steven had a look of awe upon his face as she revealed these things to him.

"Well then why? Why did you make me wait so long?" He asked after a moment.

"You weren't meant to wait." She began as she placed her hand on his face to console his increasing sob. "You were supposed to be with us the night of the accident, but then it was seen fit for you to stay behind. After that I couldn't let you come with your heart the way it was. You had to find happiness again."

Steven took one last look at Carrie and knew that she was the happiness that he had found. He wished that he could stop her pain in that instant, but he knew that he had to go.

He looked back to Brooke and stood as she stood also. He took his sister's hand and walked with her into the still-present light and in death, he realized that he had spent the last year and a half of his life living to die.

About The Author

L.B. Kelly was born in a small Mississippi town. A former courier at a local community college, he is now self-employed. He lives in a rural area of Mississippi with his wife, Amanda and two young sons, Lukas and Layne.

L.B. has always dreamed of writing a novel. "Living to Die" is a fictional completion of one of many short stories that he has written in the past. You will be able to identify with the characters in this story and forget that it is a work of fiction. "Living to Die" is only the first in what should be a long line of intriguing novels and promises to make the author's name well known.

Printed in the United States
41200LVS00001B/3

9 781418 497903

Steven Harris is a young man living in a small Mississippi town. Life before this small town seems so far away, remnants of a family and no one to care that he was on the brink of suicide. The journey that brought him here was filled with loss, pain, and fear.

Steven begins to build a new life for himself in this small town. He finds love and hope and even begins to heal. What no one knows is that on this journey Steven bore witness to murder. Through a strange twist of fate Steven is brought face to face with the murderer and is forced to live and work along side this man unable to tell anyone what he knows.

Events unfold that lead Steven and those around him to an unexpected conclusion.

authorHOUSE™

ISBN 1-4184-9790-8

90000

9 781418 497903

$4.99

348102
a26-
296-G